D1476567

The Spirit Keepers

By J. K. Winn

This book is dedicated to my new New Mexico family,
Jonah and Chris.

May the Spirits be with you.

Chapter One

San Anselmo Pueblo, New Mexico - August, 1994

A sudden gust of wind raised dust. Ben Rush halted his hike atop Rainbow Mesa to wipe grit from his eyes. He ran his tongue over cracked lips as dry as the desert floor. With his backpack open on a flat rock, he made a scrabbling search for water and drained what was left in his bottle.

When he glanced back up at the wind-scoured plain, a tall funnel of dust caught his attention. He shaded his eyes with a hand and squinted into the distance - a dry sea of clay soil dotted with green brush and the occasional crimson butte. A small line of people approached the mesa.

Strange. He rarely ran into anyone this far from the pueblo.

Through raised binoculars, Ben watched the procession of men in white shirts and dark pants come closer. The gleam of sun on silver reflected from squash-blossom necklaces. The flash of red on foreheads indicated headbands. One member of the group stood out. Although the same height as the others, that individual was a boy, one of Ben's senior students, Virgil Chavez. Others carried an object wrapped in a blanket. A body. No mistaking it.

In the last month a handful of people had come down with what was described as the flu; two children had died from it. One was the Chavez child. A pity she had died so young, his heart hurt for Virgil and his family.

The group had reached a site directly below him when a maroon pickup truck careened toward them. It stopped nearby and a short, heavyset man jumped out. Virgil's dad, Albert, peeled away from the procession and strode up to the newcomer, striking a belligerent stance. The wind picked up murmurs, but even with voices amplified in anger, Ben couldn't make out what was being said. Albert Chavez's scowl quickly turned into an expression of rage. He vehemently shook his head, then raised his fists. The other man lifted his arms in front of his face and, for a moment, it looked as if Albert would punch him.

Slowly Albert relaxed his fists, and the other man lowered his arms. Ben watched while the two men conversed, then released a long-held breath, relieved the confrontation was winding down. About to turn back to his hike, he saw Albert step forward and poke a finger into the other man's chest, causing him to stumble. Before the man could recover, Albert shoved him. The stranger staggered, lost his balance, and fell. He slowly rose while the others watched. Ben fully expected him to return the attack. Instead, he dusted himself off and turned to leave, head down.

Ben's stomach cramped. Disturbed by what he had witnessed, he waited until the stranger had trudged back to his truck before lowering the binoculars. *What the hell was going on?* People on the pueblo were typically cordial. Even upset or unhappy, they rarely said anything to your face. He didn't for one second like what he had seen. He had come to the pueblo to get away from trouble. He hoped it hadn't followed him here.

A long ribbon of highway stretched as far as Sandy Jacobs could see. Low-lying scrub speckled gritty soil. Barren hills rose all around. She raced her *Tercel* along the highway, windows rolled down. The wind twisted and knotted long strands of her hair, blew them across her face. She repeatedly wiped them away with the back of her hand, along with the moisture that beaded her brow. She was heading into a vast empty unknown. Of landscape. Of life.

Anxiety and anticipation had become her twin companions the moment she crossed the state line into New Mexico. Unsure of how to locate her destination, which didn't exactly put her at ease, she couldn't imagine what she'd find when she arrived. Menacing dark cumulonimbus clouds accumulated on the horizon. Black sheets of rain fell on faraway hills.

Awesome, she thought at the unexpected sight. As quickly as that thought came, a second followed. Would her dreams, like the rain, always be off in the distance? Far beyond her reach.

She closed her windows and drove straight into the downpour. Lightning etched the sky; sizzled in the air. Her wipers failed to keep apace of the water sheeting down the windshield and forced her to slow to a crawl. She inched her way toward her destination, the pueblo of San Anselmo.

When Ben lifted his binoculars again the maroon pickup truck was turning onto the main road. The group had moved to the side of a granite outcropping and was placing the wrapped body in a rocky crevice, pointed to the east in San Anselmo Indian fashion. Weather-worn rocks came together in a womb-like trough where they laid the body. *Fitting.* It was being returned to its source.

"Ha nah, ha nah, ha nah, ha nah," rose the chant along sandstone walls. One by one, the men went over to the blanketed body, sprinkled it with what had to be cornmeal, cupped their empty hands over their lips and breathed deeply into them.

After each man had completed his turn, they scattered out along the edge of the mesa, picking up rocks and returning to place them over the wrapped body. When the body could no longer be seen, they chanted one last time and shuffled with heavy, measured steps, single file, back toward the pueblo.

Ben immediately scooped up his backpack and started down the mesa. On his way home he would stop by to visit his friend and mentor, Kwinsi. He wanted to find out all he could about what had happened to that child. There had to be a reason for all the commotion today.

At the truck, he noticed rain clouds gathering on the horizon. A downpour would soon follow. While he hadn't been raised on the reservation, or the southwest for that matter, he knew the area as well as anyone around. With his native instinct unaltered by a childhood far from his people, his ability to strike out and survive on his own had become both his strength and his weakness. It illuminated his independence, and the loneliness that gouged canyons in his soul.

Unable to put the funeral out of his mind, and wanting to get out of the storm, Ben turned his truck toward the village.

By the time Sandy saw the sign, *San Anselmo, 30 miles*, the rain had lightened. Sun streamed out from behind thick dark clouds. Shadows stole across the desert floor, but she could still make out the silhouette of distant hills. At the exit sign for the pueblo she eased her car off the main highway and followed the arrow past a small outcropping of old adobe buildings.

She continued on the one paved road for what seemed an inordinately long time. She had yet to meet another car. She wondered if she was even heading in the right direction. To double-check her bearings, she pulled over and consulted the map spread across the passenger's seat. It showed a number of side roads heading west. Taking any of them appeared to lead into the hills.

She decided to take a well-deserved break before turning back to the cluster of dilapidated buildings for directions. Exiting the car, she made her way toward the trunk for refreshments, but lost her footing on the terra cotta soil that had turned to orange slime during the rain storm, and slid to her knees.

Mud seeped over her shoes, into her socks, under her jeans. She rose to find pants, socks, shoes and skin stained a bright red-orange. Damn, she was a mess. After retrieving a towel from the trunk and wiping herself down, she hoisted herself onto the hood and yanked off her shoes and socks to dry.

The sun blazed off something white at the base of a distant hill. She shielded her eyes and focused on the object, a small herd of sheep grazing on shrubs. Behind them, the hills rose jagged and worn. With her free arm levered against the sun-warmed hood, she leaned back to enjoy the bucolic scene.

A man emerged from behind a large boulder. Assuming he must be a shepherd because he carried a long stick, it didn't surprise her when he raised the stick and pointed it at the sheep. Then, to her horror, she heard gunfire and saw animal after animal topple. Shocked, she squelched the urge to scream, because she didn't want to become the marksman's next target.

Into her peripheral vision, a truck hurtled toward the flock. The gunman in the field must have noticed the truck too, because he dove behind a large boulder.

The truck stopped near the dropped sheep and the driver jumped out. He bent over the fallen animals, looked around, then took off in the direction from which he came.

Sandy was too stunned to move. She couldn't believe what she had just witnessed. Why would anyone shoot sheep?

Rather than sitting there slack-jawed, she had better find her way into town to report what she had seen, or she might be next. She beat out the worst of the caked mud from her clothes, which had dried quickly in the New Mexico sun, and was about to climb into the car when a Crayola-red pickup truck rounded a bend in the road. Relieved, she waved her arms to flag it down.

Ben maneuvered his *Ranger* across from the *Toyota* stationed at the side of the road. A woman, with long, ebony hair that framed one of the sweetest faces he had ever seen, stood at its side. Her bright, blue eyes looked distressed. Why was she waving him down? Had she run out of gas? If she was in trouble, he might be her only hope of help for hours out here.

She started toward him with a slight limp. Nothing obvious, but a small drag on her left leg that caused a hesitation when she walked. Was this something she had inherited, or had she been injured in an accident? Too bad she was just one of the many tourists who passed through the pueblo all summer long, because he'd sure like to find out more about her.

The roar of the red pickup pulling up across from Sandy's *Tercel* sounded like salvation to her. A rough-hewn man with long legs in denims and cowboy boots unfurled from the driver's seat, took a couple of strides and came up alongside her.

Sandy shielded her eyes and gazed up at the Native American with his copper-colored complexion, easy smile, and long, poker-straight, chestnut-colored hair.

"Something wrong, Miss?"

"Yeah, I'd say." She tried to calm the rising tide of panic so she could remain coherent.

"You run out of gas?"

All at once she realized this stranger might not be any safer than the man with the gun. What had she been thinking when she stopped him? She hadn't been thinking at all.

He narrowed his eyes. "What is it?"

Too late, she was in too deep. "I just saw a man shoot a bunch of sheep over there." She pointed in the direction of the hill.

A startled expression blanketed his features. "You gotta be kidding."

"I know. If I hadn't seen it with my own eyes, I wouldn't believe it either. Do you have any idea where I can go to report the incident?"

He squinted into the sun. "It's not your problem. I'll check it out and let the authorities know."

"Actually, I'm a witness. I really should go with you."

He lifted a hand. "Not in this case. You're an outsider. It would be better if I take care of this myself."

No use debating him. "There was someone else who witnessed the result of the shooting. A man in a pickup came upon the dead sheep."

"What color was his pickup?"

"Maroon."

"Interesting."

"Why's that?"

"Something I saw earlier. Nothing to do with you."

He deliberately looked her over from head to toe until she flushed. "Looks like the mud had its way with you." He pulled a bandana from his pocket and handed it to her.

When his hand grazed hers, their eyes met. She quickly turned away and began to scrub at her jeans. "Thanks."

"First time here?"

"You must have seen my Pennsylvania plates."

"That, and any local knows not to pull off the road and risk being stuck in the mud."

She felt herself blush. To hide her reaction, she glanced down at the reddish-brown splatter. "I'm trying to find San Anselmo. Could you point the way?"

"Sure. It's become a popular destination. I've had to help a dozen other lost tourists locate it this summer Must have been that June article in New Mexico Magazine."

She could set him straight about her status, but since she was still unsure about him, she decided against it.

He gestured over her head at a couple of large rock formations. "Head back in that direction. It's around sixteen miles south."

She must have passed the turn-off miles back. If she didn't move on she might not find the pueblo before dark. "Are you sure I can't be of help?"

"Nah, don't worry about it. I'll take it from here. You did enough letting me know."

"Good," she said, grateful she had encountered a man she could trust. "Nice chatting with you, but I guess I better be going." With a wave, she ducked back into the car and made a U-turn.

A glance in the rearview mirror showed the stranger watching her. His age was difficult to determine. The creases in his face deepened into crevasses when he smiled, as if his face, like the terrain beyond, had been etched by the elemental forces of sun, rain and wind. While his high cheekbones and square jaw held onto the linear planes of youth, he wore the ravages of a hard life. He didn't in any way resemble the polished city men she had known.

"Thanks for taking care of this," she called out the window.

"No *problema*." He waved.

She remember the bandana and held it out the window. "Don't forget your bandana."

He shook his head. "Keep it. You may need it again."

"Are you sure you won't?"

"All I need is another of those beautiful smiles of yours to think about until we meet again."

Would they meet again? Probably not.

As he pulled away, she heard him shout, "If you intend to do any hiking, watch out for rattlesnakes."

Another glance in the rearview mirror caught

him smiling after her.

"And be careful if you pull off the road."

"I think I've learned my lesson," she yelled, before driving off with the tall, mysterious stranger on her mind. From what he had said, he must be from around here, but with distances as they were in the southwest, he could be from anywhere, even the town on his license plate holder, Grants, forty miles west of the pueblo. Better he not be a local, he was too darn attractive.

And she was definitely not available.

When Ben arrived back at his haunt, a fresh gathering of rain clouds hid the sun. He threw his daypack onto a chair and a sage leaf slipped out. He rubbed it between thumb and forefinger. The leaf, rough yet velvety against his calloused hand, gave off a pungent scent. During his climb to the top of Rainbow Mesa, he had collected juniper berries and Indian paintbrush-used by the locals for dye- evening primrose-prized for its medicinal qualities-and sagebrush.

He removed leaves and flowers from the pack and placed them in glass containers. With a bag of evening primrose in hand, he headed across the arroyo to a small, partially-melting adobe brick hut. A grizzled old man answered his knock. "Clancy" to the white traders with whom his daughter did business, the old man was known to his friends by his tribal name, Kwinsi. Ben stood in the doorway and looked in at the old Indian whose wrinkled face told of ninety years of hard work and struggle.

"*Kyimme*, I am surprised to see you again today," the old man said.

"I'm sorry to bother you, Kwinsi, but I have a question."

He handed Kwinsi the bag.

"Come in, Nephew, and ask." Kwinsi motioned Ben into the two-room adobe.

Ben had to stoop to pass through the squat doorway. He took a seat on a sofa in the low-ceilinged, dimly lit room, adeptly avoiding a spring popping its way through worn plaid.

"I was just over at Rainbow Mesa and spotted a procession burying the Chavez child. I was wondering if you knew anything more about it."

Kwinsi bobbed his head and Ben waited respectfully for his reply. Over the two years Ben had lived in San Anselmo he had developed a close friendship with Kwinsi, freeing him to reveal information rarely leaked to outsiders.

"It is sad, *Kyimme*. The little Chavez girl only saw six harvests in her life. Such a small time to live." Kwinsi hesitated a long minute. His eyes brimmed with sadness. "She was even too young to be initiated into a clan."

Ben frowned. "I've never seen a child buried here before. Why did they place her body in a crevice rather than a grave?"

Kwinsi cleared his throat, making Ben wonder if

he had overstepped his bounds. He was about to change the subject when Kwinsi answered.

"An uninitiated child's body is always placed in a crevice, in hopes it will return home."

"People are saying she came down with the flu, but this isn't flu season. Do they know what happened?"

Kwinsi pondered a long moment. "No one knows for certain."

"Maybe it's a different virus."

"Perhaps..." He stared at the floor for several seconds before he looked up at Ben. "Some people think she was witched."

Ben raised an eyebrow. "I hadn't heard that. Is that the best explanation they can come up with? Who do they think witched her?"

"Rumors walk through the village. I try not to hear them. They start trouble. You will know all rumors before long, if you listen."

"I will listen, but I won't swallow rumors. I'm more concerned that she might have had a contagious disease."

"We will know in time."

"I wonder if these rumors have anything to do with an argument I saw between Albert Chavez and another man at the funeral today."

"More than likely, Nephew, but you should forget this whole thing. No use plowing another man's field." Kwinisi's firm voice and stern advice surprised

Ben.

He wanted to tell Kwinsi about the sheep shooting, which he had already reported to the tribal police on his way home, but could see the old man wasn't up to it. Another time. Ben rose and approached Kwinsi. "It's late to be bothering you. We'll talk again soon." He shook Kwinsi's age-roughened hand and left, closing the loosely-hinged screen door behind him.

Rain was falling again. With head lowered to avoid the drops, Ben crossed the arroyo and entered his apartment. A damp pall greeted him. The only sound came from a solitary clock on the top bookshelf. He had the same nagging sense of emptiness he'd been feeling more often of late.

He flicked on the television to shut out the feelings, but the only three channels he received showed inane sitcoms at this time of day. *A Tale of Two Cities*, plucked from among the many books on the cinder-block shelves, held no appeal for him, nor did the CDs on the lower shelf. He had listened to each one until he could hear them in his head without playing them.

The day's events had left him ill at ease. Wistful. Like that body among the rocks at the foot of the mesa, he had been left behind for time and the elements to modify. Unlike that body, a dynamic force had begun to stir within him, creating a sense of restlessness, compounded by his chance meeting with that tourist today.

Much like the sun's shadow across the face of the mesa, his emotions had recently shifted. The light had not totally burned out in his heart; his hormones played their familiar bluesy tune. A desire to move on had recently replaced his lingering grief. He had moved to San Anselmo to heal his wounds. It appeared the treatment was working.

Long after dark, he sat with his feet propped up on the walnut coffee table, a cup of coffee in hand, thinking over the events of the day. What really happened to the Chavez girl? Kwinsi's version left too many unanswered questions. Even more distressing was the implication that a tribal member had a role in her death.

Lost in thought, he almost missed a figure flashing past his window until he heard the splashing footsteps. Whoever it was had covered half the distance between his apartment and the adjacent school building before Ben reached his door and stared at their retreating back. What was the hurry at that time of night?

"Can I help you?" he called. The figure quickly disappeared behind a building.

He turned to see if anyone was in pursuit. Seeing no one, he scratched his head in confusion. This kind of incident was uncommon for San Anselmo, especially on such a strange day.

And he had to wonder where this all might lead.

Chapter Two

At a ramshackle building labeled *General Store*, in the midst of the outcropping of decrepit-looking adobe buildings, Sandy dashed through drizzle and ducked inside. She approached the clerk standing behind an old cash register. Thunder rumbled in the distance. Everything smelled damp. Everything felt damp. Humidity hung like a wet blanket in the air. She shook the drops from her shoulders and ran a hand through her soggy hair in an attempt to look more respectable to the woman watching her so closely.

"I'm afraid I'm lost. I'm looking for San Anselmo."

The woman smiled broadly. "You found it."

That stopped Sandy cold. She glanced around the pathetic little mercantile with its meager supplies. "This is San Anselmo?"

"Lived here my whole life and unless things changed while I was working today, this is it."

After the principal's emailed description, Sandy didn't know whether to feel foolish or simply deflated. This place bore no resemblance to the pueblo she had envisioned in her mind. She had imagined a multi-storied structure, rising up toward the sun, like the photograph of Taos pueblo she had hung in her Philadelphia classroom. Instead, she stood in a dingy little low-ceilinged store, in the midst of a gaggle of squat and squalid huts clustered along a lonely road. Her heart sank, but she put on a brave face.

"Is the weather always so bone-dry around here?"

"Nah, it's usually a whole lot wetter." The woman laughed. "Actually, we don't see much rain this time of year except thundershowers. You're lucky to be bringing the rain." She had a slight accent Sandy couldn't place.

"Lucky?"

"The dancers spend all summer trying to bring the rain and you just up and bring it with you."

Sandy liked the woman's warm brown eyes and straight ebony hair, so close to her own hair color. On closer inspection, she guessed they were about the same age, twenty-nine. "My name is Sandy Jacobs."

"Luci Tsabita."

"Is this your store?"

"My mother's. I run it for her. She's getting too old to stand all day long. Can I get you anything?"

A dog barked in the distance. A tang of smoke filled the air, unusual but not unpleasant. "Anything? Everything. I'm a new teacher and I'm moving into an apartment near the school. I'm sure my cupboard is bare."

"Look around and let me know if you need any help."

The door opened and a short, fat woman entered the store. She glanced over at Luci and quickly turned away. "I...I am here for milk. I did not have time to go into Grants."

Luci sent the woman an exasperated look. "Find your milk and get going. I have another customer."

Sandy was about to tell Luci not to hold back on her account when she noticed the look in Luci's eyes and thought better of it. She tried to act busy, checking out a label, but she couldn't help watching the interaction between the two women from the corner of her eye. The customer hurriedly removed the milk from a refrigerator, paid Luci, and left with a slam of the door. The tension was thicker than moisture in the air. After what happened with the sheep and now this, she had to question what intrigues might be going on in this sleepy little town.

With Luci's gaze following her, she turned away and wandered up and down the three short grocery aisles looking for labels she recognized. Her attention was drawn to all the sacks of *masa* flour, cans of hominy, and the large bin of green chiles. She had definitely stepped into a cultural time warp. Since she hadn't the slightest idea how to use such exotic food stuffs, she scoured the racks for the pueblo equivalent of low-fat food, filling her basket with cleaning supplies and canned staples, beef stew and Tex-Mex chili. With a pinch at her waist, she noted she could use the opportunity to lose a couple of pounds.

Luci rang up the purchases. "What, no green chile? You're a full-fledged *gringa*, that's for sure."

Sandy shrugged. "I wouldn't know the first thing to do with chiles."

"If you're going to stay around here, you'll come to appreciate fry bread and chili stew. Everyone learns to digest it after a time."

"Whew." Sandy swiped her brow in relief. "For a moment there I was worried I'd be the odd one out."

Luci had a warm, open smile. "Need anything else?"

"Just directions to the elementary school."

"Two streets north. Take the dirt road at the trailer house with the three beehive ovens next to the corner. Turn east and it is just behind the yellow house on the right. Can't miss it."

Sandy grimaced. "Easy for you to say. I just hope I can find it."

"It's not as hard as it sounds. You'll soon learn the native landmark system." Luci shut the cash register drawer. "What made you choose San Anselmo?"

"I was taking a class at the local college and saw a recruitment flyer from the school. I really needed a change in my life and thought I might like the challenge of teaching in a new place." Sandy shrugged. "Looks like I found one."

"Where are you from?"

"A suburb of Philadelphia."

Luci's smile revealed a gap between her front teeth. "Yep, you found one all right."

Sandy picked up the paper sack Luci handed her and began to back toward the front door. "I better be locating my living quarters before it gets any darker. Thanks for the help." She released the battered screen door behind her, climbed back into her *Toyota Tercel*, and, with Luci's directions, quickly located the school, a nondescript, one-story brown building with a small blacktop playground. With evening edging its way toward the pueblo, the schoolyard was empty.

The teacher's quarters, flat, brown and bereft of surrounding vegetation, sat directly adjacent to the school grounds. Her apartment was number three. She pulled her car to a halt before the front door and sat staring at the dismal building, horrified by the principal's downright deception about the pueblo. His description had lacked the pertinent details. The dirt parking area. The broken rain gutter. The peeling paint. If he had been this dishonest, what else hadn't he told her?

Rain poured down hard again and pelted her windshield. When it slowed she darted from the car to door Number Three, which had been left ajar. She entered the apartment and saw, even before finding a light switch, the basic brown sofa, the old wooden table surrounded by an assortment of unmatched chairs, and a faded western landscape print in a primitive frame on the far wall. The place was the defining picture of dreary.

Sandy ditched her overnight bag by the door and looked around for any redeeming features. Tightness filled her chest, and she had to swallow hard to staunch the tears that burned at the back of her throat.

But she couldn't waste time feeling homesick for long. She had to unpack the car while there was a break in the downpour. She raced to the passenger's door, carted groceries into the pantry-sized kitchen and hoisted the bag onto the scratched Formica countertop.

Alongside the counter the empty refrigerator gaped idiotically open. With a sponge she had purchased at the general store she scrubbed the refrigerator out before unpacking the bags and plugging it in.

As she worked, she recalled her grandmother's favorite saying: *You must take the risk to reap the rewards.* She had failed to stand up for what she wanted once and still lived with the emotional repercussions of that decision. Her life seemed to be heading nowhere...at least nowhere she wanted to go. She felt purposeless, frozen. She needed to find a way to thaw out. She had to give this move a chance, no matter the cost.

Her teaching career in a fancy Philadelphia suburb had seemed doomed to babysitting rich kids who had it all, who knew it all. The entire last school year, tension headaches had plagued her on a regular basis. The school nurse had attributed them to burn-out and ordered her to find a different profession, but to leave teaching altogether was out of the question. It played too large a role in her life. Her connection with children, rewarding in itself, helped to ease the pain of losing her son.

Children raced past the principal's office. Squeals followed. Inside, Arnie Sloan fingered the frayed ends of his bolo tie. "So let me get this straight, Ben. You want Emilio Onakee's vice principal position when he retires next year?"

Ben nodded. "Exactly what I said."

"Why you? What are your qualifications?"

Ben knew Arnie was baiting him. "I've taught school for years longer than any other teacher on the pueblo. By my own calculations I'm next in line for a promotion."

Arnie sat back and watched him through beady eyes. "You no longer want to be on the front lines? Tired of the kids? Maybe this job is too much for you."

Ben stifled his rising anger. The principal loved to provoke his staff to prove his power. Ben didn't want to fall for the trap. "You know better than that. I love these kids. Just because I move up to an administrative position doesn't mean I'll be any less involved with them. It's just time to do something new."

"I'll tell you what. I'll take your request under consideration, but only if you do one thing for me."

Ben tensed. Whatever Arnie's angle, he knew it wouldn't be in the best interest of anyone except Arnie. "What's that?"

"I want a piece of land to use for my own recreation. Since I'm not a member of the tribe, it's hard for me to find anything here. Maybe you can ask around?"

Since Ben wasn't a tribal member either, his chance of finding a piece of pueblo property was as good as the principal's. With his obvious Indian blood, Arnie might be confusing him for a San Anselmo. "I can do that, but I can't promise you anything."

"And one other thing." Arnie twirled the tie. "Your job doesn't include helping the Ortiz family on their sheep farm or lunch money for the Adakee girl."

He sat forward. Where had Arnie heard that? "I didn't know I was limited in what I could do for these kids."

"We're not running a social service here." Arnie rose. "Now I have to take care of a couple things before school starts. Is that all?"

Ben rose too. Although Sloan was often unpredictable, Ben couldn't understand why he would give a damn one way or the other about what Ben did in his free time or with his spare dime.

Arnie maneuvered him toward the door. "I'll run your request by the school board and get back to you, but keep your nose clean in the meantime."

Until this meeting, Ben hadn't known it was dirty.

Sunlight roared through Sandy's bedroom window, shimmering against the opposite wall and waking her. Disoriented, it took her a minute to remember where she was. When she did, she pulled the covers over her head, willing herself back to sleep so she wouldn't have to face all she had to do that day. But it was too late. Her mind had lit up with the room.

Galvanized by the sunlight and newfound optimism, she was ready to unpack the rest of her belongings. As soon as she had dressed and gulped down a cup of weak instant coffee, she tackled the task. By late afternoon her many personal treasures—a framed Monet, sprigs of dried flowers in a blue glass vase, and souvenirs from her trip to Spain—disguised the ugly, functional furniture. A spritz of Mountain Meadow air freshener banished the musty smell. Finished, she stood in the doorway between bedroom and living room to appraise the results and found herself humming. The apartment had been transformed from dreary to cheery.

She scooped out the last of the low-fat yogurt she had picked up in Albuquerque while trying to read over information the school had sent her, but the pueblo beckoned. She put on her walking shoes and headed out the door.

On her way through town, she passed Luci locking up the store. Luci signaled her over. "I'm going to a rain dance. Want to come along?"

Though intrigued, Sandy considered how to politely refuse. She still had work to do polishing up her apartment and preparing for school. "What's a rain dance?"

"You are a newcomer, *gringa*. The *Kachina* dance many evenings during the summer at the old pueblo to bring the rain."

"I have so much to do this evening."

Luci took her arm. "You'll do it later. This will be worth the wait."

Sandy reluctantly let Luci lead her toward the old pueblo. "Could you tell me more about the *Kachina*?"

Luci released her arm. "The men put on masks and outfit themselves to impersonate the spirits. Then they dance as an offering to the spirits to encourage them to send us rain."

They walked behind a building and up a hill. "Are you sure it's all right for me to be a part of your ceremonial? I'm not exactly a tribal member."

Luci chuckled. "Could have fooled me. You worry as much as the elders. Would I invite you along if it wasn't okay?"

At the crest of the hill, Sandy looked down into the courtyard of a two-story building and realized she was standing on its roof. Dirt had built up over the years on the side of the old pueblo until it had become one with the earth. Below her, a crowd sat in lawn chairs around the edge of a plaza, the rest lined the rooftop along with her. Luci pointed to an empty spot and Sandy trailed her to it. They crammed in among others along the rim. The sound of chanting voices and beating drums grew louder. Anticipation and a wondrous, but unfamiliar, odor filled the air.

A group of men in white shirts and bandanas entered the courtyard in rhythmic unison, followed by a line of men in kilts and masks. Their red and white bandanas reminded her of the one in her tote bag, donated by her rescuer. By a trick of fate, he might be in the crowd. She glanced around, hoping to spot him, but returned her gaze to the dancers when she didn't.

The beat of the drums followed by chanting echoed in the stomp of the dancers' feet. Their masks of turquoise-painted wood had black slashes for eyes. Huge spruce ruffs wreathed their necks. A few wore long sable wigs and counterfeit beards. Others had elaborate feathered headdresses. Turquoise and coral jewelry adorned their painted bodies. Each man carried rattles, which shook and clattered as he pranced in a circle in the center of the courtyard. Sandy caught a whiff of the same exotic aroma she had smelled before.

"What's that odor?"

"Burning piñon pine," Luci whispered.

She looked out over the heads of the crowd and noticed the vistas extending to infinity in every direction. In the distance, clouds formed huge cottony balls against the darkening blue sky. She sensed the spirituality of the surrounding hills and valleys, their ageless serenity settling over her like a blessing. Surrounded by the scent of sage mixed with piñon, any earlier doubts about her decision to move to the pueblo eroded like the ancient sandstone hills. Determination replaced her reservations.

As the sun sank over the western mountaintops and the light dimmed, the mesas in the distance turned startling shades of coral and burgundy. The intensity of color combined with pulsation and aroma in a hypnotic convergence of sight, sound and smell. Sandy was grateful to be at that precise intersection of time, space and events.

A flash of feathers caught her attention. A row of dancers strutted directly below and reminded her of where she stood: on the precipice of this pueblo, on the threshold of a new life. The beat of the drum echoed the beat of her pulse when she considered the possibilities opening to her. Anything was possible in her life. Anything at all.

Luci had moved off to join a group of people, her arm draped over another woman's shoulder, leaving Sandy alone. She thought about the effort she had made over the past couple of years to find her son; the frustration she had encountered. She had to leave open the possibility that one of her leads would pan out someday and she would be reunited with him. She had tried every avenue she could: approached County Social Services; searched internet databases and genealogy sites; even petitioned the state.

While all her efforts until now had only led to dead-ends, she would drop everything and return to Philadelphia at the end of her year-long contract if she could be with him. It would be unfair to make any long-term commitments or attachments. She might be a short-timer. No matter what happened or what opportunities presented themselves to her, she had to keep that in mind.

Chapter Three

The following morning, Sandy set out to ready her classroom for the first day of school. Halfway down a long hall with classrooms on both sides she spotted a man with long straggly gray hair and a green bolo tie.

"Excuse me," she called to him, "I'm looking for the principal's office. Could you point me in the right direction?"

He stopped in front of her "I bet you're our new fourth-grade teacher. I've been expecting you since yesterday." His handshake was clammy. "I'm the principal, Arnold Sloan, but everyone around here calls me Arnie." An unctuous smile plastered his pale face.

A stale odor emanated from him and turned her stomach. She tried to remove her hand, but he held onto it.

"I'm glad to meet you in person. I've been looking forward to discussing the new curriculum with you."

"Great," she said, "but I have so much to do today to get ready for my class. Can I stop by another time?"

Much to her relief, he released her hand. "Anytime..." he said with a wink.

Something about him made her cringe. "Would you point the way to my classroom?"

"Number six, down that hall."

She said her goodbye and took off at a fast clip,

as eager to get away from him as to find her room. Once inside the classroom she encountered exactly what she had expected, vacant shelves and barren walls that cried out for immediate attention. Without delay, she went to work placing desks and chairs in rows, arranging the files in a drawer, and enlivening the bulletin board with magazine pictures and dried oak leaves carried all the way from Philadelphia. After a couple hours, her handiwork represented only a fraction of what needed to be accomplished before the room was ready for the first school day. One of the fluorescent lights had burned out. A chair wobbled on unstable legs. Possessing neither light bulb nor tools, she braved the hall in search of a janitor.

The school reverberated to the sound of her footsteps on linoleum tile which bounced off the buff-painted cinder block walls. Halfway down the hall, she looked into a room where a tall man in jeans, forest green tee shirt and baseball cap stood on a ladder fixing another light. From behind and below she could see his shirt stretched across the muscular back and upper arms of someone who performed physical labor. She might have found her man.

"Excuse me," she called up to him. "I have a problem with the overhead light and a rickety chair in my classroom. Could you help me out?"

He stretched on tippy -oes to reach the wiring, and in a strained voice said, "I'll be by as soon as I'm done here."

"I'm in room six when you're ready."

Sandy made her way back to her classroom. As

she stapled the last leaf to the bulletin board, a noise behind her caused her to glance over as the stranger from the road incident sauntered into the classroom. She almost dropped the stapler in surprise.

"What are you doing here?"

"I've come for another beautiful smile."

She tried to tone down her enthusiasm. "*You* were the guy in room fifteen?"

He flashed a wide, white-toothed grin that flattened the sensuous curve of his upper lip. "Ben Rush, at your service."

"You're the janitor?"

Ben laughed.

"You're *not* the janitor?"

The familiar playful twinkle lit up his eyes.

"I'm the science and social studies teacher for the upper grades." Ben looked down at her from a good six inch difference in height. "I guess I'm not what a big eastern city girl like yourself expects in a teacher."

"The Marlboro Man look threw me, but I can get used to it."

Ben gave her a crooked smile. "That's not the only thing you'll have to get used to around here."

"Like what?"

"I overheard your first meeting with our fearless leader. He makes quite an impression on the women faculty. Don't let him get to you. It's just his policy to offend female staff members."

Voices in the schoolyard distracted him and she followed his gaze out the window to a couple of kids on swings. When she turned back, Ben studied her through wise eyes.

"Then there's the cultural differences you'll have to face. This isn't Pittsburgh—"

"Philadelphia," she corrected.

"Yeah, that's close enough. These kids are different than the ones you're used to. And our equipment is a generation behind."

She went over to perch on the edge of her desk. "So how different can these kids be?"

He leaned against the wall, folding his arms across his chest. "They're quieter, more submissive than city children."

"That might be a nice change."

"I sure hope so. It's hard for most outsiders to handle."

With his light cocoa-colored skin and deep-set brown eyes, she wondered if he was a local in more than tenure, and was about to ask, when he pointed toward the burnt out bulb.

"What needs fixing besides the light?"

"A utility chair, but I don't want to take you away from your own preparations. Do you know where I can find the janitor?"

"Yeah, but I'm here and can probably help you faster than he can."

"If that's not a problem."

"I'd tell you if it was."

She liked his straightforward manner. It made him seem like someone she could trust. She showed him the broken-down chair and he disappeared, returning with the ladder he had used in room fifteen, a screwdriver in his jean pocket, and four fluorescent tubes still in sleeves.

He handed her the screw driver. "Use this to tighten the chair."

While she did that, he changed the light tubes. Finished, he wiped his hands on jeans and climbed down to where she was finishing her chair repair.

"Let's see how you did." He applied all his weight to the chair. It stood firm. "Not a bad job for a city girl! What other talents do you have?"

She gave him a small smile. "I'll let you discover them for yourself."

The gleam in his eyes hinted that he might be interested, but she wasn't about to succumb to his charm.

She might not know much about the pueblo and its culture, but one thing she knew for sure: she had better watch herself around him.

Chapter Four

"Good morning, class," Sandy said. Prepared, yet aware she was far from Philadelphia, she took a deep breath of courage. The first day of school—with all its mystery and possibility—had arrived. "Please take out your notebooks."

The scrape of chairs on linoleum filled the room. The slap of notebooks against wooden desktops followed. Then silence. Sandy glanced around at the rows of perfectly aligned desks that held unusually quiet, attentive students. She wondered at such calm curiosity, not tinged with hell-raising plans to bring her down. Ten year olds could not be expected to sit quietly for long.

Wanting to test the students knowledge of current affairs, she asked, "Who is the President of the United States?"

In the front row, a boy, in what appeared to be a homemade plaid shirt and elastic banded pants, lowered his eyes. No one in the room raised a hand. Since this was a sovereign nation within a nation, maybe this was something outside their knowledge. She decided to try a question closer to home.

"How about the tribal leader?"

Again, no one raised a hand or shouted out a name, but the children surely knew the answer.

Sandy consulted the roster and called on a girl in the back row. "Who is it, Sadie?"

A couple of the children giggled?

"Joseph Quam." Sadie had answered so softly Sandy had to ask her to repeat herself twice.

"Very good, Sadie." Sandy turned back to the rest of the class. "Now, what's the capital of New Mexico?"

Again, no one volunteered an answer and she had to pick a name from the roster.

Sandy continued to ask questions at large, but they failed to penetrate the wall of silence that stood between her and her students. And the subject matter made no difference. Minutes turned into hours, only broken by morning recess. No matter what she said or did, these children continued to sit placidly behind wooden desks stained with ink and markers. Their behavior was a large leap from the front line trenches in Philadelphia, where shouted-out answers and mean-spirited pranks were the norm. Would that make her job easier or more challenging?

By late morning, frustration at the lack of spontaneity had begun to drive her mad. She could hardly wait for the noon bell to ring so she could consult with Ben about this unusual behavior.

When the bell sounded, the children rose almost in unison and shuffled out of class in a self-imposed line to the cafeteria. Since the route to the cafeteria led directly past Ben's room, she poked her head through his door and spied him at his desk. She immediately noticed he had pulled his hair back into a sexy ponytail, which was most appealing. He glanced up from the book he was reading and caught her stare.

"How's your first day going, teach?" He motioned her into the room.

"Not as well as I had hoped. You were right about one thing. These kids never raise a hand or answer a question without my having to pull teeth."

"That's not the pueblo way." He gestured toward a chair. "Sit a minute, why don't you, and tell me what's going on."

She pulled the chair up to his desk. "I'm about to tear my hair out. I can't get a single one of these kids to volunteer anything."

Ben patted the hand she had placed on the corner of his desk. "This is a small community. Everyone's under pressure to conform. The idea is to fit in, not stand out. No one is supposed to rise above the crowd. If you do, you can get yourself into big trouble. Kinda the opposite of Philadelphia."

She heard a commotion in the hall and saw another teacher separate two squabbling kids. She was relieved to see kids behaving normally.

"No one here wants to show off or act like a know-it-all. It's our job as teachers to get a response out of these kids that doesn't violate their customs."

"But how do we do that?"

"I can only tell you what I do. I plan the curriculum so that they're up on their feet and participating. But why am I telling you this? You're experienced. You'll figure out what works best for you. It just takes time."

"I only hope I figure something out before I go bald."

Ben chuckled. "At least bald is in." He removed a bag from under his desk. "You'll definitely need strength. So how about half a sandwich for starters?"

After school, Sandy had to pass by Ben's room on her way out of the building. She peered in to see a lanky teenager erasing the blackboard while a huskier lad set up desks.

"Sandy," Ben's voice came from across the room. "I was hoping you'd be by."

"I just stopped in to say I was leaving for the day. I didn't mean to interrupt..."

He strode toward her. "No problem. Virgil and Thompson were just helping me put this room back into some semblance of order. Have you met Virgil Chavez?"

The thinner boy turned to stare at Sandy. He stood unusually tall for a high school student in San Anselmo, but he looked gaunt; his skin color a shade sallower than the bronze tone of most San Anselmos. "How thoughtful of you to help Mr. Rush out, Virgil. He certainly can use all the help he can get."

"As you can hear, Ms. Jacobs is my greatest defender," Ben quipped to Virgil, then indicated the other boy. "And this is Thompson."

She nodded in his direction.

"If you can wait a couple of minutes, Ms.

Jacobs, for us to finish up what we're doing, I'll walk you home." Ben flashed her a grin. "I'll even carry your homework."

"That's a deal, but I can carry my own books, thank you."

"Even better."

Sandy took a seat on an empty chair at a desk well-carved with initials and waited until Ben finally excused Virgil and Thompson. He indicated his readiness to walk her to her apartment. "I'm glad you had a chance to meet Virgil Chavez."

"Why's that?" Was he about to confirm her impression that the boy's health was suspect?

"He's the brother of a girl who died a few days ago. She's the second of two children who have died lately of mysterious causes."

Sandy's heart clenched at the thought. No wonder Virgil looked so poorly.

"I taught his older brother, Duane, who graduated last year. The sister's death has been a real blow to the whole family."

"I can imagine." Sandy halted, looking over at him. "Is it safe to assume the school nurse has already checked to be sure the little girl's illness had no connection to Virgil's looking sickly?"

Ben's expression altered in a subtle way. "I think he's more miserable than sick, but you're right, I should have him checked out."

Sandy walked on in heavy-hearted silence. She

understood the trauma of losing a child, and to lose one to death must be impossibly difficult. "How are the parents holding up?"

"Not well. Virgil's dad has been drinking around the clock. His mother sits and stares blankly at the television all day long. This kid has been pretty much abandoned since the death."

Sandy could sympathize with the girl's mother, but she still had two sons who needed her. They were suffering too. "No wonder Virgil looks so wan."

Ben escorted her to her front door. The late afternoon sun cast shadows across his face. In the dull light, he too looked wan. "You worry about them, don't you?"

He nodded. "Sometimes."

"They must be good friends."

"It's more than that."

An inflection in his voice stopped her. "What do you mean?"

"Just call it a sense something's out of place, but it's based on what's been going on around here."

"What kind of sense?"

He hesitated, twisted his key nervously in his palm. "It's just a hunch something's brewing, but I can't put my finger on it. I don't know, it's just a feeling things are worse than they appear."

A knot formed in her gut.

"It's probably nothing. Most likely I'm chasing

shadows. I do have a wild imagination." He began to back away, but she stopped him with a hand on his arm.

"I hope I didn't put you off with all my questions. I didn't mean to pry."

"It's not you," he said and gave her a reassuring hug as proof. "I'll see you tomorrow."

She watched him walk away. A feeling of foreboding followed.

The next morning Ben stood outside Sandy's door, his truck idling in the lot. His demeanor had changed overnight. He looked relaxed. Bright. Perhaps she had worried for nothing.

"I have to go for a ride. Want to join me? I'd love the company."

Sandy self-consciously threaded her hand through her uncombed hair. She had yet to wash up, still wearing her Saturday morning grubbies-a long white tee shirt over black spandex bicycle shorts- and had a ton of preparation to do for the following week. "I don't know..." She hesitated. The idea of exploring new territory with Ben was stronger than the desire to finish her work. "Okay, I'll go as long as you can have me back by late afternoon."

"*No problema.*"

Why not go? An adventure might be exactly what she needed right now. And it might give her an opportunity to pick Ben's brain about his concerns, which still nagged at her. "So, where would you be taking me?"

"A pueblo outside of Socorro. Some of their science books were mistakenly delivered here. I've been asked to return them to their proper address."

"How about something to eat first?"

Ben glanced at his watch. "Since you're pressed for time, let's stop at a neat little restaurant I know outside of Socorro after the delivery. Can you be ready in twenty?"

"Sure." With just enough time for a quick shower, Sandy closed the door behind her and went directly to the bathroom, where she reveled, although briefly, in the hot water and frothy foam that sluiced over her breasts and belly and ran down her thighs. After putting on denim shorts and a violet scooped-neck knit top, she scarfed down a banana and made her way over to the truck.

As soon as she was securely belted into her seat, Ben took the road that led onto Interstate 40 toward Albuquerque where he converged onto I-25. There the land became flat and arid. The many mesas that clustered around the I-40 had all but disappeared. What was left was the scrub-speckled desert floor. They traveled through country where the only sight worth seeing was the occasional long stemmed-Yucca flower or a spindly-armed Ocotillo. Although Ben kept the windows rolled down, a furnace blast of wind battered her and heated the cab. The air was so dry she had to repeatedly clear her throat to breathe.

Over an hour had passed since they left the

pueblo. Her throat had parched and her stomach was beginning to rumble.

Ben must have noted her discomfort because he reached over and patted her shoulder. "Hold on. I'm having a little trouble with my air conditioner, but haven't been able to get into Gallup for repairs. It's not much further. The pueblo is northeast of Socorro and the last sign we passed says Socorro is twenty-four miles ahead."

"Good, because I'm ravenous."

"There's nothing to eat around here, but I'll have you at that restaurant in Socorro in no time. Trust me." He squeezed her shoulder.

Ben lifted a piece of paper off of the dash and handed it to her. "Could you tell me the name of the exit?"

She read it over. "It says Florida."

"It's Floor-*ree*-dah because it's Spanish here."

Fifteen miles farther down the road she saw the exit sign. Salvation was close at hand. "There it is."

Ben took the exit ramp and turned left onto a paved road. They rode for another ten minutes without seeing another sign. Sandy studied the sheet.

"We'll need to drive ten more miles before reaching the turn-off to the pueblo. Once at that turn-off, it's another fifteen miles to the school."

Ben set the odometer. The sun beat relentlessly down on the truck roof, heating the cab to the temperature of the desert floor. Sandy fanned herself. It felt like her blood was boiling. Her throat stung. The rumble in her stomach had turned into a roar.

At ten miles, they spotted the turn-off, a dirt road. Ben took a sharp right onto the road and Sandy held on to the seat for dear life as the truck wheels caught in the washboard ruts, jostling her about. She laid her head back against the seat and closed her eyes. Perhaps when she opened them, she would be in an air-conditioned restaurant sipping a margarita and munching on a handful of nachos. The thought gave her a moment's relief.

But it didn't last long. A wave of nausea whipped about her like the wind over the desert floor.

She opened her eyes to the blinding light. The road stretched out dusty and barren before them. "I don't see any signs of civilization anywhere."

"We'll find the Pueblo soon," he reassured her.

"To pass the time, perhaps you can tell me a little about yourself." She felt his eyes fix on her. "What are you staring at?"

He turned back to the road. "Your eyes. They're almost the color of the sky."

Her face flushed. "I can't argue with the fact the sky goes on forever. I suppose natives to this area, like you, take all this for granted."

Ben laughed. "Is that what you think, that I'm a native?"

"You're not?"

"Technically, I would qualify, but I've only lived here a couple of years."

She studied him skeptically. "Where are you from?"

"I was born on one of these reservations, but adopted out as a toddler." He cleared his throat. "Guess my mother didn't want me, because she didn't bother to keep me and never had the inclination to look for me."

Too close to home. Sandy grimaced. "Perhaps she had to relinquish you."

"Yeah, sure. If she really cared, she would have found a way to stay in touch."

Her throat clenched. "You don't know that. It's not easy to find an adopted child."

Ben stared straight ahead. "It's hard enough accepting the fact I wasn't loved or wanted, I don't really need to hear any excuses."

"But—"

He flashed his palm in front of her face and said firmly, "I really don't want to speak about this. Let's change the subject."

"Okay. No problem. So where did you grow up?"

"Kansas City."

"What brought you back here?"

He shrugged. "Long story there. The bottom line is I don't belong in the city any longer. I wouldn't go back if you paid me. I'm a confirmed southwesterner now."

"Kansas City's lovely."

"For some."

"But not for you?"

"Not quite. I was groomed to be a corporate lawyer like my dad, but I left Missouri right after completing my bachelor's at Washington University in St. Louis."

She cocked a brow. "A corporate lawyer?"

Ben smiled. "I know what you're thinking. With my jeans, boots, and long hair, I'm about as far from corporate America as New Mexico is from the ocean. I'm a long way from home and I choose to be. I never had any interest in advanced degrees and hobbling social restrictions. I'm a throw-back to my genes. And that doesn't make them or me necessarily happy." He slowed the truck. "Could you check those directions again?"

She picked up the paper, but reading the small print made her queasiness worse. She swallowed hard. "I'm afraid it still says the same thing."

"I'll pull over and take a look myself." He veered the truck off to the shoulder, read over the directions she had handed to him. "We can't be far from the pueblo according to this. Let's just forge on."

She draped her arm over her stomach in an attempt to quiet it. "How about turning back to that little gas station we passed for directions? Maybe we took the wrong road."

"That will just waste time when you're hungry. I want to see that you're fed— soon. We'll push on."

He pulled back onto the road. Ten minutes, and a two degree rise in temperature later, steam started to pour out from under the hood. Ben swore under his breath and pulled the truck to the side of the road.

"What's going on?" she asked.

"The engine's overheating." He grabbed a jug from the back seat, lifted the hood and, after letting the engine cool, poured water into the radiator. Back in the cab, the engine started smoothly. "Now we'll *have* to find that Pueblo because we'll need more water."

Five miles further, the engine again overheated.

"Wait here." Ben left the cab and threw open the hood. Against orders, Sandy climbed out and stood by the side of the truck trying to decide if it was hotter outside or in.

She heard him slam the hood shut.

"Damn! She blew a hose."

Sandy had the urge to groan but suppressed it. Ben had to deal with enough without adding to it. "Is there anything we can do?"

"Not without an extra hose. We'll just have to wait for help."

She leaned back against the truck and shaded her eyes. The sun's glare seemed as endless as the emptiness in the distance. Sun and sand was all she saw.

She crawled into the cab to dodge the relentless rays. Already her arms were turning hot pink. Ben slipped into the driver's seat beside her.

It looked less and less likely she would be back in time to do any work.

He wiped the sweat off his brow. "Just relax. We could be out here awhile."

Her mouth felt like the arroyo bed alongside the road. Dry. Dusty. "You don't happen to have a few drops of water left, do you?"

"No, but I know something around here that will quench your thirst and your hunger."

"What's that?"

"Prickly pear cactus."

Sandy couldn't believe what she had heard. "What? They look more dangerous then delicious."

Ben reached behind his seat and rummaged through his backpack, withdrawing a *Swiss army knife* from a pouch. "Don't knock it 'til you try it. I'll be back in a flash with refreshments."

She sat back while he fished around beneath a patch of cactus at the side of the road.

Back in the cab, he placed them on top of the dash. "Lunch is on me."

She stared at the hard little round red fruit he held out to her.

"You might change your mind once you've

tasted this treat." He tugged at the outer skin of the fruit and deftly separated flesh from peel, then stroked his fingertips along the length of the fruit, unraveling its spiny, green overcoat. A mass of pulp and seeds was revealed. He held it out to her. "Take the heart."

"What about the seeds?"

"Eat them too. It won't hurt."

She leaned over and took a bite from the pulp he held out to her, surprised by the succulent taste. "Why it's as sweet as a mango."

He peeled back more of the skin, and she took another bite. The juice ran down the back of her throat as cool as if it had come from a refrigerator. "What about you? I'm being a pig. You must be starved."

"Don't worry. There's more where that came from. I wanted to resuscitate you before I gathered more produce from this amazing garden." He wiped a dribble of cactus juice off her chin with a thumb.

A cool warmth spread through her.

The putter of a pick-up startled her. A green '59 Chevy truck moved up alongside theirs. The lone occupant rolled down the passenger's side window. "Need any help?"

"I'm afraid we've blown a radiator hose." Ben said.

The passenger leaned out the driver's side window. "I have water, but the nearest auto parts place is in Socorro. Let me take a look."

The truck pulled in front of theirs and its driver jumped out. Although the stranger's voice proclaimed her a woman, she wore the attire of a man; jeans with a fringed shirt and cowboy boots. Wisps of desert dry, gray hair wormed out from under a cowboy hat.

Ben lifted the hood for her and she took a look at the engine. "*Si, señor*. You need a hose all right. I will have to give you a lift into Socorro."

"How far are we from town?" Ben asked.

"Forty miles as the crow flies."

The idea someone would be willing to drive them that distance surprised Sandy. She couldn't imagine anyone in Philadelphia putting themselves out like that. Gratitude swirled up inside her much like the dust devil on the road beyond.

"Where were you heading today?" the woman asked while absently wiping her soiled hand on her jeans.

"The Pueblo of Abo," Ben informed her.

Her hand paused. "Are you still going there?"

Ben nodded.

"You better be careful. I've heard from the postman they've had an outbreak of a mysterious illness. A handful of people have been pretty sick. I think someone actually died."

Ben caught Sandy's eye. "We've had a problem on the San Anselmo Pueblo, but—" he shrugged, "—it's probably unrelated."

Worry etched lines around the older woman's eyes. "Don't take any chances."

Ben brushed off her concern with a hand. "We're not going to be there long enough to run into any problems."

He sounded so confident. Sandy could only hope he was right.

Rosa introduced herself to Sandy and Ben and then drove them to Socorro to purchase the hose. She stayed by them on the road while Ben replaced it. Before they drove off, Ben offered Rosa money for her trouble, but she refused to take it. They said their goodbyes to Rosa with a hug, promising to visit some time if ever around, and pointed the truck in the direction of the pueblo.

Much to their relief, they reached the Pueblo of Abo a little after dusk. After the books were safely in the hands of the school janitor, they turned back toward San Anselmo.

Back on the road, Sandy turned to him. "Do you think the outbreak in Abo has anything to do with what's happening in San Anselmo?"

Ben stared straight ahead, gripping the wheel. "Hell if I know, but it sure sounds suspicious."

"It makes me a little uneasy..."

"You're not alone." He took the ramp onto the highway.

"Is that what you meant yesterday about your ominous feeling?"

"That, and a sense there's something awry on the Pueblo. As I said, I don't know what's going on, but I feel it in my bones."

"Is any of this related to the sheep being shot?"

"Perhaps..." He patted her arm to comfort her. "Why don't you take a little rest. We've had a long day."

She laid her head back against the seat. "Let me know if you need me to take over the driving." Her eyes drifted closed.

Back at the apartments, he gently shook her awake. "We're here."

Sandy sat upright, rubbing her eyes. "Sorry. I didn't think I would fall asleep. I've been a rotten companion."

"Just the opposite. It's been a long day, but you've been a real sport, Sandy. I'm glad you were there. I wouldn't have wanted to do this without you." And he meant it. Not everyone would have been so calm and uncritical under the circumstances. The more he got to know her, the more he liked and enjoyed her. He wanted to know her better.

She smiled up at him, a smile that lit the dark cab. "I'd better get real sleep in a real bed." She gave him a small salute and dragged herself from the truck toward her apartment door.

Ben slipped from the cab and came up behind

her. He waited while she fumbled her key from her daypack and gave her a quick hug. She turned to enter the apartment.

Even though the outing had not gone according to plan, all and all it had turned out to be a truly wonderful day. With a small smile she would never see, he wished her a goodnight, and stood by as she quietly closed the door behind her.

Chapter Five

The three-ten bell sounded. Sandy finished writing the homework assignment on the blackboard and turned back to her desk. Kids milled about, searching for misplaced jackets and lost lunch pails. In the commotion, the room took on the appearance of a bustling subway station. It never failed to surprise Sandy when they finally filed out in their usual orderly fashion.

Alone at her desk, she eyed the paperwork pile before her with plans to finish all her grading at school for once and leave herself one free night at home. No distractions. No thinking about Ben.

She leaned back in her chair before beginning, arms behind head, elbows wide, and took a moment to marvel at how quickly she had entered the rhythm of life in San Anselmo. Things were coming together at home and at school. More comfortable in her new life with every passing day, she rarely missed the restaurants or movies or even the theater she used to attend on a regular basis. She had learned to satisfy herself with simple pleasures; cooking, reading and listening to the CDs she bought on her occasional trips into Albuquerque. She had even figured out ways to coax responses out of her students, which made teaching on the pueblo so much more gratifying.

She sensed a presence in the room and glanced up to see a boy in the back row with straight bowl-cut brown hair and almond eyes. She checked her roster to remind herself of his name. "Dixon Edakee?"

He stared down at his desk.

"Dixon, it's time to go home."

"I can't..." he mumbled. Tears spilled over the rims of Dixon's expressive dark brown eyes and trickled down his cheeks.

She swiftly approached him and took a seat on a neighboring desk. Ungraded papers forgotten. "What's the matter, Dixon?"

Dixon continued to stare down, lips sealed.

"Please tell me what's bothering you."

She was met again with silence. Something really bothered this kid and he wasn't about to spill it.

"Would you like me to walk you home?"

He raised his eyes to hers and nodded with enthusiasm. "Yes, please."

For the first time since arriving at San Anselmo, a pueblo child was coming to her for help, and she had an opportunity to make a different type of contribution to his well-being. She'd certainly put her grading aside for that.

"Do you have what you need to take with you?" While he gathered up his notebook and pencils, she collected her briefcase and stuffed papers inside. When she turned to leave, Ben stood in the doorway.

"Looks like my timing's a bit off."

"I was just on my way to walk Dixon home."

"Would it be okay if I came by your place later?" he asked. "I have something I'd like to share with you."

"Sure. I'll be home after five."

He saluted her and left.

She turned her attention back to Dixon. "You'll have to show me where you live."

"This way." Dixon took her by the hand and led her out of the building past the mound which interred the old pueblo. Just beyond the pueblo, they made a left onto a dirt road. On either side of the road, houses had been built haphazardly with no apparent concern for consistency in color or design. Packed earth replaced lawns and old trucks sat where trees normally stood. The absence of any greenery, the overriding pervasiveness of browns and beiges, and the crumbling stucco facades created a mood of deprivation. The street, like the children she taught, wore the tattered apparel of rural poverty.

Dixon turned toward a stained and faded yellow stucco box of a house. A shiny new maroon pickup took up most of the small front yard. It stood out against the somber backdrop. A short, heavyset man met them at the front door and motioned Dixon in.

"Thank you," Dixon mumbled before he disappeared down a hallway.

Sandy extended her hand to the man. "I'm Dixon's teacher, Sandy Jacobs."

"Come in. Come in." He had a strong grip. "I'm Dixon's father, Tonito."

Sandy entered a small, dark room behind

Tonito. With all the curtains drawn, it took a moment for her eyes to adjust to the dim light. When they did, she noticed the room was furnished with a torn overstuffed brown velour sofa, dotted with pale, cotton-like filling poking out through seams like custard from a donut, and fronted by a 1950s style scratched brown coffee table. In one corner, a wide-bodied, twenty-five inch television sat on a giant telephone cable spool. The thick, beige, pleated brocade drapes could have been a throwback to an earlier era. Only the television was a relatively late model. Leaning up against the far wall stood an elaborate feathered altar with eye-catching vibrantly colored snakes and rainbows.

A work table filled an alcove off the living area. Scattered on it were turquoise and coral-colored stones. "Do you make some of that lovely pueblo jewelry I've seen around town?"

Tonito beamed. "Yes. Besides ranching that is what I mainly do. I sell the jewelry to traders in Grants and Gallup."

"I hope this isn't an imposition, but I'd love to watch you work sometime. I've never seen jewelry made."

"Come now and see."

"Are you sure this isn't a bad time?"

"Any time is a good time for jewelry."

Tonito approached his work station and flipped a switch on a grinder. Sandy moved up behind him and watched as he polished a large blue stone, scattering a fine blue-green powder.

"What kinds of jewelry do you make?"

"*Heishi* and *squash blossom* necklaces and rings." He glanced over his shoulder at her. "Whatever people want." He continued to grind the turquoise into rounded stones.

He seemed so absorbed in his task she was surprised when he spoke again.

"Did you have to walk Dixon home from school?"

Sandy heard a noise behind her and turned to see a woman as broad and round-faced as Tonito in the doorway of what appeared to be the kitchen, a toddler clutching her chunky leg. She knew the woman from somewhere, but where?

Then she remembered. She was the woman Luci had snubbed at the general store her first day in San Anselmo. She acknowledged the woman with a nod. The woman nodded in return.

"He wouldn't walk home on his own. He seemed to be afraid of something...or someone."

Tonito abruptly stopped his work. "Yes, he has told us boys were waiting after school to fight him." His expression had turned deadly serious. "We are grateful you helped him today. We do not want him to be fighting. He was right to come to you."

The child could have been badly battered. "If there's a problem, you should let the principal know. He can take care of it."

Tonito flashed his palm in front of her face.

"This is not a problem for the officials. This is our problem."

"Are you sure the school can't help? I won't always be there to walk him home. How do you plan to stop the bullying?"

Tonito turned back to his work. "Dixon's brother walks him home, except when I need Quinton to work on the sheep ranch after school, like today."

The woman came forward. "We raise sheep on a ranch a few miles outside the pueblo, as is our way. I am Cecilia, Dixon's mother. Can I offer you a cool drink?"

About to decline because of her promise to meet with Ben, Sandy noticed Cecilia's expression and changed her mind. "Sure, I'd love one."

"Please have a seat." Cecilia smoothed a clean handwoven blanket over the ripped portion of the sofa.

Sandy gingerly took a seat, concerned the stuffing would overflow under her. Her gaze followed Cecilia into the kitchen, which was a good deal larger than the living room. Judging by appearances, a long narrow Formica table in the middle of the room acted as catch-all and work station. A huge, old-fashioned cast iron stove took up most of the back wall.

Cecilia disappeared for a moment and then reappeared in the doorway to the living room followed by the wobbly toddler. She handed a tall glass to Sandy, who took a sip of the cool mint tea.

"Mrs. Edakee, do you know the reason someone would be out to harm your son?"

Cecilia looked down, much like her son had when questioned, and refused to make eye contact. "For this and that. You never know with kids. They are always fighting over something." She glanced over her shoulder toward her husband. "Tonito, could you turn that infernal machine off for a minute so I can talk to Dixon's teacher?"

The motor ceased and Tonito Edakee ambled over to join the two women. "Sorry, I should never have started."

"Actually, I'm to blame. I got him going," Sandy said in his defense.

Cecilia Edakee flapped her hand. "We cannot blame you, you are our guest. That jewelry is Tonito's life. I have trouble getting him off the machine to do anything else, even take care of the livestock."

Tonito's smile was sheepish. "There are things I get off the machine for." He cocked his head at Cecilia, who wagged a finger at him.

"Remember our guest." Cecilia glanced at Sandy's half-empty glass. "Are you ready for more tea?"

Sandy took a sip. "I'm fine. But about Dixon's problem with the bullies—"

"We appreciate your help," Tonito abruptly interrupted, "but all will be okay. His brother will walk him home tomorrow."

"You have been so kind," Cecilia said. "Can you join us for supper?"

"Thanks, but I can't stay. I'm meeting a friend."

"Maybe you can come back another time?" Cecilia picked up the toddler who was tugging on her skirt.

"Are you certain the school shouldn't be doing anything else for your son?"

"No. We can take care of the problem ourselves. Please do not worry yourself about it." Cecilia took the empty glass Sandy handed her.

Sandy stood, bewildered by the reticence of these people to seek outside intervention to remedy their son's situation. Most parents would jump at the chance for aid from a teacher or an administrator. Why were they being so evasive?

From Dixon's house, Sandy took the main street home so she could pass the general store. She hadn't seen Luci in days and used the opportunity to stop in for a visit.

Luci sat behind the cash register reading a magazine from the rack. The moment she saw Sandy, she shoved it beneath the counter. "Hi, stranger, where have you been?"

Sandy shrugged. "I haven't had time for anything but school since it started."

"So I noticed Saturday when you and Ben roared out of town," Luci said in a mock scolding tone. She shook her head at Sandy, and when she did, multi-stoned silver earrings swung from side to side in dangling snake-like coils.

"Those are the most unusual earrings I've ever seen," Sandy said. "Where did you find them?"

Luci fingered one of them. "In Zuni. My cousin married a silversmith over there. He made them for me. One of a kind."

"I love them." Sandy had the urge to flick one of the earrings with a finger and watch the snake slither away from her touch. "Do you think your cousin's husband could make me a pair like yours?"

"I could ask him, but they wouldn't be exactly the same. I would see to that." She touched the earring. "And I'd make sure he puts better backing on yours. Mine are always slipping out of my ear. So what brings you in today?"

Sandy automatically reached toward a package of cream-filled cupcakes next to the counter, remembered the calorie count on the side of the box, and withdrew her hand. "Just checking in. How are things in the retail business?"

Luci sneered. "Slow as ever. Why not buy something and help us starving Indians out."

"I will, but first I have a question for you."

"Shoot. Oops, I'm not supposed to talk about shooting in the store." Luci grinned from ear to ear. "Ask away."

A car door slammed outside the store and she hesitated, fully expecting another patron, but no one entered the building.

"What do you know about Tonito and Cecilia Edakee?"

She could swear she saw a shadow pass over Luci's face. "What do you want to know?"

"Why anyone would want to beat up their son, Dixon?"

"You like the tough questions, *gringa*. Wait a minute." Luci nodded toward the door as a young girl walked in. They waited while she picked a can of beans off a shelf, paid for it, and left.

Luci turned back to Sandy. "Around here they say the Edakees are witches."

"Why would anyone think such a thing?"

"I don't know the whole story. How do you know them?"

A man stumbled noisily into the store. Sandy looked over in time to see him tilt into a shelf and knock over cans of soup and boxes of cereal. He righted himself and marched as resolutely as he could toward the counter. She'd seen a few drunks in her time, but this guy was soused.

Luci reached under the counter and, much to Sandy's surprise, pulled out a pistol, placing it in front of her. "What do you want, Tony?"

"Ja..m..m." The man's voice wavered.

Luci wagged a finger at him. "Find what you want, buy it, and get out of here."

The man muttered under his breath as he passed Sandy. She managed to step out of his way, but not fast enough to avoid the rotten and festering odor that clung to him. He picked out a bottle of standard brand strawberry preserves, paid for it with a clatter of change dredged from his pockets, along with lint and string, and lurched past her to the door.

As soon as he disappeared, Luci put the gun away. "Can't be too cautious with Rodriquez Ukestine around. He's harmless enough when sober, but mean when drunk."

Sandy stared dumbfounded at Luci. "You pack a pistol?"

"This is the wild west. I've had the bad fortune to be robbed a couple of times. I keep a hunting rifle at home, but it's too bulky to keep in the store. I picked this toy up for protection. I didn't want to shoot Ukestine, just scare him sober. But, if I had to shoot, I would."

The snub-nosed pistol looked nothing like a toy to Sandy. "You're a woman of surprises with a secret side."

Luci chuckled. "No secret. I'm just not going to let my property get away from me again." Luci's unwavering stare suggested she wasn't kidding. "Now what was it you asked me?" Luci frowned in concentration. "Oh, yes. The Edakees."

"Their son's in my class and I had to walk him home today. I just came from there."

"Wow," Luci said. "You've been here a short time and already you're hanging out with bad company. You better watch yourself."

Luci's reaction surprised Sandy. "What in the world?"

"Hang around with witches, you might get witched."

"Do you mean they might place a spell on me?"

"Right. So be careful, *gringa*. The Edakees have many enemies, including that mean drunk you just met."

"Why him?"

"Tonito excluded him from a clan gathering because he was drunk. Ukestine has never forgiven him for that slight."

She didn't believe in witchcraft, but just in case they were up to no good, she had better be cautious around them. "Those people look pretty ordinary to me."

"I hope you're right, *gringa*, but watch your back anyway."

"Don't worry about me." Sandy paid for a granola bar she found among the *Twinkies* and turned toward the door. "I have homework to do. I'll stop by again soon."

"Don't be a stranger," Luci said to her back.

Exhausted after the unexpectedly long day, Sandy spread out on the sofa for a short siesta the moment she arrived home. She let herself sink back into the pillows and closed her eyes.

The rhythm of a drum beating filled her head. She searched for the source of the sound and caught sight of a coven of witches dancing in a circle, chanting an unintelligible verse. The beat of the drum grew louder and louder and persisted even after the witches disappeared. She awoke with a start and sat bolt upright, tingling from head to toe.

The pounding came from the front door. Ben's voice carried through to her. "Anyone home?"

Sandy shook off sleep and stretched. "Just a minute." In slow motion she lazily made her way over to unbolt the door. "I must have dozed off." She yawned. "I had a really strange dream."

Ben entered behind her. "What about?"

"Witches. You know, the kind with long black robes and pointed hats."

He took the seat she indicated on the sofa. "What would make you dream about that?"

"What happened today. Remember that kid I walked home from school, Dixon Edakee? Someone's out to beat him up. Luci thinks he and his family are witches."

"I heard about the Edakees."

"What else did you hear?" Finally, someone who could tell her the full story. She took a seat facing him, all ears. "Why in the world would anyone mistake them for witches?"

"Remember what I mentioned about two children dying mysteriously in the past couple months?

Since then five more people have taken ill and two others have died. No one knows who or what to blame for this epidemic so the Edakees are taking the rap."

The unfairness of this irked her. "Why them?"

"Besides ordinary scapegoating—quite common in this type of situation, where people are afraid and looking for someone to blame—it's pure jealousy. Tonito has made quite a bit of money from his jewelry in the last couple of years. He bought a brand new pickup and a bunch of sheep. Rumor has it his good luck is because he's a witch." Ben paused to remove his jacket. "When two neighbor kids die, whammo, the whole family is labeled."

Sandy snorted. "They're not labeled, they're libeled. I don't understand why someone, a minister or priest, or the law, doesn't stop this insanity in its tracks."

"Doesn't work that way here, I'm afraid. If anyone tries, they'll be ostracized too." He rubbed his brow. "Remember the sheep you saw shot?"

"How could I forget?"

"They belonged to the Edakees."

She covered her mouth with a hand. "How awful."

"That type of retribution is extreme in San Anselmo, but watch yourself. This is exactly what I came to talk to you about. I knew Dixon was in your class and you'd be drawn into this somehow. Be careful."

"Everybody seems to be saying the same thing."

"That's because everybody is concerned. It's better to let the locals handle this matter."

"If they would..."

"They'll do it their way." He frowned, seemed to be searching for words. "Too many whites come here thinking they have all the answers for the natives. I hope you're not one of those types."

Her defenses rose along with her temper. "First of all, I'm not interested in being stereotyped..."

"Neither are the San Anselmos."

"And secondly, I'm not planning on doing anything, but I'm not about to let any of my students be harassed."

He shook his head. "The pueblo culture has been around a long time. These people are steeped in their ways. They've had the same system of beliefs for centuries. You're new here. Sit things out for a time and absorb the culture. It takes at least six months to learn totally new customs. Don't think you can change these people the white way."

What did he know about her expectations? He might be damn attractive sitting here across from her in his tight jeans and tooled cowboy boots, but he had no right to make such a facile assumption. "My main concern is the welfare of Dixon. Don't tell me..."

Ben stopped her with a raised hand. "Just give it time. Get to know what you're dealing with."

"But..."

"Let's drop the whole thing. I stopped by to share a beer with you, not a debate." He reached into the bag he had brought and removed two beers. "Smuggled in from Grants by yours truly to facilitate a mild orgy."

She laughed to defuse the tension between them. She found him more appealing the longer she knew him; she really wasn't up for an argument either. "Is that the nearest place to buy beer?"

"As you may have noticed, this is a dry reservation. No booze allowed. We're officially breaking the law by drinking these."

"What about the town drunk? Where does he get his hooch?"

"Ukestine? You've already met him?"

"In Luci's store today."

"Ukestine's harmless enough, but the stuff he makes from cactus apples isn't. Much stronger than these." He held up a bottle of *Heineken*.

"I'll get glasses." She left to fetch a couple from a kitchen cabinet, unsure his evaluation of Ukestine was even close.

Ben popped the tops on the beers and poured each into a glass, one of which he handed to Sandy. He watched her study the amber liquid before taking a sip. "You know what else would be nice? Since it's beginning to get chilly these nights, I think we should make a fire in the Franklin stove."

Sandy glanced at the black wood-burning stove lording over a corner of the room. "To be honest, I've never started a fire myself. I'm rather leery of the thing."

"You needn't be. Franklin stoves are so efficient the teachers staged a rent strike last winter to force the school board to install them after a really bitter December. Count your blessings."

Sandy shrugged. "I hope all that effort's not wasted on me. I don't even have wood."

"But I do. I'll be right back." Ben left her apartment, returning moments later with an armful of kindling and logs. "Have any paper?"

Sandy gathered sheets of the Albuquerque Journal and wadded them into balls, allowing Ben to build a fire. In minutes, the chill had been chased from the room, a comforting warmth taking its place.

"Isn't this better?" he asked.

"Of course."

The effect of the fire, the alcohol, and Sandy's company combined to lull him into a pleasant mood, even after the tension between them. The Edakees were obviously a touchy subject.

He looked over at Sandy. She too had let down her guard and was curled up on the sofa next to him. "I better throw a few more logs on the fire." When he sat again, he moved a little closer to her. "I can't think of anywhere I'd rather be at this moment than right here beside you."

She sipped her beer and placed it down. "My sentiments exactly."

Heat not created by the fire ignited in him. He snuggled nearer, hoping she wouldn't pull away. She didn't. He glanced over and found her studying him. Staring into her beautiful blues made the urge to kiss her almost unbearable. But when he started to lower his lips to hers, she pulled back.

"I'm sorry...I can't."

"What's the matter?" His voice sounded husky.

"I told you before. I don't know if I'm going to remain on the pueblo beyond this school year. It's not fair to start something I can't finish."

"Why? What would make you leave?"

"Unfinished business in Philadelphia."

Did she mean another man? His peaceful mood crumbled like corn kernels on a grinding stone *metate*. The fire waned in the stove as well as in his loins. Disappointment replaced desire. "I see." All at once it became difficult to breathe. He needed fresh air.

He crossed to the wood stove, swung open the grate and stirred the flame. The small logs had burnt down to charcoal. He was grateful for an excuse to put distance between them.

"I better run by my place and get more wood or we'll run out."

Back in his dimly lit, chilly apartment, Ben shrugged into a down-filled vest and searched in his gadget drawer for the extra long matches. As he clawed his way past screwdrivers and a socket wrench set, he thought of what Sandy had said. He could still smell her perfume on his shirt, feel her in his empty arms. It pained him to consider her leaving San Anselmo within the year. But what had he expected?

His fingers touched a cold, round object and he palmed it. His wife's locket. He turned it over in his hand and studied it. Even after all these years, he had not been able to part with it. Gold with delicate filigree trim, the locket had been Gabriella's favorite treasure. She had worn it faithfully whenever she went out. Until the night they took her away. Now it was all he had left of her.

With a constricting ache in his chest, he slowly opened the locket. Gabriella smiled up at him, her eyes wide and shining. But all he could picture was her eyes the night they hauled her out of the house and out of his life forever. He sensed then what was later confirmed: it would be the last time he ever saw her. He ached all over thinking of her. He was to blame for what happened in El Salvador and he had to live with the guilt of that night for the rest of his days.

He placed the closed locket back in the drawer and quickly closed it. He couldn't face another loss just yet. He had only begun to heal from the last one.

After Ben left for more wood, Sandy took the empty glasses to the kitchen sink and found herself gripping the edge. Her knuckles white with tension, sick at the thought she might lose Ben because of her uncertainty. He had come to mean so much to her, and she had begun to depend on him as a friend and fellow teacher—and something else she didn't even want to name. Too bad she couldn't offer him what she knew he wanted, but it was impossible. The consequences would be too great.

Or would they?

How long had it been since she had let herself go with a man? What was it that frightened her so much? Of course she might move back to Philly if she had the opportunity to be with her son, but was that really the reason for her reticence? Or was it something else?

She didn't know how long she stood by the sink before she heard the slam of the door and Ben's voice calling her name.

By the time she wandered back into the living room, Ben had stuffed the stove full of wood and was stoking the fire. While warmth filled the room, a chill had descended between them. Even though he rejoined her on the sofa and they continued to make small talk, Sandy could sense something was amiss. Not long after returning, Ben excused himself, saying he had to be up early to help the Sanchez family rebuild a fence.

Sandy remained on the sofa long after Ben left, mulling over what had happened. In the last hour their relationship had shifted shape. A barrier had been erected between them. Would she have the nerve to take the risk and raze this impediment? And what would be the consequences of letting herself go with him?

Chapter Six

Sandy turned her attention away from the blackboard, where Sadie Martinez labored to solve a multiplication problem, and scanned the room to see if Dixon waited for her as he did whenever his gangly brother failed to appear outside the door after last bell. The sight of Dixon's soulful eyes, full of hope and trust, touched a nerve deep inside of her and made the job of walking him home from school a purposeful one. But today he was nowhere to be seen. He must have left with his brother when she was preoccupied.

She finished up with Sadie and was wiping the blackboard clean with a damp towel when Dixon stumbled back through the classroom door with a torn shirt, a black eye and various scrapes and scratches. He looked like he could have been a victim of the historical pueblo uprising against the Spanish. She immediately went over and took his face in her hands. His breathing sounded ragged. His eyes held the fixed stare of panic.

"What happened to you? Who did this?"

"They hit me, but...but...I got away." Tears ran down Dixon's bloody face and etched streaks in the dust on his cheeks. He trembled with terror.

She wrapped her arms around him and drew him close, comforting him with murmured words. Finally, the shaking subsided. She checked him over briefly, but most of the abrasions appeared to be superficial.

"Wait here while I get something to clean you up." She went to the sink and soaked down a paper towel. "Who are '*they*,' Dixon?" She turned back to him. "I need to know."

He trembled. "I do not know them well. They are big kids."

"What are their names?"

"I do not know names, teacher."

"Could you point them out to me?"

Dixon looked at her more terrified than before. "No... They jumped me from behind. I could not see them well."

It became apparent he wasn't about to reveal the kids' identities and it would be futile to try and force an answer. Instead she busied herself soaking up blood that seeped from his nose.

Patches of blood had dried on his upper lip and chin. She had to scrub harder to remove them.

"Ouch!" he said, and shoved her hand away.

She stepped back, giving him a moment to catch his breath. "Sorry, I hate to hurt you, but I have to clean you up before your parents see you like this. I'll try to be gentler this time."

She dabbed and blotted up the blood until most of the external signs of the massacre were erased from his face and upper body, then she took Dixon's face in her hands. His wide eyes were still wild with fear. Her heart went out to him, and his parents. How would she feel if this were her own son under attack? She calculated quickly. He would be close to the same age.

The thought that someone would harm this

child, or her child, or any child, infuriated her. Tenderness for Dixon waged war with her indignation; one moment anger inched out sympathy, the next love replaced fear. She couldn't allow this violation to continue while she was on watch. She gave Dixon a protective hug, which he greedily accepted.

"Come on, I'll walk you home."

On their way to the Edakee house, yellow and red leaves crunched underfoot and clung for life on the cottonwood trees that lined the arroyo. When she knocked on the front door, Tonito Edakee opened it and immediately gathered Dixon in his arms, carrying him off to the back of the house. Sandy waited in the doorway until Tonito returned, followed by Cecilia.

Anxiety was written all over Cecilia's face. "Did you see what happened to Dixon, *Tsila*?"

"No, but I wish I had. He showed up in my room in even worse condition than you see him now, saying a couple of big kids had beaten him up. But he wouldn't say who. Most of the damage is a bloody nose, but I don't think it's broken."

"Where was Quinton?" Cecilia ruminated. "Dixon should not have tried to leave without his brother." She took Sandy's arm and led her into the living room. "No matter. Dixon is going to be fine. We will do our best to find out what Dixon knows of the boys once he has settled down. For now we want to thank you for helping him today, *Tsila*. We owe you a great deal."

Tonito stepped forward. "Cecilia's right. It brings us peace to know you are there to help him home."

Sandy accepted Tonito's outstretched hand. "I wish I could have done more to protect him."

"You have done all you can, *Tsila*," Cecilia assured her.

"Why do you keep calling me T...tila?"

Draping an arm around her shoulder, Cecilia chuckled at her pronunciation. "*Tsila*," she explained, "means 'aunt' in San Anselmo. We have adopted you into our family for helping us out with Dixon. You are our aunt now."

Sandy watched the look that passed between Cecilia and Tonito and saw the tenderness and understanding they shared. It moved her to see so much love. "I'm honored, but, if I'm your aunt, doesn't that make me older than you?"

Tonito's rich, full-bodied laugh came right from his belly. His openness and authenticity always disarmed her. "No, *Tsila*, not in San Anselmo. It does not matter how young you are, you can still be our aunt."

Even though a part of her sensed she should be careful since she hardly knew these people, another part swelled with gratitude. She had never expected to find a family in San Anselmo when she couldn't even find her own son in Philadelphia. "I'm touched by this honor and will do my best to live up to the title." She smelled something burning and sniffed the air.

"Oh, the stew..." Cecilia rushed back toward the kitchen, but managed to call over her shoulder, "The first thing you can do is join us for dinner."

A small commotion arose from the kitchen. Cecilia's voice carried back into the room. "Don't worry, the mutton's okay, but the sauce boiled over onto the burner." In the doorway, Cecilia motioned Sandy. "Come and join me. We can talk while I finish cooking."

For the first time Sandy became aware of a conspicuous absence. She looked around. "Where's Maria?"

"Down for a nap," Tonito said. "Go with Cecilia. I will wake Maria when we are ready for supper."

In the kitchen she found Cecilia lifting a large kettle off the burner. She scooped up a dishtowel and helped her place it on an iron grate. "Now that I'm part of the family, I insist on helping with the meal." Sandy washed her hands under the kitchen faucet.

Cecilia smiled. "Then could you take this knife over to the chopping block and slice up that onion?"

Sandy did as ordered. She began to peel the onion. "Where do I put the skin?"

Cecilia opened a door under the sink to expose a large black garbage pail. "In here." She stood back and watched Sandy work. "*Tsila*, I have a request for you."

Sandy stopped in mid-slice and looked through watery eyes at Cecilia.

Cecilia gnawed at a knuckle, obviously hesitant. "I would like your help. I worry about Dixon and what he has been going through. I worry about all of the children."

Sandy put the knife down. "What more can I do for you?"

"Take care of Dixon when he is with you. Make sure he is safe. We have no friends left on the pueblo except my aunt and uncle. I do not know where to turn for help."

Sandy studied the distraught woman, who reminded her so much of her generous and loving sister, Peggy. How she missed her sister, the only real family member she had left. How delightful to have met someone so like her. "I'd be happy to be there, but I do have thirty other pupils." She caught the look in Cecilia's eyes. "I'll do what I can." She wiped her hands on a towel Cecilia handed her. "I don't mind helping out at all, but there are other people in authority who could do more for you."

Cecilia shook her head. "No, *Tsila*. You do not know our ways. No one will help us now." Her mouth lifted again in a small smile, but her eyes remained sad. "I see something special in you. I see it in your eyes. I hear it in the beating of your heart. I know it is in your breath. I can trust you. You will be there when we need you."

Cecilia reached out for Sandy's hand. Her hand was as warm and soft as a baby's. How could she turn this poor woman down when she could see so plainly her fear and pain? "Of course. I'll do everything possible.

When supper was ready, Cecilia invited the family into the kitchen, and they took their seats at the gray speckled Formica table. Dixon was last to appear and was helped to the table by his elder brother, Quinton. Blood no longer dribbled from his nose and bandages covered most of his abrasions. When everyone except Cecilia was seated, Sandy took the empty chair Tonito slid out for her.

Cecilia rubbed her hands against her apron and approached the table. "Quinton, where were you today? You were supposed to walk Dixon home."

Quinton lowered his head. "I went to the sheep ranch. I thought you needed me there."

Tonito raised his hands to gain Cecilia's attention. "There was just a miscommunication. It is all my fault."

Cecilia sighed. "We all need to know who is walking Dixon home from now on. Then there will not be any more problems like the one we had today."

Tonito nodded. "It is time to put today aside. It will not happen again. I promise." Tonito waited for Cecilia to take her seat. *"Naakwee Tonaawe,* Grandparents, let's eat," he said.

At that invitation Quinton picked up a serving spoon and began to ladle stew onto his plate. Suddenly the room came alive with silverware clanking against ceramic plates, glasses clinking against the tabletop, and raised voices requesting the salt or the chili.

Sandy took a modest spoonful of the sheep stew offered to her and cautiously brought it to her lips, hoping she would be as enthusiastic about it as the others. A taste of it reminded her of the lamb chops her mother had grilled for her as a child. She polished off her bowl and pleased Cecilia by accepting a second one.

Tonito finished his meal before anyone else, sat back in his seat and folded his arms over his prominent belly. "After each meal, *Tsila*, we honor the Corn Maidens, who give us our bread, by saying a prayer and sprinkling their gift of cornmeal upon our altar." Tonito rose, stepped over to a rainbow-colored, pyramid-shaped shrine, took a pinch of cornmeal from a bowl, said a few words, and sprinkled the meal over the raised structure. Then he blew into his hands. "The Corn Maidens are glad to have a home in San Anselmo, and so are we. This is our home always. We will never leave our land."

"Thanks to you, I'm beginning to feel at home in San Anselmo, too." Sandy took the cornbread Cecilia offered her and considered the fine handiwork of the Corn Maidens in addition to Cecilia's fine culinary skills.

A shout from outside sent a sudden chill through the room, chasing away the warmth and camaraderie. Everyone at the table froze mid-meal—forks held high, bread only partially broken—except Cecilia, who reached down, scooped Maria into her arms and held the toddler protectively to her chest.

Sandy listened as loud voices shouted harsh words that pierced window panes and boomeranged violently against white walls. They drowned out all other sound. While she couldn't understand what was being said, it was apparent by the tone and manner of their delivery, as well as the way everyone reacted, that they were threats.

The yelling stopped almost as abruptly as it had begun, but no one at the table moved for a couple of long minutes. Behind her, Tonito began to robotically pace the room. Then Quinton sprang to his feet and went to the back door, opening it a crack. He slammed it shut and tore out of the kitchen in a rage.

Sandy sat forward, still a little breathless from the attack, but unable to control her curiosity. "What was that all about?"

Cecilia placed Maria down and sighed. The toddler waddled closer to her, clinging to her skirt and whimpering. "It is the *Kachina, Tsila*. They have been in the habit of coming to yell at us lately."

"What in the world?"

Cecilia distractedly tousled Maria's hair. "We have upset them, made them mad. They keep coming around to let us know of their anger."

Sandy wondered if this upset had anything to do with what Luci and Ben had mentioned. "Any idea what you did to annoy them?"

Cecilia glanced at Tonito, whose expression had closed in on itself like a clenched fist. His frown drew deep lines around his mouth. "They say we have killed two children, but it is not true. Still, there is nothing we can say to change their minds. They will not believe us."

The superstitious injustice of what was

happening broke Sandy's heart. "Why doesn't anyone do anything to stop this? Can't you go to the police for help?"

"No, *Tsila*. They will not help us." Tonito's frown had frozen on his face. "We must handle this ourselves."

"But there has to be something you can do..."

Maria whimpered louder and pawed at Cecilia's dress. Cecilia picked up the crying toddler and carried her into the back room. Dixon had moved into the corner where he cowered against the cabinets. His brother paced the living room like a caged tiger. The air was so thick with tension she had difficulty breathing.

"I don't know how you can stand this. It would drive me batty." Even though the wood-burning stove threw off warmth, she found herself shivering.

"It is, *Tsila*. It is." Tonito made his way toward the door. "I better check on the pickup truck. Make sure they did no damage."

Cecilia insisted on driving Sandy home that evening, even though it was only a short walk. During the drive, Sandy tried to make small talk to lighten the mood, but nothing she said seemed to dispel Cecilia's distress.

At the apartments she spied a light in Ben's window. Although she hadn't seen much of him since the night he dropped by with the beers, he was the only one she could turn to for answers.

She waved goodbye to Cecilia and, as soon as the truck drove off, knocked on Ben's door. A moment later the door opened and, much to her relief, Ben's surprised expression quickly mutated into a smile. He invited her in.

She stepped past him into a living room almost identical in layout to hers, yet entirely different. The look was distinctly male with a dark walnut coffee table in front of a gray sofa, a large Navajo sand-painting on the wall behind. Cinder-block bookcases on the opposite wall held innumerable books stacked in careless piles. A southwestern landscape of an orange and red rock-walled canyon in rough pallet knife technique floated over the wood stove.

"Sorry for stopping by so late, but I have something I want to run by you." She paused, searching for the right words. "I felt funny coming to you, since I haven't seen much of you lately, but I didn't know where else to turn."

Ben tensed at Sandy's implication that he had been avoiding her, but, as much as he liked her, he wasn't about to become involved if she had someone waiting for her in Philadelphia. It would be too difficult to let her go. "What is it?"

"I just had the strangest experience at the Edakees'. They were visited by a couple of really belligerent *Kachina*."

"What did these *Kachina* look like?"

"I don't know, I never had a look at them, but

they sounded mean as hell."

"You might be describing the bogeymen *Kachina*."

She sent him a curious look. "The what?"

"The bogeymen. They're sent to keep children in line if they've been mischievous. The parents put in a request for the bogeymen to help them out when a kid is out of control. They always come at night to scare the kid into obedience."

Her laugh sounded high-pitched. Nervous. "There really are bogeymen here? That's wild. Sounds like something my parents would have threatened me with."

"It works as a form of discipline."

"I bet. The Edakees certainly took them seriously. They were scared to death and never left the table or spoke the whole time those *Kachina* were out there."

"I've never heard of the bogeymen coming to intimidate adults. They usually save their venom for those under twelve. I'll have to ask Kwinsi about this."

"Who's Kwinsi?"

"He's a repository of tribal information. At nearly a hundred years old, he knows as much about San Anselmo as anyone alive."

"I'd love to meet him sometime. I have a ton of questions I'd like answered." Sandy kneaded her hands. "Ben?"

He cocked his head, listening.

"What do you think I should do about this?"

How endearing but naive of her to think she could do anything to help these people. He knew better after El Salvador. He had been in her shoes once—had put himself on the line to help others—and had lost much more than his dignity in the process. He lost a large part of his life. He didn't want to see her destroy hers. "I know how worried you are about this kid and his folks. I am too. But there's really nothing you can do."

"But they're being harassed by these *Kachina*. They're paralyzed with fear. I can't just sit by and watch."

As much as he thought of her as kindhearted and conscientious, he wanted to discourage her from interfering. It would only lead to trouble. "I wish you could do something, but you're an outsider. Anything you do might place you in danger, and the Edakees at greater risk." He took a seat on the sofa. "Respect their ability to solve their own problems."

"I do respect them."

"Then let them deal with this."

"I wish they would, but they don't seem capable of acting."

She looked distraught. It bothered him. "I have an idea. I can ask Kwinsi what he thinks we ought to do."

Her face relaxed. "That would be great. I would really like to have insider advice."

Good to hear her use sound judgment.

She brushed back her hair in her characteristic way. "I just hope this thing blows over soon."

With all his heart he wanted that too. But he doubted it.

Sandy made her way over to the sofa, her limp more evident than usual. "Damn this leg."

Ben watched her progress. "Would it be rude of me to ask where you picked up that limp?"

She flushed, looking down at the offending limb. "I was hoping it wasn't too obvious."

"It usually isn't."

"I hope not." Sandy worried her bottom lip. "A few months before my eighteenth birthday, I was in a car accident. My boyfriend, Adam, was driving when a car rammed us from the rear. We never saw it coming. Our car burst into flames and I was barely able to escape."

Ben patted the sofa and she took a seat next to him. "Is that the guy you're thinking of going back to?"

"Hardly." Sandy swallowed hard, tears filled her eyes. "Adam died in the accident. I was pregnant at the time and a few months later gave birth to our son, Tim. My mother said there was no way I could remain at home and keep the baby. She said I was too young to take care of him and she wasn't prepared to be a mother all over again."

The look of anguish in her eyes caused him to reach toward her, but she brushed away the hand meant to console her. "I begged her to let me keep Tim; tried to convince her I could handle him, but she wouldn't listen. I had to make up my mind. I wasn't ready to leave home, to live on my own. I wasn't even finished with high school and still recuperating from the accident. Without support, I felt I had no choice but to give Tim up. It was one of the hardest things I've ever had to do."

He couldn't believe what he was hearing. "Shit, Sandy. I'm so sorry. I would never have told you about my adoption if I had known."

"I don't want you to hold back on my account. That wouldn't be fair to you." She patted his hand. "I often wonder if my son feels the same way you do about your mother, if he thinks I didn't want him."

He didn't know what to say.

"I have always regretted my decision."

"What else could you have done?"

She shrugged. "For the last eleven years I've been trying to convince myself he's perfectly happy with a perfect family, living the perfect life that I couldn't give him."

She looked up at him, the pain evident in her eyes. "When you told me about those children dying, all I could think about was what if something like that happened to Tim and I never saw him again?"

He hated to see her suffer like this, but it made him wonder whether his own mother's motivation for relinquishing him was more reasonable than he had thought. That perhaps she hadn't been the cold, unfeeling witch he believed her to be. Maybe there was more to the story than he realized. "Your son's probably fine."

"I wish I knew for sure..." Her voice broke. "You have no idea how many sleepless nights I've spent thinking about him and how it must be for him never to know me. To believe that I abandoned him. To think I want nothing to do with him. I've tried everything I can think of to contact him, if only to see him and make sure he's all right, but I've only been met with sealed records and disappointments. If there's ever a chance I might be able to have contact with him, I'd be back in Philadelphia in a heartbeat."

So that's who was beckoning her back. "Is your family still there?"

"Not much family left. My mother died of breast cancer a few years back and my father remarried a year later. He's so involved with his new wife and her family I haven't seen much of him since." She patted her leg. "The limp I was left with on the outside doesn't compare to the one I feel inside. I lost everything. I lost my first love. I lost my first child. And I lost my way."

She hesitated, spooling her hair around a finger, deep in thought. "Even though I'd like to blame my mother for the adoption, I made the final decision. You can say I ran away...from my son, from myself and from any sense I ever had of being safe in the world. Maybe that's why I'm so stubborn at times. I gave up on one child and it changed everything. I'm not about to give up on another."

"I had no idea." At that moment he yearned to

hold her, to comfort her. When her eyes searched his, the sadness in hers made him want to kiss away her pain and shame with a kiss that was soft and warm and eminently healing. All the hurt, all the longing, all the loneliness would coalesce in that one kiss. All he would feel was her lips pressed against his. And his staggering need for her. With a finger he wiped a wisp of hair off her cheek.

The shrill whistle of the kettle pierced through his trance. What had he been thinking? Was he really prepared to face another loss if she moved back east? His indecision proved he wasn't, even if his body suggested otherwise.

"I better take care of that," he muttered and rose to fetch the coffee.

Chapter Seven

Ben waited on Kwinsi's threadbare sofa for the tribal elder to speak. He had stopped by, as he did every day after school to see how Kwinsi was doing, and had taken the opportunity to share with him what Sandy had witnessed.

Kwinsi's rheumy eyes stared off in the distance. "I worry about what is happening, Nephew."

He wasn't alone. "In what way?"

"I sense someone in the tribe wants to make harm for this family."

Ben studied Kwinsi's lined face. As an elder, Kwinsi knew more about what was going on in San Anselmo than an outsider might suspect of a feeble, partially blind old man. With his shamanistic powers, he could identify a problem long before it was apparent to others.

"Do you know who it might be?"

"That is not clear, Nephew, but we will know in time." Kwinsi looked in his direction. "I need your help, Nephew."

"What kind of help?"

Kwinsi spoke slowly, pronouncing each word separately, which seemed to give it special significance. "You must be my eyes and ears. Whatever happens must be done in a tribal way. It is important no outsiders are invited into our tribal troubles."

Ben wasn't sure what Kwinsi was getting at, but

he would never let his friend and community down. "Just tell me what to do."

Kwinsi smiled, exposing yellowed teeth. "You will know what to do when the time is right. Do not allow anyone to interfere in our traditions. Otherwise disaster will follow. Somebody will get hurt."

Ben's throat tightened, thinking about Sandy and the Edakee boy. Kwinsi had confirmed what he already suspected. "I'll do everything I can, Kwinsi. I promise." And he planned to keep his word.

After school, Sandy crammed a pile of freshly minted history papers into her briefcase and made her way to Luci's store to pick up a few items for dinner. Just before turning the corner onto Main Street, she spied the town drunk, Rodriquez Ukestine, reeling across the street, a nasty scowl on his unwashed face. Preoccupied with watching him, she carelessly allowed a report to drop from her satchel onto the dirt road. After he lumbered behind a building and out of sight, she stooped to pick up the file, prepared to move on, when she overheard one of two men standing across the street mention 'witch'. Her interest piqued.

"We do not want witches here," the other man said.

"What do we do then?" the first man asked.

"We must move them."

She straightened in time to see the first man point in the direction of the Edakees' house. He was tall and thin, the other short and squat, the San Anselmo version of Laurel and Hardy. The short one was gesturing with animation. Sandy quickened her pace toward them.

The tall one facing her looked as morose as her last superintendent of schools. He had a dour expression on his long, angular face. From all appearances it seemed her reception would be mixed at best, but she took a deep breath, threw her shoulders back, and approached them anyway. "Excuse me, but I couldn't help but overhear your conversation."

"Yes?" asked the tall one with an arched brow. "Why does that concern you?"

She swallowed hard, ill at ease under his impatient glare.

"I thought I heard you say something about witches."

The thin man's already small eyes narrowed further. "What are you talking about?"

She felt a flush rise under his gaze, much like it used to bloom under her mother's critical stare. "I thought you had mentioned witches..." she mumbled.

The heavyset man flanking her burst into laughter. His jowls shook. "We did not talk of witches. We talked of ditches." He wagged his finger at her in a good-natured way. "That's what happens when you eavesdrop on the conversations of others. You tend to misunderstand."

Heat rose in Sandy's face. Could she have been that mistaken? "I'm sorry. You're right I shouldn't have butted in. I must have misconstrued what you said."

The fat man held out a hand. "And you are...?"

She shook it. "Besides deaf and dim-witted...I'm Sandy Jacobs. The new elementary teacher."

"Welcome to San Anselmo. I am Robert Tsabi and this is Harley Dista. We are both tribal council members who are trying to decide where to locate a drainage ditch."

Sandy had rarely been this embarrassed. "I'm so sorry, I can't think how I..."

"We do not concern ourselves with witches, Miss Jacobs. We run the tribe," Harley said, looking down his long nose at her in a supercilious manner.

"Please forgive me for interrupting you."

"We all make mistakes," Robert replied. "But now if you will excuse us, we must get on with our job. Nice meeting you, Ms. Jacobs."

The two men returned to their conversation and Sandy trudged past them with as much grace as she could muster. Once out of their sight, she slowed and reconsidered. She could not shake the sense that somehow she had not been totally mistaken. An eerie chill at her nape, reminiscent of one she felt when the chalk screeched across the blackboard, had settled in place and remained.

"Luci?" Sandy called as she poked her head around an aisle in the general store, surprised to find her friend missing from her usual seat by the cash resister. When no one answered, she called again, but to no avail.

Rather than waiting for Luci to make an appearance, Sandy busied herself picking out a box of low fat milk and a can of tomato soup she needed for dinner.

She glanced up at the sound of Luci entering from her house behind the store.

Luci looked surprised. "How long have you been here, *gringa*?" she asked. "I didn't hear you come in."

"Only a couple of minutes."

Luci took her seat behind the counter and checked out what Sandy had placed in her basket. "Is that all you came for?"

Sandy added a box of bran cereal and hoisted the basket onto the counter. "Just this and some information."

"You always want to know something. What is it today?"

"It's the Edakees again."

Luci rolled her eyes ceiling-ward. "What now?"

"They're being harassed by a couple of bogeymen *Kachina* because of that ridiculous superstition you mentioned. Can you tell me anything more about it?"

Luci whipped her hand back and forth in front of her face. "The Edakees' business is none of mine."

"Do you mean you haven't heard anything at

all?"

"Do I have to repeat myself?"

"I thought gossip's the big thing around here. So, how come you haven't heard a thing?"

"I'm not saying I haven't heard anything. I'm saying I don't want any part in it. I know what talk does to people. I've learned to ignore it."

Sandy leaned forward. "Then you *have* heard something?"

"No more than you. I really don't want to know. I mind my own business." Luci began to ring up Sandy's purchases.

"You sound like Ben, but I'd sure like some answers about what's going on here."

"Ben's right." Luci placed the cereal in a plastic bag. "You will stir up nothing but more trouble if you bake bread in someone else's oven. You owe me seven dollars and twenty-five cents."

Sandy handed her a bill and accepted the change. "Why are you so suspicious of the Edakees?"

Luci sighed. "Alright, *gringa*, I'll tell you something that ought to make you reconsider what you think about the Edakees. Twenty years ago my father lost our grazing land to Tonito Edakee in a card game, and Tonito has refused to give it back."

"Why should he if he won it fair and square?"

"Because it wasn't my father's to give. Land in San Anselmo belongs to the women. My father was drunk. He didn't know what he was doing. In my opinion, Tonito took advantage of my father's condition and stole that land from us. I will never trust that SOB, and I advise you to do the same."

Perhaps Luci was right. Again she was reminded to keep her eyes open with the Edakees. "That was a long time ago. Perhaps Tonito has changed."

"Not from what I can gather." Luci crossed her arms over her chest and stared straight ahead, stonily silent.

Which did nothing to ease Sandy's anxiety, or quell her concerns.

Back at her apartment, Sandy was stashing her purchases in a kitchen cabinet when she was summoned to the door by a firm knock. She opened it to Ben, who held a small plastic bag in one hand and a large key attached to a wooden stick in the other. He handed her the bag.

She sniffed the sack and caught a whiff of sage with its sweet exotic odor. "Umm, nice," she said. "Where'd you find this?"

"It's the wild sage growing at the base of Rainbow Mesa."

"What a treat. I'll put it in my potatoes tonight." She placed the sack on the kitchen counter. "So besides this wonderful delivery, what brings you by today?"

"Nothing special, except to see you." He jangled the keys. "I was on my way home from my part-time job inputting tribal land records into a computer program and noticed you were home."

"Wow, I had no idea you had a second job. You're a busy man."

"Keeps me off the streets. The tribe wants to organize all their old files, but I could really use a break from all this good clean fun. How about joining me for a shopping trip to Grants this Saturday? I need to stock up on supplies."

She could use a few items herself. "Sounds like an offer I don't want to refuse."

Because of their late start Saturday afternoon, the shopping trip into Grants turned into a dinner date as well. After loading the truck with groceries and school supplies, Ben suggested a nifty little place on the way out of town where they could grab a bite.

Lights strobed into the cab and bathed Sandy in an intermittent glow as the truck meandered past dilapidated motels and old-fashioned coffee shops. Neon lights lit up the night. On the outskirts of town, they made a turn onto a narrow road and drove past a decrepit gas station with a couple of dusty barns. Further along, a handful of adobe houses rimmed the roadside with bundles of red chiles hung drying in what Ben called *ristras* from porch railings. She inhaled the comforting piñon smoke permeating the air.

Ben veered off onto a rutted dirt road and drove up to a small adobe building with '*Eddie's*' labeling the front. He escorted her into what must have once been a living room in the rundown house. Dust motes floated in the dim overhead light beams. Aged rough-hewn wood covered the walls. The knotty wood bar to her left looked as if it could have been used in a John Wayne western, and the table Ben led her to was made from an antique wooden door. She pulled a wobbly ladder-backed chair up to it.

He took the seat across from her. "What would you like to drink?"

"A glass of Chablis."

"One Chablis and one *Bohemia, por favor*," he shouted to a balding, older. hippy-type man behind the bar.

"Coming right up," yelled the bearded man.

The drinks arrived and Ben raised his glass to hers. "*Salud.*" Sandy toasted his and took a sip of wine. The Adagio by Albioni played over a couple of Precambrian speakers behind the bar; the strings filled the air, the drink her head. Before long, the ambience of the bar began to seduce her. Besides being unpretentious, it shimmered with a sense of serenity rather than the typical hustle of an urban club. Her muscles, her joints, even her cells released their saddlebags of tension. A fuzzy feeling she took for gratitude replaced her stress.

"It's lovely here," she said, clanging her glass against his one more time.

His eyes never left her face until, self-conscious, she lowered hers.

"I'm glad you like it."

After munching on the chicken enchiladas Ben had recommended, she preceded him past the bar where he paid the bill and bantered for a minute with the bartender. Outside the cantina a sliver of moon sliced a narrow path through the darkness and lit the way to the truck.

Inside, Ben put a disc of Baroque music in the deck. "...to maintain the mood," he said.

Sandy sat back and listened as strings filled the air with their celestial sound. Uplifted, she could not remember the last time she had felt such peace. Reaching back, she rubbed Ben's shoulders as he drove. As his muscles melted under her fingertips, she became aware of his rough wool shirt and the warm skin beneath. Longing heated the cab.

Closer to home, Sandy silently debated the wisdom of inviting Ben in for a nightcap. The night, while wonderful, seemed incomplete. She studied his profile in the dashboard lights and was about to make the offer when the truck pulled into the apartment lot and there, in the headlights, she spied the lone figure of Dixon Edakee huddled under the portal.

Abruptly, the spell shattered.

What was he doing here at this hour?

She flipped quickly through a list of possible reasons, but the only answers she came up with filled her with dread. The truck screeched to a halt near her door and she ran over to the shivering child.

"Dixon, are you all right?" He looked as startled as a deer they had passed on the side of the road. "What are you doing here so late?"

Dixon's eyes were wide. "My mother sent me to ask you for dinner. She worried you were not home."

"Your mother must be more worried that *you're* not home. Get in the truck. We'll take you there."

Dixon crawled in between Ben and Sandy and they drove him directly home. They had barely pulled up to the house when Cecilia flung open the front door, raced over to the truck and reached over Sandy to gather Dixon into her arms.

"Where were you, Dixon? We were worried!"

"He was waiting at my apartment for me to come home," Sandy said.

Cecilia led Dixon into the house, while beckoning Sandy and Ben inside. Tonito and Quinton waited in the living room.

"I sent him to your house earlier to ask you to dinner," Cecilia said. "When he returned and said you were away, I sent him back with his brother to find you. After that, they were to go to the sheep ranch to check the sheep. I thought he was with Quinton, but Quinton came back alone a few minutes ago saying he dropped Dixon off in town and thought he had gone home."

"It appears he stayed behind to wait for me."

Tonito set his hands on his hips. "He has definitely adopted you, *Tsila*, but—" he turned toward Dixon., "—you worried your mother, boy."

Cecilia shooed Dixon down the hall. "Go to your room and get ready for bed. I'll be in to say goodnight in a little while." Then she took Sandy by the arm. "Since it's too late for dinner, stay and have a cup of tea with us."

Sandy shook her head. "I wish I could, but Ben needs to be somewhere early. I'll take a rain check for another night."

"Then both of you come for supper Tuesday night before the rain dance."

"I'd love to," Sandy said. "See you then." Glancing at the clock and noticing the late hour, she began to urge Ben toward the door.

"I'm afraid I have practice Tuesday," Ben said on his way out. "Another time."

They backed out of the driveway and had only gone about fifty yards down the road when they spotted the flashing light of an ambulance in front of a manufactured home. "That's the Chavez house," Ben said and pulled over. "I'll run in and see what's going on. Wait here."

Ben rushed up the dirt path to the house. The front door opened and he disappeared inside. Sandy strained to see what was happening, but could only make out the silhouettes of people, looking like Indonesian shadow puppets, moving past the picture window.

She put her head back on the seat and must have dozed because Ben woke her when he opened the door. "Bad news. Virgil and Duane's dad Albert died about an hour ago from what looks like a massive hemorrhage. It's a mess in there."

Although drowsy, Sandy went from sleepy to alert in seconds. "So sudden? What happened?"

"I think I mentioned he's been drinking steadily since his daughter died. A blood vessel burst in his esophagus. He bled to death."

Sandy grimaced. "Oh God, Ben. That's terrible."

"Yeah," he said, looking miserable. He sat ramrod straight, his eyes pinned ahead.

Sandy wanted to reach out, to comfort him, but where all evening he had grown closer, he now seemed as far away as Philadelphia. "How is the family faring?"

He frowned. "Yola Chavez is beside herself. Within the last few weeks, she's lost her daughter and now her husband. She was so hysterical the paramedics had to give her a sedative."

"How sad. How about the boys?"

"Those boys have been through too much."

"Is there anything I can do?"

"Not tonight. The extended family's there and the medics have things under control. We'd just be underfoot." Ben clutched the wheel. "I'll take you home to catch some sleep, because you'll need it. Things will be wild in the classroom tomorrow after word gets out. The funeral is tomorrow night." He looked over at her. "Would you come with me?"

His obvious shock and pain sparked her empathy. She ached for Ben. For the Chavez family.

For the children at school who would blame the Edakees for their classmate's tragedy. For the Edakees' added trouble. "Of course I will."

At dusk the next evening, Ben escorted Sandy to the Chavez house. Clouds streaked the sky in purples and grays, creating an ominous mood, foreshadowing the hours ahead. An autumn chill filled the air. Before they reached the front door they were met by a chorus of wails from inside. Unsure what to expect, Sandy hesitated at the sound of the mournful choir, before cautiously following Ben inside.

A group of women in black dresses, their heads covered by shawls, stood in a circle in the middle of the room. Behind them, men sat on chairs against the walls, chanting to themselves.

She looked around for Virgil Chavez and spied him in the corner, looking more gaunt and guarded than ever. The fact that his eyes appeared to have sunk into his head and were underlined by deep charcoal circles worried her. Next to him stood a husky young man who Ben said was Virgil's brother, Duane. In contrast to Virgil's sorrowful stare, Duane's scowl was fury-filled. They both watched closely as Ben made his rounds, introducing Sandy to the family and offering condolences. When he nudged her into the woman's group and joined the men against the wall, she was relieved to be out from under the boys' apparent scrutiny.

An older woman standing nearby graciously took her arm and guided Sandy into the circle. At the center she saw the body of the deceased laid out on the floor, dressed in a white shirt and dark pants. His face had been covered with a coating of finely ground cornmeal, which gave him the appearance of a mime. Sandy half expected him to rise at any moment and shift position. The women around him howled their pain at ritual intervals, sounding more like wild animals caught in steel-tooth traps than any mourners she had ever heard before. Sandy instinctively joined in.

How much later, she was not sure, the trance she had joined was broken by a tug on her arm. Ben maneuvered her outside the circle. "We can leave now."

She nodded her agreement, they said their goodbyes, and slipped out of the house, seemingly unnoticed by everyone but the Chavez boys. Side-by-side they trudged silently through the village toward home.

Nearer her apartment, Sandy found her voice again. "What happens next?"

"They bury the body tomorrow morning after his wife's sister washes him and wraps him in a blanket. Then the men carry him west of the village where he'll be buried along with a number of his worldly possessions to take with him to the *Kachina* Village."

"Does the Chavez family believe in the Christian afterlife or a San Anselmo one?"

"Both. Since they bury their dead so quickly there's no time for a circuit priest or minister to be part of the ritual, but many families will have a more traditional Christian service within a week."

She had to take two steps to each of his to keep pace.

"The mourning continues for three days. On the fourth, they'll take black cornmeal and toss it to darken the road. That way the spirit doesn't return to take anyone with him."

A slight breeze picked up a strand of her hair, brushed it across her cheek. She fancied Albert Chavez's spirit hovered nearby; watching; waiting. She rubbed her arms to comfort herself. Seeing this, Ben draped an arm over her shoulders. "Then it's time to go back to life as usual."

"It won't be too easy for those boys to go back to anything that resembles normal."

Ben nodded. "You're right. They're in for a tough time. And the Edakees as well."

Ben waited impatiently outside Sandy's classroom for all the children to file out before he entered to find Sandy at her desk packing her briefcase with reports. She was so preoccupied he had an opportunity to watch her at work. Her slender fingers clasped the plastic covers. Her ebony hair framed a cameo face. The serious expression in her blue-green eyes provoked a longing he often felt around her. How he wished he could let himself go, be close to her. But he knew better. He cleared his throat and she looked up.

"With everything going on these last couple of days, I forgot to run by you my ideas for the joint assembly on Friday."

"Oh..." she said, but she seemed a thousand miles away. "I forgot all about it."

He picked a book off the desk top and handed it to her. "Since the winter solstice ceremonies are just beginning, I thought we could do something to parallel the tribal rituals. What do you think?"

"I'm sorry. I have so much on my mind... I didn't hear the last part."

He could see she hadn't been listening. "What's going on?"

"The children have been avoiding Dixon the last couple of days. It breaks his little heart."

"I was afraid that would happen."

"I've been trying to make sure he's included in group activities, but I can't insure they treat him kindly when I'm not around. I do my best, but it's not enough." She frowned. "What was that you were saying?"

"It's about the all school assembly. Come on. I'll tell you about it on the way back to the apartments."

The moment they started toward the door, the principal stepped into the room, a sheaf of papers in his hand. "I stopped by to see you, Ms. Jacobs, but I see you have company."

Ben didn't like the tone of Arnie's voice. Against his will, he tensed. "We're on our way out. Is there something you need to tell Ms. Jacobs that can't wait?"

Arnie narrowed his eyelids until his eyes

became mere slits. "It's important enough." He looked directly at Ben. "May I speak with you alone?"

Ben sensed what was coming. He turned to Sandy. "Excuse me for a moment?"

"No problem. I have to organize a few things for tomorrow morning."

He followed Sloan into the hall. "Can you tell me what this is about?

Arnie again narrowed his eyes. "About you and that administrative position you've been hankering after."

The unstated threat in Arnie's voice was plain. Instinctively Ben balled the fist by his side. "And?"

Arnie led him out of Sandy's hearing "Fraternizing with other employees will not endear you to the board. I'm only suggesting you consider the implications of getting too cozy."

Ben's fist tightened. "Where is it written that teachers can't be friends?"

"It's an unwritten law around here that you should be aware of, especially with your ambitions."

"Are you threatening me, Arnie? Because if you are, you might as well come out with it."

"Just a word to the ambitious," Arnie said, judiciously backing off, and none too soon.

Ben would have liked to take a poke at him, but knew better.

While Ben had his own personal reasons for

avoiding a relationship with Sandy, he resented Arnie's intrusion as much as he wanted the administrative position. "I won't be intimidated, Arnie. I'll make my own decision about this."

"I'd reconsider if I were you." Arnie kept his narrowed eyes on Ben as he backed his way to Sandy's room. At the door, he called to her and, when she appeared, handed her the papers before moving off down the hall.

Ben had to take a number of deep breaths to calm his anger before reentering Sandy's room. "Are you ready for that walk?"

She glanced up from the paperwork Sloan had handed her with a shrewd expression in her eyes. "What was that about, or should I ask?"

"It's nothing. Arnie and I just had a little disagreement over some school business."

"By the tone of your voices it sounded like more than a minor disagreement."

"Nothing for you to worry about. Now let's go for that walk."

Sandy gathered her book bag and led him out of the building.

"So," she said as they approached the apartments, "what about this ceremonial thing?"

"In the next three weeks, everyone in San Anselmo will be busy cleaning and preparing the village for the new year. The old year is ritually removed and a new fire is kindled for the new one.

Omens are read for the coming season."

"After what's been going on, I hope the omens are good ones."

"All I can tell you is the ceremonies close with the village being purified and protected for another year."

She gave him a small smile, although he could still see the sadness in her eyes. "I could certainly get behind that."

So could he. "Now let's talk about that school assembly."

Chapter Eight

As promised, on Monday the Edakees sent a note to school with Dixon inviting Sandy to attend the rain dance informally scheduled for Tuesday evening. Sandy accepted the invitation with a gentle ruffle to Dixon's hair.

Shortly after the rain dancers filed out of the plaza at sunset on Tuesday, Sandy walked alongside Cecilia and Tonito to their home. At the front door, she had a strange sensation of being watched and turned to see Virgil and Duane Chavez standing across the road, huddled together, watching her. An invisible, but palpable, dark cloud of pain hung over them. She waved, but they didn't wave back. She thought it odd, but dismissed it as a symptom of their obvious grief.

Once inside the house, Sandy took a seat on the sofa and sipped on a cup of chamomile tea Cecilia had given her just before leaving to tuck Dixon into bed. She rubbed the back of her neck with her free hand and stretched her sore legs. Closing her eyes, she leaned her head back against the sofa cushion.

Angry, raised voices startled her upright. Her stomach immediately cramped as the tea turned to acid in her gut.

Threatening shouts came from outside the house. As the shrieks grew louder and more menacing, Sandy's agitation turned to rage. She had to do everything in her power not to yell for them to stop. A hard object, perhaps a rock, smashed against the exterior wall.

She told herself the harassment would end soon. They would tire of this intimidation and go away. Instead, the violent tirade seemed to escalate and intensify, draining any remaining joy right out of her. When she could no longer stand it, she sidled over to the window and eased the curtain aside. The voices were partially drowned out by the blood thudding in her head.

Her breath caught in her throat. The full moon illuminated two of the most hideous masked creatures she could ever imagine, with long black hair and bulging eyes, stamping back and forth in front of the house. Red splashes resembling blood covered their black tunics. In their hands they carried blood-stained knives and yucca whips. They spat out native words in blood-curdling howls while thrusting their weapons in the direction of the house.

When the one with a large feather in his hair stopped abruptly and pointed his whip at Sandy, she suddenly became aware that a single-paned window was the only thing standing between her and their fury. The feathered one glowered at her and screamed at the top of his lungs. She instinctively jerked back and dropped the curtain, praying she hadn't been identified. The *Kachina* continued to rant, but now she could make out one phrase repeated many times, "*Weat, Weat, Melika.*" A chill traveled down her spine.

Another bout of taunting followed. Then dead silence. She turned to see Cecilia and Tonito behind her surrounding the children like a shield. No one moved or uttered a word until Sandy broke the silence. "What were they saying?"

Cecilia tip-toed over to pull the window drapes tighter. Tonito turned on a lamp. A bead of sweat traveled his cheek.

"They called you a crazy white woman, *Tsila*. This is not good."

"I went to the window to see what they were doing. I'm sorry...I..."

A deep crease had formed on Tonito's brow. "I hope you do not have any trouble from them on our account. Those *Kachina* are *attanni*." His voice trembled.

Sandy rubbed her arms with clammy hands. "What does *attanni* mean?" she asked, although she thought she already knew the answer.

"It means dangerous, *Tsila*. They are said to have cut off a boy's head once for offending them." Tonito ran his index finger across his neck to demonstrate his words.

Her stomach lurched. She reached out to the window ledge with a shaky hand for support. "I don't believe they'd do anything like that to me."

Tonito went to the window and peeked outside. "I hope not, but you must protect yourself."

She cleared her dry throat with a cough. "I'm not worried. I'm an outsider. What can they do to me?" In answer all she got was a worried stare. "What else do they say when they shout at you?"

"They tell us we must leave town. They say we are not wanted here," Cecilia said.

How horrible. She hated to see these people made to feel any more unwanted than they already felt. "Have you thought about what you can do?"

Tonito shook his head soberly. "All we know, *Tsila*, is that this is our home. We will never leave it, no matter what happens."

"Those *Kachina* sounded serious. You have a family to care for—"

Cecilia flashed her palm in front of Sandy's face. "We are serious too, *Tsila*. We are not leaving. They will not scare us away. We are grateful you are here to help us. You are a teacher and you are wise. Together we will know what to do."

Sandy appreciated the compliment, but it wasn't yet deserved. "I've handled my share of problems at school, but this is different. I think we should call the police."

Tonito wagged a finger at her. "We trust you, *Tsila*, and no one else. The police will do nothing for us."

"If it's just pride that's keeping you-"

"In time you will understand. Right now you must respect our decision."

What were they keeping from her?

"We are alone in this, *Tsila*. We must fight our own battles."

Dixon cowered beside his father. Next to him, Quinton looked wound up enough to go after the perpetrators and was only restrained by Tonito's hand on his arm. Cecilia took a step forward to line up in solidarity with her husband. "Enough for now, *Tsila*. We are all tired."

Cecilia turned to Tonito. "You better drive Sandy home tonight. I do not trust she will be safe out there alone."

"Yes, that is right." Tonito trudged over to the coat closet where he wearily shrugged into a gray wool parka that looked about one size too small.

"Wait here," he said to Sandy, then stuck his head out the door and looked around. All clear, he indicated they should go.

Although Sandy protested, she was actually relieved when Tonito insisted on driving her home. Now that the *Kachina* had identified her, she couldn't be sure what lay in store for her. Or for the Edakees. The only thing she knew for certain: it would not be anything that any of them would have wished on their worst enemy.

The next day, the Indian Health Service hospital sent a doctor to address her class on how to use their services. Dr. Neil Kramer had a pale, scholarly-looking face surrounded by curly salt and pepper hair and wire-rim glasses perched on the bridge of his crooked nose. Behind the glasses, she could see piercingly dark, kind eyes.

After his lecture, he waited at her request for the children to rumble out of the room. He was studying a posted book report when she approached him.

"I wanted to thank you so much for taking the time to come and speak to my class."

Dr. Kramer smiled warmly. "I was glad to do it. I enjoyed your students. They were so well behaved."

Perhaps too well behaved. "Do you speak to classes often?"

"Every year since I've been in New Mexico. We want the children to know about our services and not to be afraid to use the hospital when they need it." He glanced at his watch. "I have an appointment, but can I walk you to your car?"

She laughed. "I live just across the yard."

"Oh," he said. "Then you can walk me to mine."

She walked with him to a white *Jeep Cherokee* and stood back while he opened the door. "How long have you been in these parts?"

He laughed. "I should ask you that question with your accent. New York?"

"Philadelphia."

"What a surprise. I'm from Philly too. It's rare to find one of Philly's Finest out here."

"What brought you here?"

"Adventure, primarily." He checked his watch again. "Wish I could chat longer, but I have to run. Tell you what, I'd love to speak with you about our common homeland. Perhaps you have time next week for a quick cup of coffee?"

Why not? She could sure use a friend outside

the pueblo right now. "Where shall we meet?"

"How about the hospital cafeteria in Acoma? Not exactly *Starbucks*, but they have decent java."

"I'm heading to Albuquerque one afternoon next week and could stop by on my way. Would that work for you?"

"I'll give you a call at the number you left." He sent her a salute and ducked into the cab.

She watched Kramer drive off and turned toward home, grateful to be through her long day of multiplication tables and topographical maps, only broken by Kramer's talk. Between the busy day and a restless night's sleep, she could certainly use a rest.

She rummaged in her briefcase for her key, but, before she had a chance to locate it, she glanced up to notice that the front door of her apartment was slightly ajar. That stopped her. Hadn't she locked it when she left that morning? Or had someone made an unexpected—and unwanted—visit?

She knew she shouldn't go inside alone. She should find a phone, should call for help. But rising rage at the thought that her sanctuary may have been disturbed galvanized her into action. Even knowing someone could be lurking inside—waiting, watching, threatening—did not stop her.

Her hand trembled when she pushed the door open and stepped inside, immediately sensing the apartment felt different. It even smelled different. A burnt odor—cedar or pine—hung in the air. She scanned the room, mildly disoriented, feeling as she did after her car had been serviced and there was a minor shift in the seat position, or a slight repositioning of the mirror. Everything looked just like she had left it that morning, yet everything seemed slightly off-kilter.

Before she could determine what made the familiar so different, she sensed whoever had been there was gone. Relieved, she released a long-held breath, before making her way through one room after another seeking signs of damage or disappearance. The longer she looked, the less she saw anything that alarmed her. Nothing looked out of place. Cabinet drawers remained closed. Books were still alphabetically arranged on the shelves. Plates and pans housed in the usual place.

She grabbed the fireplace poker in case her instincts proved wrong and cautiously approached the bedroom. Every muscle tensed. She pushed the door open so hard it would have slammed anyone behind it against the wall.

The room, while empty of intruder, had been turned upside down. All her bureau drawers had been pulled out and dumped haphazardly on the floor. Underwear and socks had been tossed to the floor, shirts and slacks strewn on the bed, jewelry littered the dresser top.

She stood back in horror, sickened by the knowledge her personal belongings had been manhandled in this way by some vile creature. When she was able to calm her racing heart and gather her courage she approached the dresser, fully expecting to find missing pieces of jewelry. She lifted the jewelry box off of the floor and began to place earrings, bracelets and rings back in. Much to her relief she found every prized piece, even her grandmother's marvelous diamond brooch, under the dresser.

Puzzled she had found nothing of value missing, she began to pick up the scattered clothes and place them in the laundry hamper to be washed before wearing. What had the intruder been after? If they hadn't taken anything, what was the purpose of the break-in? She mentally inventoried everything several times before realizing the only item unaccounted for was a green paisley silk scarf she had purchased years ago. She hardly ever wore that scarf, but it had such a distinctive pattern, its absence was evident. *Of all things, why would anyone lift that silly scarf?*

She heard a car pull up to the curb outside and hurried to the living room window to watch Ben step from his truck with an armload of grocery bags. She threw open the sash and called to him.

He immediately ditched the bags on his stoop and came over. "What's up?"

"I had an uninvited guest in my apartment today."

A dark scowl spread over Ben's features. "What kind of uninvited guest?"

"The kind who comes in while you're away from home and helps himself to something."

The frown lines around Ben's eyes deepened. "What's missing?"

She raised her hands in a gesture of confusion. "That's the strange part. From what I can see, the only thing they took was a really old scarf."

Ben's scowl didn't soften at all with the news. "Are you all right?" When she nodded, he said, "If it's okay, I'd like to take a look around."

She stood aside and watched while he paced the entire apartment, checking the ransacked closets and noting her trunk with its contents emptied on the floor. She took a seat on the living room couch, elbows on knees, forehead resting in her palms.

He soon joined her. "Whoever was here seems to have made quite a mess. Are you sure the scarf's all that's missing?"

"As far as I can tell. They didn't take any jewelry, even though the diamond brooch is worth something. I looked as thoroughly as I could through my kitchen cabinets and drawers, but they don't look as if they were touched at all."

"Do you have any idea where they came in?"

In her upset, Sandy hadn't even considered that. "The front door was open, but it hadn't been wrenched or pried. I can't believe I didn't lock it though. I do it automatically after living in Philadelphia."

"I'll check around."

A moment later, she heard him call from the bedroom,

"I think they came through the side window because it's wide open. I better secure all these windows for you so you don't have any more unwelcome visitors. I'll be back in a flash."

While he was away, she called the police and moments after he returned, they followed. While Ben wedged dowels into her window frames, locking them shut, she gave her report. After he finished and the police had left, Sandy poured them both a glass of wine from a bottle she had picked up in Grants.

She took a seat next to him on the sofa and handed him his glass. He placed his down on the coffee table and turned to her.

He opened his mouth, but before he had a chance to lecture her, she said, "You don't have to say anything. I know what you're thinking. You believe this whole break-in was just meant to scare me with a witch doctor pins-in-effigy kind of thing?"

"I hope that's all it was. But it seems to me, whoever broke in meant business. Breaking into your place in full daylight is too big a risk without serious intent."

Sandy placed her wine glass down. "Those awful *Kachina* were at the Edakees' again the other night. I think they may have identified me."

"Shit, Sandy. I don't like this at all. I know how things work around here. If someone develops a vendetta against you, they don't seem to have any back-off. I'm worried about you."

"I'm a big girl." She ignored his skeptical stare. "I don't think this has anything to do with witchcraft, even though someone wants me to believe it does. Those *Kachina* want to run the Edakees off the pueblo. Maybe they want to run me off as well."

"And maybe they intend to do more than just scare you. They may be out for blood. Not yours, of course, but the Edakees'. You're possibly a pawn."

His worried look bothered her. Behind his eyes was a wisdom that could only be acquired through experience. She longed to learn what lessons lay there, to share in his secrets. The thought stirred a flutter in her chest. Part attraction, part foreboding. "Ben, I saw the Chavez boys outside the Edakee house only minutes before those hideous *Kachina* made their appearance. Could they be involved in this?"

Ben frowned. "Virgil and Duane? No way. Those boys have enough to deal with without sticking their noses in this mess."

He obviously didn't take her instincts too seriously, but she wasn't so sure. "They have reason to be upset with the Edakees if they believe the family was behind their sister's death, and maybe their father's too. They have the most compelling motive of anyone I know to want to scare them off."

Ben brushed away her argument with a hand. "I can't believe they'd cause this kind of trouble. They were always good kids in school, not troublemakers. I can't see it."

She couldn't hope to convince him otherwise so why argue with him? "Maybe you're right. There seems to be so many who would like to get rid of the Edakees. It would be hard to tell who's behind those masks."

Ben set his drink down next to hers. "I don't want anything to happen to you. Why don't you stay away from the Edakees for a while?"

She stiffened. The prolonged silence that followed was emotionally deafening. She fiddled with her fingers, recalling the last time she had stayed away from someone in need. Her cousin had been one grade behind her in the same middle school and had quickly become a magnet for every bully who walked the halls and ate lunch in the caffeteria. And, while glaringly obvious, Sandy had ignored his suffering in the interest of protecting her own vulnerable position with the one group of girls who accepted her. She still cringed when thinking about the moment she learned he had killed himself. She had never forgiven herself for being such a wimp and had promised herself then she would never act that way again. Here was a chance to keep that promise. "Ben, you don't understand. They've adopted me. I can't desert them now. Everything will be okay."

He leaned toward her, his dark eyes capturing hers in an impassioned stare. "For Christ's sake Sandy, your apartment was broken into today. You could have been hurt. I don't even want to consider what could have happened."

She couldn't exactly debate his logic and was not about to scoff the shine off their developing friendship by arguing with him further. The break-in had taken the wind out of her. All she wanted now was to find a peaceful place inside herself. "I have a favor to ask of you. I'd really like to know more about these *Kachina*. Could you take me to visit your friend? You know, the old man you mentioned to me."

"You mean Kwinsi?"

She nodded.

"Be careful here, Sandy. You could be stepping into quicksand. You're a good friend and I don't want to see you hurt."

Sandy took his hand. "I just need some information."

He considered her request. "All right, I'll take you to him. But promise me you won't do anything foolish, whatever you learn." He squeezed her fingers.

"That's a promise. Now, how about another glass of wine?" She reached for the bottle. "By the way, what should I call Kwinsi? Is that his proper name?"

"It's actually Clancy Otero."

She picked up the bottle and was about to pour him a glass when she noticed how tense he looked. "Everything's going to be all right. You'll see," she reassured him.

He held out his glass. "I hope you're right. But if what's been happening is any indication, this may be the beginning of bigger problems."

Her stomach cramped at his words. Only the beginning? Then what would follow next?

At Kwinsi's crumbling adobe house, Sandy stood aside while Ben knocked. She could hear the scraping of furniture inside and waited for what seemed an eternity for the old man on the other side to reach the door. When it opened, a man browner than the hills and more leathery than an armadillo stood before her. He stared at her through rheumy eyes. Eyes almost identical to those of an ancient seer's in a picture book she had read to her students more than a year ago and a world away.

His benevolent face and wide smile invited them in.

Ben made the appropriate introductions before Sandy seated herself on the sofa next to him. Kwinsi took a full minute to cover the distance between door and chair. He lowered himself cautiously into a seat across from them. The simple act of greeting and seating them caused him to wheeze like shutters rattling.

When he finally caught his breath, he asked, "What brings you by again today, Nephew?"

"A serious matter upsets my friend Sandy. She asked me if she could speak with you."

Kwinsi eyed Sandy and laughed, a deep throaty laugh that ended in a phlegmy cough. He continued to stare at her through unseeing yet all-seeing eyes. "You look like one of us, sister."

With her long straight black hair she supposed she might be mistaken for Native American from a distance, but that wasn't the case here. Sandy could see the milky film in Kwinsi's eyes and knew cataracts compromised his vision. How long could a person look upon the misfortune of others before their eyes clouded over? Intuitively, she knew she could trust this man.

"Thank you, Mr. Otero, I'm complimented."

"What do you wish to ask of me?"

"The family of one of my students here in the pueblo is being visited by bogeymen *Kachina* on a regular basis. Ben says you know just about everything there is to know about the pueblo. I was hoping you could help me understand what's going on, and why."

Kwinsi considered the question a long time. "Bogeymen usually visit the children one or two times to make them obey their parents."

"This is different. The bogeymen are coming every few nights to scare this family away from the pueblo."

Kwinsi shook his head slowly from side to side. "This is unheard of, sister. I cannot remember this going on in my lifetime."

"But it has happened before?" Ben asked.

"In myth."

Kwinsi sat silent for such a long pause that Sandy thought he would say no more, but he cleared his throat.

"My ceremonial father once told me of a *Kachina* who ran a boy off the pueblo. That was long before my breath came into this world. No, I have heard of nothing like you tell me since that time."

"Is there anything I can do to help these people? They're scared to death." Sandy glanced over at Ben, who was frowning.

Kwinsi again sat in silent contemplation. "The *Kachina* are powerful...supernaturals who take care of us. They bring the rain, which brings the food. But they are temperamental and need to be pleased. If someone has displeased them, there is little you can do."

"But they're only human beings wearing masks. Isn't there something that can be done?"

"You do not understand, sister. When a person puts on the mask of a *Kachina*, he becomes that spirit. He is no longer himself. He is the *Kachina* he impersonates. You cannot interfere with what the spirits decide."

"Is there anything that can be done?"

"No, there is nothing to be done. If you interfere in the workings of the spirits, or break their laws, only misfortune will follow you. You are a mere mortal. It is not your place to rise above the gods."

Disappointment, and a feeling Sandy could only describe as sadness, mingled inside her. The deeper she delved into the situation, the fewer answers she found. After a few more minutes of small talk with Kwinsi, Ben signaled that it was time to leave. They excused themselves, insisting on letting themselves out so they would not disturb the old man further.

On the way back to her apartment, Sandy stared down at the arid, unyielding ground, feeling more defeated than ever. She had placed her hopes on Kwinsi's knowledge to help her find a solution for the Edakees. Instead, all he did was give Ben more ammunition to support his contention she should leave well enough alone.

When they were within arm's reach of her apartment door, Ben stopped Sandy with a hand on her forearm. He turned her toward him. Rather than the triumphant expression she fully expected, his mouth was set in a frown. His eyes solemn.

"Listen to Kwinsi and don't meddle. You might create more problems than you solve."

Sandy took a deep breath. "Kwinsi didn't specifically say I should just leave these people to their fate, Ben. He said there was little I could do to help them. I won't look the other way when they're in obvious danger."

Sandy heard footsteps behind her. Her whole body froze. When she glanced over her shoulder, the English teacher strode past, giving her a short wave. She relaxed, surprised at the intensity of her reaction. She must be more on edge than she realized.

"Let's talk about this where we won't be heard." Ben tugged her just inside her apartment door. Frustration etched the lines more deeply around his eyes and mouth. "You don't seem to realize this is a foreign culture to you, with its own ways. It's not right for you to be judge, jury and police force all rolled into one."

"What are you saying? That I should just sit back and do nothing? I couldn't be so callous."

"You said you recognized your limitations. Stay out of this."

"I wish I could but it's too late for that."

Ben shifted away from her. "I thought you moved to San Anselmo to get away from trouble."

She got the message. While the subtle rejection implicit in his body language stung, she wasn't about to surrender. "I didn't come looking for trouble. Trouble came looking for the Edakees, and now for me too."

"Sandy, you're being pigheaded here. It's against the culture of the pueblo for an outsider to interfere."

"What do you want me to do? Stand by and watch one of my student's suffer? I couldn't be so cold-hearted."

A stricken expression, which looked like anger, but may have been fear, flickered across his features. "Are you implying I have no heart?"

The last thing she wanted was to alienate one of her only friends. "Of course not. I wasn't saying that at all. I just want this to be over with."

"This can end for you right now. All you have to do is remain neutral in a situation which is none of your business."

What she really wanted to do was end their dispute and rekindle the warm, exciting sensations she once had with him, but she could not sell out. Too much was at stake—even life and death. "I hear your advice, Ben, but I need time to think things over."

He stared past her at the Monet print on the far wall. "You can take all the time you need, Sandy, but listen to your head, not your heart. Don't let your emotions rule you."

Was he accusing her of being too emotional? "Easy for you to say from a distance."

Ben shook his head. "I'm only trying to be objective and dispassionate."

Again she heard the judgment in his words. "Are you saying I'm not?"

"In this situation, you're not. I think you identify Dixon with your lost son and are allowing that identification to color your judgment."

His words hit too close to home. Any remaining tender feelings fled. She drew back from him as sharply as if he had smacked her in the face.

"Please don't play psychiatrist," she said, still reeling from his verbal blow. "I'll certainly consider everything you said. But I'll make up my own mind."

Chapter Nine

Sandy stopped by Ben's classroom after school the following day to speak about switching hall duty. She had promised to oversee the talent show the following week and needed every spare second she could find to organize it.

When she peered through the doorway into the open classroom, she spotted Ben in the back sitting knee to knee with Virgil Chavez. The boy had his head down and his shoulders shook as though he was crying. Perhaps Ben had taken what she said more seriously than it seemed. Then she realized Ben was comforting, not confronting. He leaned forward with a hand on Virgil's shoulder, speaking to him in a low, consoling voice. She watched for a minute longer before backing away. She didn't want to interfere, but was deeply touched by his obvious concern for the grieving lad.

She could speak with him later.

Back in her classroom she bent over her desk to pick up a pile of reports and spotted her stolen scarf folded neatly alongside her briefcase. She froze, barely able to breathe. She quickly scanned the room for intruders, noting her only companions were the caged hamsters using the habit-trail on the rear book shelf. She breathed a little easier.

She gingerly picked up the scarf with trembling fingers and three chiseled arrowheads clattered onto her desk. She automatically jumped back, clutching her chest.

After a couple of deep breaths, she picked up each arrowhead and turned them over one by one. Marks etched in the flint could only have been created by primitive tools. Obviously they were artifacts from an earlier era, and probably valuable. Maybe even museum material. Yet, here they were cluttering her desk.

Anger flared in her with the suddenness of a dust devil. If whoever left these crudely chiseled specimens in her scarf to scare intended her off, they hadn't sized her up at all. This provocation wasn't grounds for surrender. This was grounds for a fight. She carefully refolded her scarf around the arrowheads and placed it in her purse, then left for Luci's store.

Sandy had to wait while Luci checked out a customer before she pulled the arrowheads out of her purse. "Someone left me a present." She placed them in Luci's hand.

To her surprise, Luci's hand began to shake. When Sandy looked up she noticed tears in Luci's eyes. "What's wrong? Why are you reacting this way?"

Luci's eyes remained transfixed on the arrowheads. "There's something bad about these. They're witched, I can feel it."

Sandy took an involuntary step back, unnerved by Luci's response. Was it possible Luci sensed a vibration trapped in these arrowheads?

Sandy's earlier resolve wavered. The thought that someone had bothered to break into her apartment to cast a spell on her caused her knees to buckle. She grasped the counter for support.

"Witched? Are you sure?"

"Someone has placed a curse on these arrowheads. It's probably those Edakees. They're up to no good."

"It doesn't make sense it would be them. I…I can't imagine it."

Luci managed a half laugh. "Don't be naïve, *gringa*. They're witches. That's what they do."

"Maybe..." Sandy couldn't help wondering if the claim had any validity. "...or maybe somebody wants me to think it's their doing. To drive a wedge between us."

"I hope that's all there is to it, but I doubt it. This seems like the real thing to me."

Sandy glanced down at the cursed arrowheads in Luci's hand. Had their shiny ebony surface taken on a satanic sheen, or was it her imagination? "What do you suggest I do about them?"

Luci didn't miss a beat. "I have a cousin who's a medicine man. If I were you, I'd have him release the spell."

"It's not that I'm normally superstitious, but in this case, I'd appreciate that."

"Good. I'll drop them by his place when I'm done work. For a few dollars, he'll be happy to help."

She fished a couple of twenty dollar bills out of her wallet and handed them to Luci, who looked at the money with approval.

"I'll come by your apartment when he's done."

"Thanks Luci. You're a real friend." Sandy gave Luci a generous hug. Halfway out the door, she took a quick glance back at Luci, who continued to stare down at the arrowheads in her upturned palm with an expression of dismay.

By the time Luci's knock brought Sandy to the apartment door mauve, peach and magenta streaked the late afternoon sky.. Luci handed her a small bundle wrapped in a dish towel. When Sandy unraveled the towel, the arrowheads gleamed in the lamp light. A strange, exotic scent much like jasmine incense wafted toward her.

"Just returning your gift," Luci said with a small, conspiratorial smile.

"Thanks for taking care of them," Sandy said. "Are these safe?"

"As safe as salt. But as you know, a little salt won't hurt, but too much of it can cause big trouble."

"Are you suggesting they're still cursed?"

"The spell has been lifted, but I wouldn't take any chances and keep them around."

Sandy sniffed. "What in the world is that pungent odor?"

"My cousin uses special herbs to treat them."

Light refracted from the multi-faceted, jet-colored stones. Now that the arrowheads didn't possess any real peril, she had to admire their symmetry and workmanship. Looks could definitely be deceiving.

"Are you sure I can't keep them? It's a shame to discard such valuable merchandise, with so much historical significance. They're really lovely arrowheads."

"Nice but nasty. If I were you, I'd bury them deep. But it's up to you. The curse is gone."

"You're sure of that?"

"My cousin knows what he's doing and he assured me it is so."

Sandy walked Luci to the door and gave her another hug. Her heart swelled with affection for her newest friend.

"Stay away from trouble. Let things take their course," Luci offered as she left. "And be wary of witches."

On his way home from soccer practice, Ben decided to stop by Sandy's apartment and see if he could mollify her after their latest argument with an invitation to dinner. The last thing he wanted to do was offend or alienate Sandy. Whether he wanted to admit it or not, she had come to mean too much to him.

He raised his hand to knock on her door when it flew open and Luci stepped out. What was she doing at Sandy's this time of the evening? Luci nodded and rushed off before he had a chance to ask.

Through the open doorway he spied Sandy standing in the middle of the room, studying her palm. She unconsciously flipped her long ebony hair over her shoulder with the back of her hand and her eyes narrowed in concentration like a scientist studying a slide. A crease formed between her brows when she was deep in thought.

"Taking up palm reading, perhaps?"

Sandy's head shot up and her eyes were wide. "Ben? You scared the hell out of me. I wasn't expecting you. When did you arrive?"

"A couple of minutes ago, but you were too engrossed in your anatomy to notice." He could certainly understand how that could happen. Her anatomy engrossed him too. Then he caught sight of the arrowheads in her palm. Concern squelched his appreciation of her charms. "What's that?"

"A little anonymous gift I received today. Only it wasn't intended as a gift." She extended her palm.

He took two long strides closer. The arrowheads lay side-by-side in her hand. "Where'd they come from?"

"They were wrapped in my stolen scarf and left on my desk at school. Luci thinks they were witched and meant to curse me. She had the curse removed."

All at once the air became too heavy to breath. Kwinsi was right. The arrowheads proved someone was stalking Sandy. He had to stop her from what she was doing before whoever left these cursed totems did. Sandy placed the arrowheads in his hand.

"I don't know what to do with them, Ben. They're too good to dispose of. I'm thinking of keeping them."

He had little concern for what she did with the arrowheads, only what she did to protect herself. This obvious intimidation worried him. If only he knew who was behind it. Any number of people thought the Edakees were witches and all of them had reason to want the family out of the way. Witches meant bad luck and tragedy on the pueblo. The people believed where witches tread, misfortune, illness, and death soon followed. Better to be rid of them.

But how to get through to Sandy. After what happened in El Salvador, he knew he had to find a way to discourage her. He once had the audacity to think he could interfere in the workings of another culture. His hubris had destroyed his life, and Gabriella's. Guilt gnawed at his gut. Turned his dinner into gastric distress. He could not allow history to repeat itself, especially after what Kwinsi had said. He wouldn't be able to live with himself.

"Why don't you give the arrowheads to a museum, or better still, the tribe? They'll know what to do with them. Leave the Edakees alone, too."

"Is that your only advice?"

"I'm just hoping you might wake up and smell the chile before you get yourself in serious trouble."

"Give me some credit here. I've done all right so far in my life."

"That is if you call bringing down the wrath of these bogeymen all right. You have no idea what you're involved in."

Her eyes flashed with fury at him. He wanted

more than anything to stop the struggle between them, to turn the anger in her eyes to longing. But he was as helpless to alter this dance they did as he was to stop the El Salvadoran military. "There's nothing more to do."

"There's something I can do." Sandy looked around the room as though searching for a solution. "I...I...I can go to the tribal police, if I have to. I won't allow this horrible harassment to continue."

His experience with law enforcement in El Salvador had been a disaster. "What do you expect the police to do? They have no better idea of who is behind this than you do."

Sandy shook her lovely head. Her long, dark hair bounced against the shapely curve of her breast. She bit her full bottom lip and looked past him as though she knew he listened to a different drum. "It's their job."

He had to convince her to remain neutral. Her life could depend on it. "The tribal police are basically the mouthpiece of the tribal council and the prevailing local sentiment. They're useless to you."

Sandy balled her fists and pressed them against her hips. If only he could get through to her. The more he wanted to help her, the more he hurt her. What a damned paradox.

She pounded one fist into an open palm. "Well, then... I'll talk to the Bureau of Indian Affairs in Albuquerque."

"Lots of good that will do you. They're more

concerned with land distribution and grazing rights than tribal disputes."

"You're not going to talk me out of doing whatever I can." She stared off into the distance. Behind her he could hear laughter and see children playing in the school playground. Innocent fun. A world apart from where they stood.

"We're educators, Ben. We know that this witch label isn't real. This is superstition working against a family's dignity, their home, their peace of mind. It's *cruel and unreasonable*! You can't possibly believe there's nothing we can do."

He tried to catch her eye, but she immediately looked away. Part of him wanted to fight and part of him wanted to flee, but all of him wanted to clasp her to him forever. Everything he said—everything he did—only pushed her farther away. Now she even questioned his integrity. "Let me look into this, but I won't promise you anything."

"What good will it do if you've already decided it's futile?"

Her eyes held his for a moment, turning from a vibrant blue to a steely gray. If only he could kiss her eyelids shut, and hide her reproach. He reached for her, but she brushed his hand away.

"Don't you care what happens to these people?"

"Sure, I care about them, but I care more about you. Won't you see I'm on your side?"

"All I see is a selfish man willing to let a small boy and his family suffer in order to protect his job."

The sharp edge of her caustic words slashed through him like a blade. Blood rushed to his head; humiliation quickly followed. "If that's all you see, I'm in the wrong place." He stared at her a moment longer before slamming out the door toward Rainbow Mesa. Only a walk would quiet the tornado churning inside.

A short distance from the foot of the mesa he felt compelled to look back. The light from Sandy's apartment illuminated her in the doorway. From a distance, she looked small and sad. He wanted to jog back to her side, gather her into his arms and comfort her, but it was too late. He hesitated a moment longer before continuing to trudge in the direction of the great mesa.

"My mother wants to know if you can come to dinner tonight?" Dixon blushed as though what he had asked might have major ramifications. Like, would you adopt me? Or could you loan me a thousand dollars?

Sandy smiled to herself. She had come to appreciate the shyness of the San Anselmo children and adore their good-natured friendliness. Especially Dixon's. "I'd love to, but aren't I supposed to walk you home anyway?"

"No, Quinton will be here. Mama says come by at seven o'clock."

Sandy's smile lasted only as long as Dixon was in the room. Once Quinton had come and the brothers had gone off, hand in hand, she allowed her heartache to resurface. Her argument with Ben the night before was still fresh in her mind. She wanted to be back in her apartment, nursing her wounds.

But before she could leave the building, she had to clean up the refuse left in the room. She had bent over to pick up the last wad of paper when she heard footsteps in the doorway and looked up to see Arnie Sloan leaning against the door frame, sneering at her. She must have been quite a show. She briskly straightened, swallowing the bitter taste that immediately filled her mouth.

"I'm glad I caught up with you, Sandy." He pushed himself away from the wall and approached her. "I have the recess schedule for this week to show you." He took up position by her side and shoved a piece of paper in front of her face.

He had a way of invading her personal space she didn't like at all. When she took a step away, he moved with her.

"Take a closer look at this."

Sandy glanced at the schedule again, immediately irritated that it had been inconveniently rearranged, without consulting her. "I thought Thursday at two was Eleanor's time to take recess duty, not mine."

"Eleanor had another appointment. She asked me to switch her playground duty. I hope you don't mind."

An inflection in Arnie's voice disturbed her. His hot breath on her neck made her skin crawl.

"I'll be around if you need me to help out."

"That's very kind of you, but the switch doesn't work for me. I had planned to work with Rainy Ramirez on his reading at that time. We've already made arrangements with his folks. It's the only time we could both do it."

"Sounds like you and Eleanor are in the same predicament. Maybe you two can get together and work this out. I'd be willing to do anything that helps you. You know I think a lot of you." To her shock, she felt his fingers grasp her right rear cheek.

She spun on him and grabbed the offending arm, thrusting it firmly away. "Mr. Sloan!"

His silly grin faded. He cleared his throat. "I didn't mean to brush against you like that. It was an accident."

He was close enough to smell the alcohol on his breath. "In the future, keep your hands to yourself."

"I certainly didn't mean to offend you. It was purely accidental."

"Is there anything else you want to tell me or are we through?"

His beady blood-shot eyes narrowed. "Don't mention this little incident to anyone." A sly glint filled his eyes. "There is one more thing." His face took on a menacing expression. "There's a rumor you've become involved in the affairs of a student and his family. Is that true?"

Sandy braced herself with hands on a desk, wondering who was behind this betrayal. "If you mean that I'm trying to help one of my students because he's being harassed after school, then you're right."

"I don't think you understand how we do things around here, Ms. Jacobs, but we try and keep our academic lives separate from our social lives. Since we live in such close proximity to our students, it's important to keep a distance between us and them. Stay out of your students' personal lives. Keep your work separate from your personal life."

Sandy's hackles rose. The man had just taken the liberty to grab her butt and now had the temerity to demand she keep her work and personal life separate. What a farce! "What I do in my free time is not a professional matter."

"I know the school board would see things differently."

So that was his game. Make her feel uneasy about what she was doing so he could hold it over her head. That way he could ensure she wouldn't turn him in for his sexual harassment. Principal or not, she wasn't about to let him intimidate her.

"I wonder how they'd look upon your actions toward me today."

The self-satisfied grin turned nasty. "I can assure you they will take what I say as a principal on the pueblo for more than a decade over the word of a newly hired and unproven teacher. Your job depends on your neutrality. If you appear to be biased toward any individual student, you won't be popular with the school board or the community." Arnie snatched the paper from her hand. "I'll get you a copy of the schedule and leave it in your box."

As soon as he disappeared, Sandy plopped down in one of the student chairs, fuming. She couldn't say anything to anyone about Arnie without him taking retribution. She had nowhere to turn.

She spotted Ben sauntering down the hall and rushed to catch up with him, but he curtly acknowledged her and continued walking as though she wasn't there. "I just had an interesting visit from Arnie," she said to his back.

Ben slowed and allowed her to catch up with him. "Oh?"

"Someone told him about my dealings with the Edakees. Do you have any idea who that someone might be?"

Ben wheeled around with an offended expression. "Are you suggesting I did it?"

"You're the one who wants me to abandon them."

"I might want you to lay off, but I'd never sic Arnie on you."

She believed him, considering what she overheard between them. "Sorry," she mumbled. "It's just that you looked like the most obvious suspect."

"Thanks for your vote of confidence. You don't trust me at all, do you?"

The line between his eyes deepened. His pained expression troubled her. "The way everything is going lately has me confused. The only thing I know for certain is that your friendship means the world to me and I don't want to lose it, Ben."

"I don't see that. You never listen to any of the advice I give you. Why do you even want me around?"

"If anything should happen, I want you there by my side." She hesitated. Apologizing was not one of her strengths. "I didn't mean what I said last night. I was just upset and angry. I shouldn't have taken it out on you. It wasn't fair of me." She reached out to him. "Please don't turn away. I need you more than ever, Ben."

"Why me? You think I'm a selfish brute."

"I'm sorry. I didn't really mean it. Please forgive me."

He studied her for a long moment, and then, shrugged. "Okay. I probably shouldn't do this, but apology accepted. Even though I believe you're diving in way over your head with the Edakees, I'd feel like a damned fool if I wasn't around to toss you a life preserver."

"I could use help now in the form of an answer."

"What's the question?"

"How come Arnie hasn't gotten himself into a whole mess of trouble before this? He just came by my room with alcohol on his breath."

Ben took her arm. "How about if we walk while we talk. There's something I've been meaning to show you."

After her encounter with her boss, she could use

a walk. "Sure."

"Come on."

She gathered her things and followed Ben out of the building and down a dirt road.

"Believe me, Arnie's been reported to the superintendent before, but so far nothing's been done. The only explanation I have is that his wife's best friend is related to a tribal council member."

More reason for her to keep the extent of what happened to herself.

They had covered close to a mile before he stopped at the edge of a tangerine-colored rock canyon. "Here's what I wanted to show you."

The canyon, lit by rays of the late afternoon sun, blazed a vibrant orange-red. The scene was a dead-ringer for the painting she had admired in Ben's apartment. "That's amazing."

He beamed at her enthusiastic reaction. "And look at this." He indicated a sizable mound at her feet.

She glanced down at what looked like any other deposit of sand, soil and clay and wondered about his interest.

He reached down and picked up a stone, ordinary except for its convex shape and smooth surface. He handed it to her and she turned the rock over. An ornamental pattern covered its concave side. "A pottery shard?"

"Exactly. They're all over this place."

She stooped and picked up another shard, and

then another. The hill was littered with broken pottery pieces, as though one of the pueblo gods, in a fit of rage, had smashed one pot after another against the rocks. It dawned on her that she was standing in the midst of an outdoor museum. "Should we be stomping through this sacred ground?"

Ben came up behind her with what appeared to be a piece of limestone and handed it to her with as much care as he would a Ming Dynasty Vase. The gouges around the rock's edge shaped it into a triangle and honed the tip to a fine point. "There's no indication this is sacred ground, but it's definitely an unexcavated ruin. Maybe an Anasazi village."

"So is it true the Anasazi were the ancestors of the pueblo people?"

"That's what the Archeologists believe. The Anasazi had settlements sprinkled all over the Four Corners region for centuries, but they vanished from the area during the twelfth century."

He picked up another rock-like object and turned it over in his hand. "Nobody knows for sure what happened to them. Enemies or drought might have driven them away. When they left, they scattered throughout the region and formed the pueblos that exist today. What you're looking at may well be museum quality."

She remembered the isolated hill on the Edakee land where the sheep grazed, and an idea was unearthed along with the shards. "Is it possible there may be other ruins sprinkled around the pueblo?"

"Sure. That seems likely. There's an

archeologist who's been poking around on the pueblo. The last time I ran into him in town he mentioned that he thinks there's another substantial ruin nearby. Didn't say where, but it's worth checking out." He placed the shard down. "With a flourishing trade in ancient pottery and arrowheads, any one of these sites might be worth a fortune." He studied her. "Why the sudden interest?"

"I don't know. I was just thinking about that hill on the Edakee land. It's isolated in a totally flat landscape. I might be way off base, but it certainly is curious."

Ben considered. "It's worth checking into. If the Edakees do have artifacts on their land, we could alert the proper people to protect the relics and them."

"Do you have the archeologist's name and number? I could contact him."

"Wish I did, but he's only an acquaintance. Next time I see him I'll get it for you." He stroked his chin in contemplation. "And if that doesn't lead anywhere, maybe there are valuable mineral deposits or uranium on the land. There's probably an organization willing to protect those resources."

For once they were on the same page.

"Looks like we have our homework to do." She turned over the arrowhead in her hand. "Wouldn't it be interesting to be an archeologist and uncover an entire civilization? To expose a living record of history."

Ben shrugged. "Interesting but tedious, if you ask me. I've watched the archeologists work. It's a slow and precise process."

She knew he lived his life in broader brush strokes, like those in the canyon painting. She glanced over at the canyon. With the setting sun, it glowed vibrant shades of coral and terracotta, as though it had been painted by Ben with his wide paint brush and palette of natural colors.

"We better head back before it gets dark," he said.

They turned to leave but had only gone a few steps when Ben grasped Sandy's arm.

A couple feet from where they stood, a sidewinder coiled and warned them off with a prolonged rattle. Hearing it, Sandy froze. The snake again sent off an ominous signal with its ringed tail, which reminded her of bacon frying.

"What do we do?" she whispered, never taking her eyes off the serpent.

"Stand perfectly still and keep your eyes open. They tend to travel in pairs." He reached for a stick with three prongs, reminiscent of a devil's trident. With it in hand, he took a step toward the snake and thrust the stick, trapping the snake just beneath the head. By grabbing the back of the snake's head and pulling it up sharply, he locked its jaw open. With his free hand, he removed the stick, lifted the snake and tossed it over the side of a nearby ravine.

Sandy was immediately at his side. "Are you okay?"

He glanced over the ravine. "I'm fine and so is

the snake. It slithered off unharmed. I didn't want to hurt it. It was only doing what comes naturally." He looked back briefly to insure their safety. "Let's get going." He took her hand and they took off in the direction of the apartments.

When they reached her apartment, he walked her to her door.. "Did you know there's an Indian myth about what just happened to us? The people in the pueblo believe that if you cross the path of a snake and escape unharmed, you're due for something else to strike you soon."

"Do you mean we escaped that snake only to be struck again? We have something to look forward to."

He looked straight into her eyes. "Maybe we do."

As she approached the Edakee house that evening, Sandy saw a pale blue *Dodge Ram* pickup truck with a white camper shell parked in front of the driveway and a stranger standing in the doorway speaking with Tonito. Even from a distance she could hear the tone of their conversation. They were definitely not engaged in friendly repartee.

The stranger raised his voice, and Tonito struck a belligerent stance. Spotting Sandy, he pointed in her direction. The other man spun around, and Sandy immediately recognized him as Councilman Harley Dista from the ditch incident. He barely acknowledged her before turning back to Tonito.

"We will talk another time," he said in English.

Tonito scowled. "It is no use, Harley, I will not budge."

"We will see." Harley started down the driveway, but stopped in front of Sandy. "You talk sense into Tonito, teacher. He needs someone to convince him to change his mind." He moved off before she could ask about what.

Tonito marched back into the house. "Come in, *Tsila*," he called over his shoulder.

By the time Sandy entered the house, Tonito had already abandoned the living room and was disappearing down the hall. Cecilia stood in the doorway to the kitchen, baby Maria at her feet. Sandy gave Cecilia a hug.

"What was that about?"

"Harley wants to buy some of our grazing land. He thinks it belongs in his family."

Maria pulled at Cecilia's skirt. Cecilia bent over to pick her up. "Tonito will not sell the land. He needs it to graze our sheep."

"Harley seemed incensed."

"He is a councilman, *Tsila*. He is not used to being told 'no.'"

Maria squirmed and reached out to Sandy. She took the toddler from Cecilia's arms. "I'm not certain he accepted what he heard."

"Harley has no choice. It is our land, not his." Cecilia went back into the kitchen, and Sandy followed, placing Maria in a highchair before taking a seat at the table. Maria pointed at a bowl of cereal.

Absently, Sandy picked up a spoon and started to feed the toddler. "Is there any trouble he could cause you?"

Cecilia stood at the work table, chopping green chile with a sharp knife, which she added to a pot on the stove. The scrumptious odor of onions and peppers wafted to Sandy and her stomach growled.

"I guess he could stir things up with the tribal council."

The spoon froze mid-air, but Maria's demanding fingers on her arm caused her to continue the feeding. "What kind of things?"

Cecilia hesitated before answering, "Just this and that. Do not worry about it. It is our problem."

"Do you think he's behind this harassment?"

"Nah. If Harley wanted something done, he would find a way to make it happen without having to harass anyone."

"I guess that's one of the benefits of power." Sandy turned her attention back to the toddler, mopping up the oatmeal she had let dribble down the child's chin when distracted.

Cecilia stirred the wrought-iron pot on the stove. "So tell me about that good-looking man who came by with you the other night."

She obviously wanted to change the subject, but she had picked the right diversion. "What do you want to know?"

Cecilia grinned ruefully. "Do you like him?"

Like him? That was an understatement. She was crazy about him. "Of course. He's a good friend."

Cecilia wagged the spoon at her. "I mean...you know...*like* him?"

She didn't know what to say. "No," she fibbed, "not in that way." Only when Maria clasped her finger did she realize she had stopped feeding her again.

Hands on hips, Cecilia pulled a skeptical expression and shook her head. "I do not know, *Tsila*, but I think you might be yanking my leg."

What could Sandy say?

A warm, rich aroma filled the kitchen. Cecilia called Tonito, Quinton and Dixon to the table while Sandy ladled each of them a steaming bowl, then joined them.

Sandy tasted hers. "This is delish. What is it?"

Cecilia beamed. "I am glad you like it."

Tonito looked up from his meal and chuckled. "This is Cecilia's favorite dish. I would never have heard the end of it if you did not like it, *Tsila*."

Cecilia shot him a look of mock contempt. "Do not make Sandy feel like she needs to compliment me."

"Why not? I do." Tonito reached over and pinched Cecilia's arm.

"Ouch." Cecilia drew back playfully.

Sandy took another taste while watching their gentle sparing. The stew was rich in flavor, subtle in texture. "I've never tasted anything like this before. What is it?"

"Tripe," Tonito said. "Stomach lining."

The spoon slipped from her fingers and clanked against the bowl.

Tonito guffawed. "Eating tripe is part of your initiation into our family, *Tsila*." He laughed a deep belly laugh.

Everyone joined Tonito in laughing at her reaction. In the midst of their amusement it took a moment for the shouts to reach them, but no time for them to slice through the gaiety with sword-like suddenness, severing all sense of camaraderie.

Outside voices rose in taunting tirades of Native tongue.

Sandy froze along with everyone else at the table, but the words tore into her as if stony points pierced her heart. The tension in the room ratcheted up slowly like the stew simmering on the stove until it reached a fevered boil. A rock smashed through the kitchen window, missed Dixon's head by a couple of inches, and crashed to the kitchen floor.

Sandy sprung to her feet, too rattled to respond to a whispered, "No, *Tsila*," from Cecilia. She flung open the kitchen door to face the two gruesome-looking *Kachina* she had seen before. The minute they spotted her, the yelling exploded into a violent rant and they thrust their blood-tipped knives in her direction.

Too furious to be intimidated, she refused to back down. "Cowards!" she shouted. "You come hidden behind masks to torment these poor people. Go away and leave them alone."

Instead, the *Kachina* spat harsh sounding words while brandishing their weapons.

"Go away or I will call the authorities."

She stood her ground against their taunts, ignoring the hammering of her heart and the cold sweat that oozed onto her brow. Finally, the *Kachina* slipped away into the darkness and she retreated into the house. Tonito watched her from across the room, a taciturn expression plastered on his face. His audible sigh was followed by a shake of his head. Everyone else sat stiffly at the table, eyes glued to her.

Tonito rose and went over to stand behind Cecilia's chair. "What do you mean about taking action, *Tsila*?"

Sandy took a seat across from Cecilia. "There must be a way to stop them. They're just hoodlums in disguise."

"You are brave but foolish," Tonito said. "They have the power of *Kachina*. Nothing you can do will change that. The river must run its course."

"I can't allow this to continue, Tonito. You asked me to help you. I plan to do just that."

Cecilia moved Maria from her lap back into the highchair. "We appreciate what you are trying to do, *Tsila*, but we worry about you. You are too little a person to stand up to the great spirits."

Sandy gave her a sad smile. "Don't worry about me. You have enough to worry about yourself." Even though she spoke with as much conviction as she could muster, the words tasted hollow.

She didn't feel half as strong and confident as she tried to appear. Beneath her brave face and bravado lay confusion and uncertainty.

Chapter Ten

On her way home from the Edakees', Sandy noticed a light shining through the tattered curtains of Luci's store, illuminating a small corner of the night. She hadn't seen Luci in days so she gave the front door a try and it slid open with a little shove. Not seeing anyone in the store, she was about to leave when she heard murmurs coming from the back room.

"Hello," she called. The voices hushed and the yellowing curtains that separated the store from the living quarters parted slightly. An older, heavier version of Luci peered into the store and then vanished. A second later, Luci appeared.

"What brings you here this late, *gringa*?"

"I was on my way home from the Edakees' and saw your light. I hope I'm not intruding."

Luci gave her a contemptuous look. "Hanging out with them again?"

"I'll go anywhere someone will feed me," Sandy quipped, hoping to avoid another head-on collision with Luci.

Luci shook her head and stepped behind the counter. "Want anything?"

"I stopped by to talk, but it looks as if you have company."

"Only my sister Ona. Since her husband's a councilman and works late, I invited her over to keep me company."

"I just met a couple of councilmen, Harley Dista and Robert Tsabi. Is either one of them your brother-in-law?"

"Harley's been my sister's husband for many summers."

Interesting. "Harley was at the Edakees' earlier this evening. From what they told me he wants to buy a piece of their land. Do you know anything about that?"

Luci shook her head. "None of my business. I keep my sheep in my own pasture."

"Not long after Harley left, those gruesome *Kachina* came by again. I can't help wondering if there is a connection between the two visits."

"What kind of connection? You're beginning to sound as paranoid as those Indians out there."

Perhaps she did, but she could no longer discriminate between fact and fiction. Paranoia and truth. She looked down at the old wood floor, cracked and splintered. She felt as fractured as the floor. She wondered whether she should take this thing any further or let it lie, as Ben was urging her to do.

"I know you're not exactly a fan of the Edakees, but couldn't you ask your brother-in-law to intervene on their behalf with the tribal council? If only someone would punish the people who are heckling them, it would end. This harassment has nothing to do with your land conflict."

Luci's laugh was dry and harsh. "The tribal council doesn't involve itself in personal problems."

"But it's more than just a personal problem when an entire family is being treated unfairly." Sandy could hear the desperation in her voice.

Luci regarded Sandy for a long, silent moment. Finally she said, "Because I like you, *gringa*, I'll do what I can."

A small glimmer of hope. "Thank you, Luci. You don't know what this means to me."

"This is not a simple request. I have to walk Ona home in a few minutes and I'll try to talk with Harley then, but don't get your hopes up too high."

Too late for hope control. She had placed all her bets on Luci. Where else could she turn?

Not wanting to delay Luci, Sandy said her goodbyes and left. Darkness and a light fog accompanied by neither streetlights nor moon closed in around her. She wrapped her jacket closer, but a chill permeated it. She couldn't see more than a few feet ahead.

At the creak of a step, she froze, heart racing. She searched the street, peering into the dark, then moved on. Slightly disoriented in the dark, she hesitated at the post office before stumbling forward.

She hadn't taken more than a couple of strides when she heard a shuffle of feet behind her. She shuddered and tried desperately to see who was there. A slender silhouette ducked behind an adjoining building. A dark ghost. A pueblo poltergeist. Shivers ran down her spine.

She thought of turning back to Luci's store, but

the light had been extinguished. Since Luci had been on her way out, the store was probably locked down.

Instead, Sandy made a dash for the apartments. She hadn't gone more than half a block before the sound of footfalls behind her propelled her to pick up her pace. Her heart pounded in rhythm with her feet.

She fumbled in her pants pocket for her key. Knowing her shaky fingers could never open her door fast enough in the dark, she targeted Ben's apartment, pounding bare palms against rough unpainted wood. The splinter that pierced her palm sharpened her sense of reality.

"Help, Ben! It's Sandy. Let me in! Please let me in!"

The footsteps slowed. A shadowy figure disappeared behind the apartment building. With adrenalin coursing, she knocked again, repeating her plea. If the door didn't open soon, the 'ghost' might make a move, bundle her up and carry her back to its ancestral home. Or worse.

The door sprung open and she threw herself across the threshold. "Close the door! Someone out there's after me!"

Ben slammed the door shut. "Shit Sandy!"

She bent over, hands on thighs, trying to catch her breath. "I was being followed."

Ben opened the door a crack and peered outside. "No one's out there..." He stepped outside and looked around, before closing the door behind himself. "Did you see who it was?"

"No. It's too dark."

He threw the dead-bolt. "But you're sure they were after you?"

"They followed me here."

He wrapped an arm around her and led her to a sofa seat. "Are you all right?"

With a hand over her racing heart, she nodded. "I am now."

Ben grabbed his jacket from a clothes tree. "Okay, then wait here. I'd better go hunt them down."

"But they must be far away by now."

"I won't take any chances. Lock the door behind me." He tore out of the apartment.

While he was gone, she paced the room, unable to sit. On one of her many passes, she noticed the key Ben had carried home from the tribal offices. She stared at the key, tempted to lift it. Torn between her loyalty to Ben and her desire to peruse the tribal land records, she debated what to do. Finally, the devil won out. She quickly sequestered the key in her daypack and took a seat on the sofa, waiting for him to return.

He did, five minutes later, an expression of distress etching lines on his forehead. "I don't see anyone around."

He removed his jacket, draping it over a chair. "I know I'm not supposed to say anything, Sandy, but these incidents are adding up . This Edakee thing has already led to your place being broken into, a curse being placed on your head, and now this. What's next?"

"I know, I know." She levered the blinds and peered out the window one last time. The parking lot and schoolyard were empty. "That scared the hell out of me."

"It doesn't exactly make me feel secure either."

What could she say without rubbing sand into a sore subject? "How about a beer?"

He studied her in the dim porch light which streamed through the partially drawn blinds, a stern expression in his eyes. "I promised myself I wouldn't say anything more about this and I'd like to keep that promise, but..."

She could sense him bite back harsh words. Her head had begun to ache. With thumb and index finger, she massaged the bridge of her nose. "I know how you feel, and I also know how Luci feels and how Arnie feels. Everyone is on your side."

Ben combed fingers through the hair falling across his face. "I'm not taking sides, Sandy. I just want you to be safe."

"I only hope Luci can do something."

Ben furrowed his brow. "Why Luci?"

"I asked her to speak to her brother-in-law about approaching the tribal council. Maybe they can come up with a solution to this trouble."

Ben's dour expression lifted. He even smiled. "Great. Let them handle it." He brushed one palm against the other as though brushing the problem away. "How about that beer?"

He returned minutes later with two beers, handing one to Sandy and taking the other to a seat next to her on the sofa. His thigh brushed hers, but she shifted away.

"I don't bite."

"But you do sting. You may mean well, but your attitude has not made things easier for me."

"I'm not trying to make things more difficult—"

"But you are. You've really surprised me, Ben. I expected you to be the kind to stand up for an underdog. I should have listened to my sister when she said expectations were just premature disappointments."

"I don't like disappointing you." He lowered his eyes and then raised them to hers. "Listen, I have an idea. I'm not crazy about involving others in this, but if the thing with Harley doesn't work out, I know someone I might be able to speak to about it."

"Who?"

"The pueblo governor. I had an opportunity to meet him last year when I organized a campaign to raise money for kids with special learning needs. I'd be willing to set up a meeting with him and see if I can argue your case. If anyone can do something to help you, he can. With him in your court, you'll probably have the problem licked."

Her spirits soared. "Why didn't you mention him before?"

"To be honest, I didn't think about it until you

mentioned the tribal council. I'm not exactly his best friend. I only met him briefly on a couple of occasions, but it can't hurt to try."

Grateful, she threw her arms around his neck and gave him a big hug. When she looked up, he was looking down at her with a gaze that went straight to her heart. "You can't imagine how much this means to me."

"I think I can, but curb your enthusiasm until we hear what the governor has to say."

Of course, he was right. The outcome was unpredictable. She picked up her beer and took a sip, but her hands still shook from fright and beer sloshed on her upper lip. Ben gently wiped away the foam with his fingertips.

The dark force that lurked behind the recent series of events seemed to be gaining a momentum of its own. An unforeseen centrifugal force was pulling her into the center of an indescribable fray. Her only hope lay in the kindness of friends and the willingness of authority.

At dusk the following day, Sandy retrieved the key she had placed in her top drawer and left the apartment. Dressed all in black, she drew her hoodie over her head and scurried off in the direction of the tribal offices. Once there, she used the key to open the main door, slipped inside and took the hallway in search of the records room. The majority of the offices were on the first floor and she quickly located the one in question toward the rear of the building. After surveying the hallway to make sure no one saw her, she stepped into the office, locked the door behind her, and flicked on her flashlight.

The flashlight beam revealed a large wooden desk along one wall and file cabinets along the other three. On closer inspection, she noticed that the drawer fronts were labeled alphabetically. She had to drop down on her knees to locate the one labeled D-F. With the flashlight on the floor, she rummaged through the drawer and found a file with the Edakee name typed on the tab. She carried the file to a nearby table and opened it, rifling through the pile of papers, piece by piece.

After combing through most of the file, she had found nothing. Most of the pages contained information that was unrelated to the land transaction and useless to her, concerning land that had been in Tonito's family for as long as there was a record. It looked as if she had taken an expedition into futility when her eyes alighted on a piece of paper folded in half. She unfolded it to discover a hand-written note assigning Tonito Edakee grazing land, signed by Harley Dista in 1989.

The paper trembled in her unsteady hand. According to the note, Harley had sold forty acres of land to Tonito Edakee eleven years earlier. This document absolutely refuted Luci's story about her father losing the land to Tonito in a card game.

She sat back, perplexed. Why the hell would Luci lie to her?

A voice just outside the room alerted her to the

presence of others. She quickly extinguished her flashlight, hoisted her daypack onto her back, and slid as quietly as she could into an adjacent closet. In the dark, she stumbled over a bucket, which scraped against the ground. She froze. Had she been heard? Sweat broke out on her brow.

The sound of a door opening reached her, then light streamed through the crack under the closet door. Her heart did a back-flip. A couple of uniforms hung on a rail at the back of the closet. She quickly and quietly slithered behind them and held her breath, afraid to move. Every muscle in her body tensed with the sound of a door knob turning. Someone she couldn't see stood inches from where she hid She prayed they didn't notice her feet only partially hidden under the uniforms.

Whoever was there took what seemed an eternity in the closet before they finally shut the door. She released the long-held breath, waiting a good five minutes after the office light had been switched off and the outside door closed to leave her hiding place. With the closet door cracked, she made sure the room was empty before reentering it.

She folded the note she held in her trembling hand and placed it into her daypack, then slipped the file back into the cabinet and let herself out of the room. Once outside the building, she released a deep breath of relief and started back toward the apartments.

But before she went home, she had one more thing to do. She knocked on Ben's door. He answered and gestured her inside.

"I was just about to make dinner but I'm totally

out of butter. Could you spare me a stick?"

He grinned. "Sure. I just happen to have one. I'll get it for you."

As soon as he was out of sight, she scrambled to locate the key in her pack, but it had fallen beneath a heavy history book and she had to dig it out. She was about to hang it on the wall when she heard Ben's voice behind her. "What are you doing?"

Her hand froze in mid-air. Slowly she turned around. "I was just looking at this key." She held it up.

He cocked a brow. "Why would it be of interest to you?"

"I was wondering why you had such an important looking key hanging on your wall."

He put the butter down on a shelf and approached her. "Don't lie to me, Sandy. I know you too well. What the hell are you up to?"

His eyes caught hers as hers flickered. Too late. She'd been caught. "Okay. You caught me in the act. I borrowed the key. That's all."

He took her shoulders in his hands. "And what did you do with it?"

She swallowed hard, afraid of his reaction. "I searched through the tribal records for information about the Edakee land."

A look she could only describe as disappointment spread over his face. "Do you know what you just did? You betrayed my trust and took advantage of our friendship. And you could have cost us both our jobs."

She could feel her face heat. The last thing in the world she wanted to do was hurt him. "I'm sorry, Ben. I never meant to cause you any trouble. I just wanted to find out if there was anything about the Edakee land that might explain the harassment."

Ben crossed his arms over his chest. "Do you realize the position you've placed me in with the tribe? Doesn't our friendship mean anything to you at all?"

His eyes bored into hers and she had to look away. "If I'm caught, I'll take full responsibility. I'll tell them you have nothing to do with this."

"Can't you see that Arnie Sloan is gunning for me? He'd use any excuse to fire me."

She looked down in shame. "I would never...I never thought—"

"Exactly my point."

"I'm so sorry, Ben. I don't know what to say." She extracted the note from her backpack. "At least take a look at what I found." She placed the note in front of his face. "I have a signed document that shows Harley sold his family's grazing land to Tonito Edakee."

Ben took the note from her and looked it over. "What does this prove?"

"It actually disproves what Luci's been saying all along, that the Edakees stole the land from her father in a card game."

"So what? People create stories all the time to

cover up a mistake. That doesn't prove anything."

She placed a hand on his arm. "Perhaps, but there's a reason Luci lied to me. I might not be a math whiz, but it just doesn't add up."

"What are you thinking?"

"I'm not sure yet, but there's something Luci's not telling me. And it might explain why Harley might want this land back."

Ben shrugged. "You're assuming it's Harley, but there are others who may want the land. How about Arnie Sloan? He asked me one time to check around for a piece of land for him." He scratched his head. "And how do we even know the land has anything to do with the harassment? There are plenty of people whose only motivation for tormenting the Edakees is to run the witches off the pueblo."

Of course he was right. She stuffed the document back in her pack. "I'm going to figure this out if it's the last thing I do."

The look in Ben's eyes made her tremble. "And that's exactly what's worrying me."

Ben unlocked the door to his apartment and let himself in. Today hadn't been a good day. He'd only seen Sandy for a minute at lunch, but the tension had been thick between them, their interaction stiff and awkward. He wished this whole Edakee thing would go away. That they could return to a time before it all began and start over again.

Thinking of her stirred up intense longing. Trying to hold onto Sandy was like trying to hold onto a wet bar of soap. The more he wanted her, the more he needed her, the farther she slipped away. The Edakee thing had driven a wedge between them, a much wider wedge than even the possibility Sandy might move back to Philadelphia.

He tossed a stack of reports on the dining room table and headed into the kitchen for a glass of milk. In the doorway he noticed the answering machine blinking. He pressed the button and Sandy's rich, warm contralto voice flowed back at him, caressing him. It filled the room and his head.

"Ben, I wanted to tell you how awful I feel about the position I put you in yesterday. I know there's no excuse for my actions. I can only hope you'll forgive me."

The machine clicked off, but her voice lingered in his mind. He replayed the tape a couple more times, then held his finger over the delete button, but didn't push it.

He'd erase it later.

Sandy dropped off a stack of paperwork at her apartment, where she changed into jeans and a turquoise knit sweater. She climbed into her *Toyota* and veered out of the lot for her trip into Albuquerque. First stop, coffee with Dr. Neil Kramer at the Acoma Indian Hospital. She turned the corner and saw Harley Dista's pale blue pickup swerve out of a parking spot and onto the street in front of her. What was his rush at that time of day?

She eased back on the accelerator and followed him at a distance to Interstate 40 where he took the ramp heading east. She stayed two car lengths behind him, continuing to keep his distinctive baby blue pickup in her sights and tailed him past two exits to the turn-off for Acoma pueblo. He pulled into the parking lot of the *Sky City Casino*, locked his truck, and entered the building.

Curious, she slipped into the casino a few minutes later and found him sitting by an electronic slot machine, pumping money into its greedy mouth. While she watched, an official looking man with a badge she couldn't read from her distance walked over to the machine and stood by. He chatted with Harley as though he knew him well, which made her wonder if Harley frequented the casino often.

Harley raised his eyes and she quickly ducked behind a machine. As soon as he was preoccupied once more, she noted her suspicions and backed out the door.

The cafeteria server handed Sandy her coffee and she joined Neil Kramer at the end of a long table. "It's nice to take a break from the pueblo once in awhile."

Neil took a sip. "Don't get away often enough? I'll have to see what I can do about that."

She smiled, but her heart wasn't in it. "My job's rather all consuming. I want to do the best I can with my students, but I often feel like I don't know enough about these kids or the culture. I feel really lost at times."

"I remember feeling the same way at first. It's a brave new world out here. But I'm sure you're doing just fine."

"I certainly hope so."

He chuckled to himself. "You can take the girl out of Philadelphia, but you can't take the accent out of the girl. I meant to ask the last time we met what part of Philadelphia you were from?"

"Lower Merion. And you?"

"Cheltenham."

"No kidding. Did you go to Cheltenham High?"

"Class of '81."

"Do you know Sandy Silverman?"

Kramer flashed a wide smile with straight white teeth. "Don't tell me we're going to play Jewish Geography in the middle of Acoma."

Sandy gave him a sheepish smile. "It's so good to meet someone from home. How long have you been out here?"

Kramer toyed with the stethoscope still slung over his shoulders. "Two years since I finished my residency at Hahnemann Hospital."

"A real homegrown Philly boy. It's hard to believe."

"And you?" he asked. "How long here?"

"Three months."

"Are you still in culture shock?"

"Been there, done that. I think I'm beginning to make the adjustment."

"You're quick," he said.

She smiled to herself, thinking of Ben. "So I've been told. What besides adventure brought you here?"

"I had student loans that needed to be repaid. If you serve in the Indian Health Service, the government pays them for you. That, coupled with the need to escape Philadelphia. I had enough of the big city. I needed something smaller. How about you?"

"I needed a change too." She put her cup down. "And I've certainly found one. That's what I'd like to talk to you about..."

Before she could finish, he saluted a bird-thin nurse passing the table. "That's Susan Taylor. Her husband Dirk is an archeologist working on the pueblos. He's spent quite a bit of time in San Anselmo. You might have bumped into him."

"Not yet. I've been too busy to get out much, but I've heard about him."

Neil took a sip. "He's an interesting fellow. Seems he's located what he believes to be a ruin under a hill on your reservation. He's anxious to get to the artifacts before the black marketers do, but it takes time to get permission to excavate. I guess it's quite a process."

"How would you recognize one of these hills?"

"From what he told me they usually stand alone and there's no other geological reason they should exist, like a nearby mountain or evidence of earthquake or upheaval. That's often his first tip-off."

Like the Edakee land. "How valuable would a village like that be?"

Neil whistled. "You can't even imagine."

Or could she? "I've been working with a family who are being forced off their land. I keep wondering why. They have a hill on their land like the one you're describing."

Neil looked interested. "If you'd let me know something about the place, I could run it by Dirk."

"I'd appreciate that, but I'd really like to talk to him myself. Could you ask his wife for his number?"

"No problem." He glanced around. "She's left, but I'm sure I'll run into her later. How about if I give you a holler when I get it?"

"That would be great." She described the land, to the extent of her memory and Neil promised to follow up.

What a relief. More than anything else she could use a friend right now—a friend who would listen to her troubles on the pueblo. A friend who wouldn't judge her. Perhaps Neil Kramer would become that friend.

Chapter Eleven

A knock stole Sandy away from the Tony Hillerman mystery she was reading. She placed the book open-faced on the coffee table and inched her way to the front door. "Who's there?"

Silence answered her. A moment later, a second knock resounded.

Still nervous after her close call with a stalker, she cautiously set the safety lock and opened the door a sliver. Light streamed through the crack and blinded her. She could barely discern a child under the porch light. A blood-and mud-covered child staring wild-eyed at her. It took her a moment to recognize Dixon.

She stifled a gasp and flung open the door. "Dixon, what happened?" she asked as she pulled him inside.

"P...pushed," Dixon answered between sobs.

Sandy bundled him into her arms and held him to her until his sobs subsided, then led him to a kitchen chair. "Let me clean you up and take a look." With a dampened towel, she gently wiped the mud and blood off of Dixon's face, neck and arms.

She took his chin in her hand and looked him over. A smattering of ugly bruises were beginning to appear as smudges on his face, arms and, when she lifted his shirt, chest. A large reddish scratch ran the length of his cheek and a deep gash had been carved like an arroyo into his forehead. Ruby-red blood oozed from the cut. She didn't need a medical degree to know he needed stitches.

After her coffee with Neil Kramer, she knew where to find the closest Indian Health Service hospital. She pressed the towel against the wound. "Hold this in place, honey." She guided him toward the *Toyota*. First stop, the Edakee house.

"Dixon's in the car," Sandy told Cecilia at the front door of the Edakee house. "He's been hurt and needs stitches. Where's Tonito?"

Instead of answering, Cecilia tore past Sandy to where Dixon sat. Sandy came up behind her. The towel she had pressed against Dixon's wound was soaked with large splotches of blood.

Cecilia drew Dixon to her and comforted him in a soothing tone before asking over her shoulder, "How did this happen?"

"He said he was pushed. I haven't learned the details. I'm not a doctor, but it looks to me like he'll be all right once he has his forehead stitched."

Cecilia looked ghost-white in the porch light. She waved a trembling hand. "I have to take Dixon to the hospital right away, but what should I do about Tonito? He is at the sheep ranch. He would be furious with me if I did not bring him along."

"Since I don't know the way to the sheep ranch, why don't I take Dixon to the hospital instead? You find Tonito and meet us there. Don't worry," she said, noticing the terror in Cecilia's eyes. "He'll be fine with me."

Cecilia's face was drawn, her eyes wild. "I will have my aunt drive me over to the sheep ranch to find Tonito. We will be at the hospital as soon as we can."

"I'll take good care of Dixon. I promise."

"I know you will, *Tsila*." Cecilia explained their agreement to Dixon, who nodded his understanding, then swiftly waddled off in the direction of the house.

Sandy hopped back into the car and veered out onto the open road, traveling as fast as the law would allow, swerving once to miss a tumbleweed, and a second time to avoid a tire tread the kind locals called a 'gator.'

In record time, they arrived at the large, faux-adobe hospital building, painted in varying shades of brown with an eye-catching United States Public Health Service sign over the front entrance. She came to a screeching halt in front of the door marked Emergency.

With Dixon in tow, she rushed past a packed lobby to the admissions desk. The admitting nurse looked Dixon over with shrewd eyes. "Looks like we have our first real emergency of the day. Follow me."

Her calm reassured Sandy.

The nurse held open a door and showed them to a cubicle with curtains for walls. She helped Dixon into a hospital gown and onto a gurney. He groaned with the effort. "You'll be fine," she said, patting Dixon on the back. "We haven't lost a kid yet from a cut on the head. I'll just go and find the doctor."

Sandy took a seat on the only chair in the cubicle, noting an antiseptic smell that made her nose twitch. The glare of fluorescent lights reflected off chalk-white walls. Next to Dixon was a silver tray with numerous instruments of medical torture: a clamp, a syringe, a kidney shaped pan. The sight of them made her jittery. It reminded her of her last trip to the hospital, after the accident.

She leaned toward Dixon. "Who pushed you? Please tell me. We can't help you unless we know."

Dixon looked down at the white flecked linoleum floor. "Some boys."

"What boys? Who are they?"

"I do not know their names."

Same old story. Why couldn't she get any more information from him? She wondered if these nameless boys had threatened Dixon or his family. Whatever had happened, it worked to silence him, but it made her livid. The idea that someone would bully him into submission infuriated her.

"Where did that cut come from?"

"My head hit a brick."

More likely, a brick hit him.

The curtain rattled open and Dr. Neil Kramer entered the cubical in a white coat. His eyes lit upon seeing her and he smiled broadly. "Well, well, well, what a surprise. Good to see you again, Ms. Jacobs. Too bad the circumstances." He shook her hand and turned to Dixon. "Let's see what's behind this towel."

He began gently prying the towel away from the coagulated blood on Dixon's forehead. Dr. Kramer's gentleness impressed her. She immediately felt she could trust him and relaxed a little for the first time since Dixon's unexpected arrival at her apartment.

"There, that's done," Kramer announced as he dropped the blood-covered towel into a basin. "Let's see that wound."

Kramer fingered the ugly gap on Dixon's forehead to a chorus of whimpers and whines.

"You're a brave boy," he said and gave Dixon a pat on the shoulder "But you need a good seamstress. Any other problems?"

Dixon shook his head, but Dr. Kramer continued to manipulate his scalp and limbs for other signs of injury. He turned to Sandy. "We're going to have the nurse wash this young man and ready him for a procedure. Please come with me."

Sandy rose, but before she could follow Kramer out of the cubical, Dixon seized her sleeve. "No! Don't go."

She pressed the small, soft hand grasping onto her jacket. "Don't worry. I'm not going far. The doctor needs to ask me some questions," she said giving his hand a squeeze, "but I'll be close by. I promise." Dixon's wide, innocent eyes tugged at her heart and she had to force herself to turn away.

Sandy caught up with Kramer by the nursing station.

He scribbled into a chart. "I take it you're not the boy's legal guardian?"

"His parents are on the way. They should be here any minute."

The doctor continued to make notes in the chart. "I'll need their permission to sew him up. Do you know what happened to him?"

"He says some boys pushed him, but he won't name names. Maybe he'll tell you." She intentionally caught his eye. "Will Dixon be all right, Doc?"

Kramer shrugged. "That's a nasty looking wound he's taken, but he'll be okay. He may have a small scar, but I'll do all I can to make the sutures neat and tidy. Now would you mind waiting outside while we prep him? We'll call you when we're done."

Reluctantly, Sandy wandered into the waiting room and found an empty seat. She was surrounded by runny noses, bronchial coughs, and minor abrasions. Old people sat stoically staring at television screens, while children played tag up and down the aisles. The word emergency lost all meaning in the hubbub of the waiting room.

She heard her name called and twisted around to see Cecilia and Tonito approaching, Cecilia still pale with shock. "Where's Dixon?"

"In the back. They want to stitch the gash on his forehead, but need your permission."

Cecilia headed directly to the emergency room desk with Tonito following closely behind. They disappeared behind the double doors. Shortly, they returned.

Tonito approached her. "Dixon is going to be

okay, *Tsila*, thanks to you. The doctor will stitch up the cut while we wait."

Sandy offered Cecilia her chair, but Cecilia refused it with a wave of the hand. "Did Dixon tell you who did this to him? He would not tell us a thing."

"Me either. Do you have any idea?"

"One of the Chavez boys. The other day we caught them taunting him and tossing dirt in his face," Tonito said. "We do not know why they pick on Dixon, *Tsila*, or why they blame us for their troubles."

An hour later the admitting nurse called to them from her desk and Cecilia indicated Sandy should follow them into the ER. They met Dr. Kramer at the nursing station.

"Your son has pulled through the procedure with flying colors. He'll do just fine, but we'd like to keep him in the hospital overnight for observation in case he sustained a minor concussion."

Cecilia groaned. "I cannot stay. I have a smaller child at home."

"You certainly don't need to stay all night. Your son will be well taken care of by our staff." Dr. Kramer inclined his head toward two nurses sitting behind the counter.

"But he has never been away from home all night. He will be afraid," Cecilia protested.

"We can go home, see to the other children and then return," Tonito suggested.

"But what do we do with Maria?"

"Why don't I stay with him?" Sandy asked. "How would that work?"

Kramer rubbed his chin. "We don't usually let anyone but the family stay, but I guess we can bend the rules this once, at least until he falls asleep. Then we have a full staff of nurses to see to his comfort."

Cecilia took Sandy's hand. Her's quivered. "You would not mind staying here, *Tsila*? That means so much to us. Dixon would feel much safer with you around."

"I don't have any other plans this evening," Sandy said. "It's not a problem at all."

"Thank you, *Tsila*," Cecilia said, her face softening with tenderness. "Every day you become more a part of our family."

"I'm glad," she said, and meant it.

Tonito and Cecilia spent a few more minutes with Dixon and left only moments before an orderly came by to move him to a room in another wing. In the room, Sandy took a seat on the far side of Dixon's bed while the nurse did what she could to make him comfortable. He had been given pain-killers in the emergency room and it wasn't long before he dozed off. Unwilling to leave until she knew Dixon was down for the night, Sandy stretched, nestled her head on her arm, and unexpectedly slipped off to sleep.

A male voice awakened her. Groggily, she opened her eyes. Although darkness lay beyond the wall-to-ceiling windows, bright fluorescent lights glared inside. Slowly, her eyes focused on Dr. Kramer.

She straightened her cramped limbs. "I must have dozed off." She rubbed her stiff neck. "What a position to be in." She struggled to rise, but a cramped leg held her back.

Kramer offered her a hand up, then poured water from a plastic pitcher into a glass and handed it to her.

She took a long drink. "That's a lifesaver! Thanks, Dr. Kramer..."

"Please call me Neil."

"Thanks, Neil. I appreciate what you did for Dixon."

"No biggy. It's my job to put people back together. Fortunately, he was only a little dented, not terribly damaged." He refilled her empty glass. "I can't stay for more than a minute because I have to check in on my other patients, but I wanted to tell you how much I enjoyed our coffee the other day. I did have a chance to speak with Dirk afterwards, but I don't have time to go over what he told me right now. Let's get together again soon and I'll fill you in." He began to move past her to Dixon's bed. "Tell you what. I'll be passing through San Anselmo next Saturday. How about lunch?"

"Sure, but I'm afraid there's only one restaurant in the pueblo, Ramona's. It's a hole-in-the-wall, but I've been wanting to try it."

"Great. I'll see you there Saturday at two."

Neil leaned over and checked Dixon's sutures, inadvertently waking him, before taking off at a clip down the hall.

Dixon bolted up and yelped like a lost pup. "Mommy!"

Sandy took a seat on the bed to assure him he was safe, but it did little to comfort the distraught child. She draped an arm around his shoulders. "It's okay. Don't be afraid. Your mom's home with Maria, but she promised to come back first thing in the morning. I'm staying here with you now."

He looked around with wide, frightened eyes. "Where am I?"

"You're in the hospital, but you're safe and sound. Lie back and rest. You must be exhausted after your scare today."

"No, I can't go to sleep. I'm too scared."

"Scared of what?"

"The bogeymen." Dixon glanced furtively at the window.

Sandy gently drew him to her. She hated to see him suffer. She wished there was more she could do. "Bogeymen can't hurt you here."

"I saw one. Over there." He pointed toward the window.

Sandy's heart skipped a beat. "When?"

"Before. When you were asleep."

All she could see beyond the windowpane was a sprinkling of stars and a sliver of a moon . "Are you sure?"

"I saw him! I did!" he whined.

Sandy slipped over to the window. Outside it was dark with low lying clouds. Lights ringed the parking lot and she saw a nurse climb into her car; heard the roar of an engine firing; caught the glare of two beams in her eyes. The car drove off. "There's no one out there. You must have dreamed you saw a bogeyman."

Dixon sobbed. "I saw it! I saw it!" He trembled all over. "Do not leave me, Miss Sandy."

Sandy still had plans to sleep in her own bed, but abandoning Dixon in his present state of mind was out of the question. "Don't worry, I'll stay with you. I'm not going to leave you alone."

Dixon sank back against his pillow, curled into a fetal position and began to suckle his fist like a baby. She waited until he had drifted back to sleep before taking a seat in a nearby armchair.

She tucked her legs under her and looked over at Dixon. The stark white bandage across his forehead stood out against his coco-colored skin like a neon banner blazing against the night sky. He looked so tiny, so vulnerable. She stared at him in the darkened room just long enough for her eyes to play a trick on her and she watched as another child took his place. Her child. The eleven-year-old she carried around in her imagination. What would it be like if he was being tormented by others? Was feeling assaulted? Was alone and afraid?

A pain as sharp as anything Dixon must have suffered cut through her.

While she could not protect her son, she would keep Dixon safe. No matter what others thought, even Ben and Luci, she would find a way to fulfill her promise and protect him.

Thank goodness Neil Kramer was on the job. She rubbed her cramped legs and again shifted her position. And what a coincidence running into a fellow Philadelphian so far from home.

Home. Funny she still thought of Philadelphia that way. The fact she felt so elated by the chance encounter made her realize just how homesick she must be. While she had settled well into the tempo of pueblo life, she still missed her old hometown more than she wanted to admit.

Dr. Neil Kramer reminded her of her past. Clean cut and professional, he was the type she dated, but never mated. The type who would make a good friend. After all of her problems with Ben and the principal, here was a man she might be able to relate to in a comfortably normal way.

Ben. Her family would certainly disapprove of this rough-hewn man with the strong independent streak. Yet, something imperceptible drew her to him. She imagined him standing silhouetted against the endless azure sky and flat crimson hills. He seemed so much a part of the land, like a human outcropping, his life intrinsically linked to the world in which he was born and now lived. She could not imagine him in another setting—especially not Philadelphia. If she had the chance to return to Philadelphia and be with her son, she might have to leave Ben behind. A lump formed in her throat.

Sandy squirmed again, her leg tingled beneath her. A nurse walking by the room must have taken notice because she poked her head through the door. "If you plan on spending the night, why don't you sleep in the empty bed? No one else will be using it."

"I can't tell you how much I appreciate that!" Sandy pulled her cramped legs out from under her, tapped her foot quietly until it came back to life, and hobbled over to the empty bed. Moments later, she surrendered to a deep sleep.

Sandy opened her eyes at the shake of a rattle. An odor of burnt sage filled her nostrils. She levered herself up on one arm to watch Cecilia and Tonito with their backs to her, standing on the near side of Dixon's bed. A lean, well-weathered man—in jeans, a plaid shirt, and white headband with a leather satchel strapped across his chest—faced them on the far side.

As she watched and listened, he softly chanted over Dixon. With another shake of the rattle, he passed three vials containing what appeared to be ground herbs over Dixon's body. The chant rose and fell in cascades of ascending and descending notes like a well-rehearsed song.

The Medicine Man scooped an herbal balm from a jar and rubbed Dixon's chest and arms, beating a tattoo on exposed limbs. He bent over and blew air into Dixon's nose and mouth. To her surprise, Dixon lay perfectly still, compliant with the treatment.

With a soft growling sound, the shaman sucked at Dixon's throat. Finally, he convulsed in a hacking cough that Sandy thought would surely bring the on-duty nurse to the door. When she glanced back, he had stuck arthritic looking fingers into Dixon's mouth. With a flourish, he extracted a ball of hair and a crumpled rag, laying them on the blanket top.

"Here are the fetishes meant to make your son infirm," he said to the Edakees. "These must be removed before he can heal. Someone wants your son to suffer."

Cecilia and Tonito glanced nervously at one another. Cecilia wrung her hands.

The medicine man chanted one more time and passed more herbs over Dixon. "We are finished for today." He packed up his supplies. "This is all I can do."

Tonito walked him to the door, leaving Cecilia behind to attend to her son. When she turned to gather his clothes, she acknowledged Sandy. "I hope we did not wake you, *Tsila*. You looked so peaceful sleeping. I know now to treasure peace."

Sandy flushed. "I'm sorry. I didn't mean to intrude just now. I awoke when the ceremony was underway and didn't want to disturb you."

Cecilia raised a hand to quiet her. "You are one of our family. You need to know our ways."

Sandy started to rise. "I'll leave you two alone so you can dress Dixon."

Cecilia offered her a hand up. "Thank you for staying last night, *Tsila*. You have become more and more important to us. We do not know what we would do without you." She smiled, but her eyes brimmed with tears.

Touched by this show of tenderness, Sandy didn't know what to say. "I'm glad I could help," she mumbled, but it sounded weak.

Cecilia hugged her. "You have helped us so much, *Tsila*."

"And I plan to continue." Sandy picked her coat up off the chair and silently left the room.

Chapter Twelve

The pueblo governor's office was located across the street from the council building. It had a certain rustic charm that always put Ben immediately at ease. He liked the comfort of the faded leather armchair in which he sat and was impressed with the display case filled with local hand-painted coiled pottery behind the governor's desk.

Narcisco Pena watched Ben through owl-like eyes staring out of a broad, flat face. A certain sense of calm authority surrounded him.

"So, Ben Rush, what brings you here today?"

Ben sat forward. "I have a friend, a fellow teacher, who's been trying to help a family in trouble. I told her I would ask you for support."

The governor scratched his chin. "This family you speak of, is it the Edakee family?"

Ben tried not to register his surprise. "You've heard about their problems?"

"Harley Dista spoke to me about them. It is not new news on the pueblo."

Ben interlocked his fingers. "No, I guess not. But what is news is that the Edakees' ten-year-old son has been attacked by bigger boys after school, and bogeymen *Kachina* have visited this family in an attempt to scare them off the pueblo. The tactics seem to be working. These people are terrified and they don't know what to do. The teacher I mentioned is trying to help them out, but she's at a loss too. We thought a word coming from you could put a stop to these attacks."

Pena tapped his desk with a pen. "I will have to consider your request, Ben Rush, and speak with Harley. The tribal governor's office never interferes in personal matters. It is not ordinarily my job."

By the stark, set look on Pena's face, Ben suddenly had a feeling he knew what Harley Dista might have said, and it wasn't in Sandy's favor. "I see." *Too well.* "I hope you'll take action before this situation spins out of control."

"I have bigger fish to fry right now. I just discovered some tribal funds are missing. An investigation will be underway next week and this should take most of my time. I will do what I can, when I can." The governor sat forward, elbows on desktop. "Please warn your teacher friend not to create trouble on this pueblo. If she does this, I will have to make sure she does not continue to live on our land."

Ben had the sense of having the wind knocked out of him. He wanted to give the governor a piece of his mind, but not at the expense of Sandy's job. "She isn't the problem. She's only trying to protect her student."

Pena rose. "It is important that she does not take sides. Tell her to back off and let the tribe handle our own troubles. It is my job to decide what is best for the tribe, not her's. I am the one who must enforce the rules. That is why I have been elected."

Had Harley bribed Pena with political favors to

win his support? Ben wouldn't be surprised. "I understand." He was tempted to turn away from the hand Pena offered him, but he thought better of it. He didn't want to alienate the governor, in case they needed him in a pinch.

"I will see what I can do," the governor said.

Ben gave the governor a perfunctory shake and left the office.

Outside, he took a deep breath of clean pueblo air and wished the air inside the office had been as pure. He had gone into the meeting hoping to dislodge an immovable object: the Edakee problem. Instead, he found the object might be glued, screwed, and encased in steel by Harley Dista. Ben's chances of effecting a change were, quite honestly, nil. His gut fluttered at the thought of facing Sandy with the news.

He started in the direction of Sandy's apartment, prepared to tell her the results of his meeting, but ready to couch his words in terms that might convince her of the futility of her actions. He had to prevent her from doing anything that could threaten her career, and the safety of the boy.

Ben stopped in front of the general store, his hands balled into fists. With an erratic swing, he smashed his right fist into the adobe wall. The radiating pain ran down his arm, but he was too angry and upset to react. He looked down at his bleeding knuckles, deciding to wipe them clean before visiting Sandy. The last thing he wanted to do was let her know of his frustration. She had enough on her mind.

"Damn it, Ben. I'm getting nowhere fast." Sandy kneaded her hands in frustration. "Every time I think I'm about to turn a corner on this Edakee thing, there's another road-block."

"I did my best with the governor, but I doubt he'll take up the cause. Besides Harley's interference, he's discovered missing tribal funds and will be busy looking into that situation over the next week or so. We might have reached a dead-end here."

She stared down, swallowing the enormous sadness that filled her. She had to play the only card she had left. "Do you know anything about Harley's trips to the *Sky City Casino*? I spotted him driving there on my way into Albuquerque this week."

"That's not news. You can ask anyone around here. Harley has a bit of a gambling addiction. He's a frequent customer at the casino."

For the first time since he told her the bad news about the governor, she felt intrigued. "How frequent?"

"All I know is what I hear around town. Word has it that Harley loves to roll the dice, but that's not unusual since they built a casino practically next door to the pueblo."

Not unusual, but interesting. She pocketed the information in case it came in handy later.

"You know what else is unusual, the *Chalaki* ceremonial is this weekend. It only takes place once a year and it's really something to see. Why don't you come with me. We both could use a break from this trouble."

"Sure," she said, "why not, even though I'd be surprised if the bogeymen ever take time off."

A blustery wind blew from the west, pressing against Sandy and Ben like a giant's hand, slowing their approach to the plaza. The wind pushed the branches of the piñon pines in on themselves as if signaling them to reverse direction. Sandy took note.

"Maybe the Gods are trying to tell us something."

"That it's gonna be one hell of a bitter night," Ben said.

"I have my down jacket. Do you have yours?"

Ben grinned. "If I forgot mine, you'll keep me warm, won't you?"

"Sure." She poked him playfully in the ribs. "I'll lend you my scarf."

"That's not what I had in mind."

They spied a band of people heading south of the plaza and tagged along. At a narrow opening between a row of crumbling adobe houses, Ben pulled Sandy forward.

Five *Kachina* walked single file into a small, enclosed courtyard. "That's the Council of the Gods led by the ceremonial father, *Saiyadasha*," Ben whispered.

The *Kachina* he pointed out was a small man in mid-calf white pants and an embroidered cape with a basket of plumes in his hand. With his ponderous tread and the rasp of his scapula rattle, he circled an impression in the ground.

Ben leaned forward. "He'll sprinkle cornmeal and toss a bundle of prayer sticks into the shrine. Then each of the remaining Gods will follow suit."

A *Kachina* with long horns sticking out of his head danced past her. "That's the *Hututu* or Long-horn K*achina*," he whispered. "The one with large ears is the *Yamuhakto* and the *Shulawitsi* or Fire God is the little black *Kachina* with multi-colored polka dots." His warm breath in her ear sent a shiver down her spine. "The blessing of the shrine always precedes the coming of the *Chalaki* to San Anselmo."

The K*achina* completed their ritual exactly as Ben had described, then exited the courtyard. After the last *Kachina* vanished from sight, people scattered.

Ben grabbed Sandy's hand. "Follow me," he said and led her up a nearby hill. "You'll be able to see the entire Pueblo from up there."

At the top, she looked down to see the Pueblo bustling with the activity of a demented anthill. Women scurried in and out of adobe houses, attending to mud-covered children and smoking bee-hive ovens. Men rode around in pick-ups or herded sheep on nearby ranches.

They watched the ceremonial preparations for a time, then grabbed a sandwich from home before joining another group of people by the Plaza. It didn't take long before the endless wait began to wear on Sandy. The late December evening temperature had dipped to a deep bone-chilling cold. She wrapped her coat closer around herself. As a recent migrant to the slow pace of the Pueblo, she had not completely adjusted to "Indian time".

"What are we waiting for?"

Ben patted her hand in a gesture of understanding. "The *Chalaki* to come into town."

The guests of honor hadn't even arrived yet. She knew there was nothing she could do but bide her time. Sandy pulled her gloves over freezing fingers and wrapped her scarf more tightly about her neck. "Where are they?"

"They're said to be on their way from a lake near Grants. It's where they believe their ancestors reside."

She already knew the routine from attending rain dances. No telling how long until the *Chalaki* made their entrance.

Finally, after what seemed an interminable wait, a drum beat coming from the west and the chanting of the priests reached her. Not long after that she spotted the *Chalaki* in the distance. When she did, her breath caught in her throat. She had never seen anything quite like the giant *Kachina* approaching the bridge. With their massive masks, the five *Chalaki* towered over their entourage.

The masks fascinated her. The *Chalaki* resembled tall, elegant birds with long blue beaks, protruding eyes, huge ruffs and crowns of feathers. She stood transfixed, watching as they advanced upon the village, passed by everyone lining the street and entered their respective ceremonial houses.

Once they disappeared from view, Sandy turned to Ben, "What's next?"

"The *Chalaki* pray until midnight. The fun begins when they start dancing."

Midnight was hours away. "What do we do until then?"

"Rest," he suggested. "We'll need it since we'll be up most of the night."

Ben led the way back to the apartments and showed her to her door. Sandy gave him a key and made him promise to wake her on time for the ceremonial before she would let him go. Shortly after midnight, he shook her awake. "Time to wake up, Sleeping Beauty."

Sandy stretched and slowly levered herself to sitting. As the blanket fell away, she shivered from the deep freeze in the air. She had to force herself to rise out of her warm bed and, with down jacket securely wrapped around her, stumbled out of the house behind him.

Ben drove down the narrow winding streets and turned onto a dirt road. He pulled up to a well-lit house far on the edge of the village. "This is one of the five houses built by a clan over the past year. The *Chalaki* will bless each of the houses tonight."

Inside the house, people stood huddled together in a large room with a half-wall separating them from the *Kachina* dancers. The *Chalaki*, with its turquoise beads and white feather headdress, ran up and down the width of the house, snapping its elongated beak at a Mudhead *Kachina*, who taunted the much taller *Chalaki* from below. When the *Chalaki* clapped its beak, the sound thundered through the house, and the Mudhead, who resembled its name, would recoil in mock fright.

At one point during the night, Sandy heard a commotion at the front door. She turned to see what was going on and spotted a couple of men pushing another man outside. On closer inspection, on her tippy-toes, she noticed the man was Tonito. Determined to intervene, she made an effort to move through the crowd to the door, but by the time she reached it, Tonito was no longer in sight. She thought about going after him, but the cold and Ben drew her back inside. She would have to comfort him another time, but the incident left a lingering aftertaste.

The *Chalaki* continued to dance until dawn, taking occasional breaks. During the down time, everyone present helped themselves to the sheep stew and fry bread offered by the hostess of the house.

At dawn, the *Chalaki* went into seclusion and Sandy followed Ben back to his apartment for a few more winks.

Exhausted, she flopped down beside him on the sofa, curled up and leaned her head against his shoulder. A moment later she slipped into welcome oblivion.

The sun sat high above the hills when noise from people passing the apartments startled her awake. She found herself enclosed in Ben's arms. She didn't wish to wake him, or leave the comfort of his embrace, but when she moved to make herself more comfortable, he stirred.

After a quick cup of reheated coffee and a leftover

biscuit, they hiked over to a large field outside the village for the foot races. Another wait ensued while all five *Chalaki* lined up in single file.

Ben's eyes shone. "Wait 'til you see this!"

The sun was beginning to warm her. She removed her gloves and loosened her scarf. "Why? What's the big deal?"

"The *Chalaki* race across the field to test their purity and commitment. They attract quite a crowd."

Within no time she knew what he meant. She glanced around at all the people ringing the field. The entire Pueblo and a couple of other communities must have been present. People stood about chatting with one another. Children ran in and out of the crowd, squealing with delight. She looked back at the *Chalaki*.

"How can they run with those huge masks on?"

"You'll see."

More people filled the road alongside the field for the event until the congregation pressed in on them. Anticipation, and what she could only describe as a nervous energy, filled the air. After another long wait, a call from the *Saiyatasha* initiated the *Chalaki* race across the field. The *Chalaki* began to lurch and sway forward on the dwarfed feet of the impersonators under the oversized masks. They scurried as fast as they could with their awkward load across the open field. The crowd cheered them onward, the excitement surging along with the racers. Halfway across the field, one of the *Chalaki* stumbled and accidentally bumped into another. Masks and impersonators tumbled to the ground in what seemed like slow motion.

Everything seemed to stand still. No one moved or uttered a sound.

Suddenly two super-sized *Kachina* with painted bird faces and huge black crow feather ruffs ran out from behind a house and rushed toward them waving yucca stick whips. A loud "OHHH!" arose from the crowd and everyone scattered like ants under foot.

Not knowing what to do or where to turn, Sandy froze.

Ben screamed, "Let's go!" and grabbed her hand. They bolted away from the intimidating figures and raced the entire way back to the plaza. Once there, she leaned over, elbows on knees, panting. Sweat dribbled down her brow. "What was that all about?"

Ben breathed heavily. "We're not supposed to see the *Chalaki* fall. They represent the Gods and the Gods are supposed to be perfect. According to local legend, if you see a *Chalaki* fall, you'll be out of luck for a long time."

"Oh great," Sandy said. "All I need is another bad omen."

Ben shook his head and said between breaths, "I didn't think all your men were bad."

Although she smiled at Ben's silly play on words, her stomach churned. "You must be delirious from lack of sleep. Let's go home." She started toward the apartments, but even tired, her head swam with an ominous feeling. Everywhere she went, she encountered mystical, inexplicable warnings as though the Universe was trying to tell her something. And whatever that something was, she wasn't sure she wanted to know.

A peculiar rustling outside Sandy's apartment drew her from the dishes. She wiped her hands on a dish towel and opened the apartment door. The parking area was empty except for a row of parked cars. Perhaps it had been a stray dog.

Sandy began to close the door when the porch light reflected off a white, feathered object lying on the stoop. Opening the door wider to view what was there, she was shocked to see a dead chicken on her doormat. The stench of it turned her stomach. She choked.

She slammed the door shut. Not only disgusted by the putrefying bird, she was sick and tired of the intimidation tactics being used against her and the Edakees. She would take care of the dead carcass later. For the moment, she felt too annoyed to attend to it.

She paced the apartment for a good five minutes in an effort to calm her rage. Then she put on a disc of New Age music, took a seat on her sofa, and waited for the urge to seek and destroy to pass.

When she finally convinced herself to clean up the decomposing chicken on the sisal mat, she was met by an odor so foul she had to pause a minute before proceeding. With a pair of rubber gloves and pinched nostrils, she prepared to remove the bird from the porch, when she heard her name called from across the parking lot. A man reeled toward her. It was the school principal, Arnie Sloan. He came to a halt directly in front of the apartment.

Damn. The last person she wanted to see was Arnie. She had enough trouble.

"Looky who's here. Whatcha doin' in these parts?" Arnie asked, slurring his words. His face was the color of clay, his suit disheveled and dusty. A large dark stain ran down his yellow and gray plaid shirt and his bolo tie was crooked. He was obviously drunk.

"I live here, Arnie. You should know that."

"Nice joint," he said and then looked down at the mat. He opened his small eyes as wide as possible. "Whadda we have here?"

"A dead chicken. Now, if you will please excuse me, I'm in the process of disposing of it."

He stumbled close enough for her to smell the alcohol rising from his pores. She retreated, but he didn't seem to notice. "Why get rid of a chicken? Why not eat it?"

Just the thought of eating it made her nauseous. "This chicken has been dead and unrefrigerated for hours. It reeks. Do you really recommend anyone eat it?"

"I was jus' kiddin'." He smiled a toothy grin at her. "Why didn'tcha tell me in the first place? A'course, you shouldn't eat it. I'll toss it." He moved closer and she backed off even farther, signaling him to stop.

"I can handle it. I've got plastic bags." She held out her gloved hands to show him they were also covered.

Arnie stumbled, caught himself, and made a feeble attempt to look heroic while straightening the plaid shirt scrunched around the waist of his slacks. "This is no job for'a lady. I'll take care of it."

"I really can handle it myself."

Too late, Arnie had already picked up the chicken by one wing. "Phew, you're right. This thing stinks."

So did he. He was near enough for her to catch a whiff of his stale breath.

Arnie lurched to the trash container and tossed the chicken inside. He staggered back toward her, a silly grin plastered on his flushed face.

Sandy winced at his tobacco stained teeth. "Thanks for the help, Arnie, but I have to go in now." She backed off, but he just kept coming closer until she was backed against the closed screen door.

"Hey, I helped you out. How about a little kiss for ol' Arnie before he leaves?" He leaned, pitched forward, and almost landed on her.

She pushed him away. "No, Arnie!"

He leaned in closer. "Now, is that nice after what I jus' did for you?"

"I have to say goodnight." She turned and reached for the door handle when he slapped his hand on the frame.

"How about letting Arnie in for a little thank you?"

Fear and revulsion crawled like lizards across her skin. "It's late. Goodnight!"

"No one's ever too tired for a little kissy face." He grabbed her with his free arm and yanked her toward him. His lips loomed large and moist above her. The putrid smell of alcohol and cigarettes descended. She wanted to puke.

Her throat tightened. "Get away!" she screamed and thrust her arms in front of her. She couldn't believe this was happening to her. It all felt surreal.

Unperturbed by her reaction, Arnie's lips targeted her. She chafed against his coiled hand, trying to break free.

Without warning, Arnie was jerked backward. Behind him, Ben stood grasping his upper arm. Stunned by the sudden turn of events, but also relieved, she mumbled, "Thank goodness you're here," but Ben seemed too preoccupied to notice.

"Didn't you hear Sandy? She said to go away." Ben's face was an angry red. His voice threatening.

Arnie tried to yank his arm out of Ben's grip. "We were havin' a good time until you came along. The lil lady was enjoying herself, just playing hard to get."

"Go home, Arnie, and sober up," Ben said. "You're too drunk to know when you're not welcome."

Arnie stuck out his chin. "Who're you to tell me

whadda do? You're just a teacher and I'm the principal. If you don' watch your step, you'll be looking for 'nother job."

"That's a risk I'll have to take. In the meantime, make yourself scarce before someone else spots you smelling of booze and slurring your words." Ben released Arnie's arm with a shove away from the door.

Arnie stumbled backward, then righted himself. "Too bad you and I have been so rudely interrupted," he said to Sandy as he attempted to straighten his disheveled shirt. He glared at Ben. "I'm not done with you yet and neither is the school board. We'll talk later." He spat his words with such venom that Sandy could see the spray through the porch light.

"I hope we do." Ben stepped aside for Arnie to pass.

Sandy trembled from head to toe, still considering what might have happened if Ben hadn't stepped in. Ben removed his jacket and placed it around her shoulders. As he did, she reached up and gave him a quick hug. "Thanks, Ben. What would I do without you?"

"Find your way into one heap of trouble after another."

She squeezed him tighter. "You do care, Ben, I know you do."

"I do, but my caring isn't sparing you." He started to move away, but turned back. "I won't always be around to bail you out of every mess."

He left her standing alone in the doorway,

staring after him until the cold drove her inside.

Chapter Thirteen

Dr. Neil Kramer stood outside Sandy's apartment door uninvited and three days early for their lunch. He wore his civilian clothes under a forest green down-filled jacket. The gleam in his eyes told of his excitement.

"How did you manage to find me?" Sandy asked.

"It wasn't hard. I stopped by the general store. A woman named Luci pointed the way. I hope I'm not intruding."

She was unprepared for company. How could he not be intruding? "Of course not. Come on in."

Neil followed her into the living room, shucking his jacket and dropping it onto a chair. Beneath it he wore a red crew-neck, lamb's wool sweater tucked into pressed khaki chinos cinched by a silver belt buckle with inlaid turquoise. His brown loafers carried not a speck of dust. Short curly hair framed his clean-shaven face. The look was decidedly city, not pueblo. She motioned toward the sofa.

He sat. "I had to run into Grants for supplies and thought I would stop by and look you up."

Sandy put away the broom she had been holding. "How nice of you, but all I can offer you is tea."

"I'd love a cup."

She placed the teakettle on the stove and returned to the living room to find Neil rifling through the National Geographic on her coffee table. He glanced up. "These are terrific pictures of the ruins in Mesa Verde. Have you been there?"

"Not yet, but I promised myself I'd visit them soon."

"How about after the first of the year? I'd love to see them again. We could drive up and back in one day."

"I don't know, Neil. I'll have to see what's happening around here." Sandy heard the pot begin to whistle. "Teakettle calling. I'll be back in a sec."

She fetched two mugs from the cupboard, placed a bag of orange spice tea in each, topped the tea bags with hot water, and returned to the sofa. Steam and spice rose from the cups, scenting and warming the chilly air. She handed Neil one and took hers to a chair on the opposite side of the coffee table.

He sipped at his tea. "What would stand in your way? I thought you were on winter break next week."

"You remember that little boy with the head wound, Dixon Edakee?"

"How is he?"

"Better, but he still has headaches."

"That's to be expected with even a minor concussion. But what does he have to do with your winter break?"

"It's his family I told you about over coffee, the ones being forced off the pueblo. With all that's being going on, I feel a need to stay close by them right now. They're considered 'witches' around here and are under attack by the religious leaders, the *Kachina*."

Neil placed his cup on the table. "Are they the ones with buried artifacts on their land?"

When she nodded, he continued, "I ran what you told me past Dirk and he said the land with the artifacts is owned by a man named Ebachee, or something like that. Anyway, he wants to talk to this Ebachee fellow, but not until he has the permission of the tribal council and governor. He's been meeting with the council members individually and plans to make a presentation soon. That's the way things work around here." He took a sip of tea. "Ring any bells?"

Ebachee certainly sounded like Edakee, but she had to be certain. "That might explain what's been going on. Were you able to get Dirk's number so I can call him directly? I really need to know if this is the right family."

"I didn't think to bring it with me today, but I'll make a note to put it in my briefcase when we meet on Saturday."

"I'd appreciate that."

He frowned at her. "You still haven't explained your stake in all this."

"It's just that everyone else on the pueblo has abandoned this family. So, I've been trying to help them out." She took a sip of tea and waited for Neil to admonish her as the others had.

"That's what I admire about you, Sandy. Your compassion. I was impressed by the way you treated that little boy at the hospital. You're obviously a caring person."

Although she heard him, his words were not what she expected. She squinted at him. "That's a different take. I've been told so many times I'm off-base, I guess I wasn't prepared for your support."

Neil cocked his head. "Really?"

"All my friends on the pueblo tell me to stay out of this family's problem. It's a relief to hear another perspective. It's lovely to get a bit of validation."

Neil beamed. "Anytime you need validation, I'm the man to call."

Sandy suddenly had the suspicion Neil was spreading butter a bit thick, and might be angling for something she wasn't prepared to give him. She wanted him as a friend. She needed his support. But she would never lead him on or make him think there could be anything more between them. "It's good to have a friend like you, Neil."

A puzzled look passed over his swarthy face. "Are you trying to tell me we have to keep this platonic?"

"That's it for now, I'm afraid. I've been seeing someone else, a fellow teacher." That was a bit of a stretch at the moment.

Neil shrugged. "I guess that does slow things

down a little, but I'm prepared to hang around and see what develops. You could use a friend right now and I'd like to be that friend." He stood. "I'm afraid I have to run. I'm on duty starting at three. Are we still on for Saturday?"

Now that she had made herself clear, Sandy felt comfortable with the arrangement. She stood to accompany him to the door. "I look forward to it."

On his way out of the post office after mailing the last of his holiday packages, Ben spied Sandy stepping out of her car. Wow. Was she a knockout. She had on a navy blue suit with high heels and nylons. He had never seen her this decked out and wondered about it.

He came up behind her while she retrieved a file folder from the backseat of her car. "What's the occasion?"

Sandy pivoted. "Ben! You always appear when I least expect you. I thought you were Christmas shopping in Albuquerque."

"I finished early and even posted the last of the packages."

Her eyes shone. "How I envy you. I still have tons to do before the holidays."

"You haven't answered my question. What are you doing this dressed up in town? Attending a holiday party?"

"Actually, I have an appointment to meet with

the tribal council."

Damn. Not that again. He had secretly hoped she would drop the whole thing once the governor had turned him down. He could guess what their reaction would be. "I thought you had Luci doing that for you."

Sandy pulled her lips into a lopsided frown. "That didn't work out. She spoke to her brother-in-law, but he refused to intervene."

Not a surprise. "How come you didn't mention anything to me about this appointment?"

She sent him a cool look. "Because I already knew what you'd say."

"But I told you what the governor said." He was only met with a blank stare. "What makes you think the tribal council will do anything if the governor won't?"

"Good question, but they're my only hope. I went to the Bureau of Indian Affairs, but they told me what you said they would. This type of thing wasn't within their jurisdiction."

He would have pointed out he was usually right, but knew her too well. She was so headstrong. The more he discouraged her, the more she would feel compelled to act. "And you know where Harley stands."

"He's only one council member, one who might have a vested interest in the Edakees' land. Perhaps the others will be more helpful."

Ben shrugged. "All right. Go ahead and make your case to the tribal council, but I'm warning you, they're a little distracted right now."

She raised a brow. "Oh?"

"It seems an audit of the tribal accounts has revealed a big discrepancy. No one knows exactly what happened, but there's going to be an investigation."

She glanced at her watch. "I better be going."

"You sure you're doing the right thing?"

"I have nowhere else to turn."

Except for a twitch under his left eye, Ben tried to keep his face immobile and not show his concern. "I think you're making a big mistake."

"Then offer me a better plan."

"With mid-term break around the corner, let's get out of town. That would take your mind off this problem. By the time we return, things might have settled down."

She guffawed. "I can't believe you'd even suggest such a thing. I can't leave the pueblo now. Whoever's after the Edakees has recently upped the ante to violence. Who knows what they'll do next?"

His shoulders drooped under the weight of his disappointment. A buzzing filled his head. It was the sound of history repeating itself. Gabriella had begged him to go away with her and forget about the petition. If only he had listened.

But he would never change Sandy's mind. "Do what you want," he said, before turning away.

Sandy stepped in front of him and blocked his

path. "Please don't be mad."

"I'm not angry, I'm disappointed. I was looking forward to spending spring break on the road with you. I'm just sad that won't happen."

She looked at him in earnest. "I'd love to do it another time. Why don't you stay here with me."

"I don't know..." He hesitated, not certain what he should do. He didn't like the thought of abandoning her when she most needed him, but he also didn't want to offer her any encouragement. What if this thing backfired? He didn't want to see her hurt.

He watched her flip her hair over her shoulder and the sudden, overwhelming urge to take her into his arms overcame all his reservations. In one swift move, he pulled her to him and lowered his lips to hers.

Then he came to his senses. With another abrupt move, he pushed her away. "I better go. Good luck in there." He strode away before he could join her. Before he could add another poor decision to his list of lifelong regrets.

Shaken, Sandy watched Ben walk away, throbbing with unanticipated pleasure and unwelcome remorse. She could still feel the pressure of his lips on hers, the path of his hands down her back.

For a moment she thought Ben might reconsider and support her. But that moment had passed quickly. She ached with the realization she would have to go it alone. A stream of loneliness ran like a river through her veins. Any uncertainty she had about what she was about to do surfaced like a thunderstorm in the desert.

She took a moment to gather her courage, smooth her skirt, fix her smudged lipstick with a finger, before she proceeded to the Council Hall, in the same dreary brown cement block building that housed the Pueblo offices. On entering a windowless waiting room, a bespectacled woman at a stained wooden desk told her the tribal council was behind schedule. Sandy would have to wait.

She took a seat on a sagging, overstuffed arm chair with a pronounced indentation from earlier users. Everything around her looked as if it had been borrowed from a secondhand store. No two pieces of furniture matched. The walnut desk didn't belong alongside pine side tables. The chairs had been fashioned from naugahyde. Sepia photos of the pueblo in a mishmash of frames hung from pewter-colored walls.

She withdrew a pile of papers from her tote, busied herself grading book reports on *Harry Potter and the Sorcerer's Apprentice.* Half an hour passed. Forty minutes, and she still hadn't been called. She approached the clerk a second time to be informed she was the next person on the agenda. Not surprising since she was the only other person present.

Her patience had been stretched perilously close to the querulous stage when, thirty minutes later, the clerk called her name. Robert Tsabi stood just outside the council room, motioning her in. She was grateful to see his broad beaming face.

Inside the council room, six men sat on folding

chairs around an oak dining room table. On the table, each council member's name plate identified him. At the head of the table was Joseph Quam, the chairman. Harley Dista sat to his right and nodded at her. At the far side of the table was one empty chair, which Robert Tsabi pointed to and she sat.

"Good afternoon, Miss..." Joseph Quam consulted a sheet of paper on the table. "...Sandy Jacobs. Is that correct?"

She nodded.

"Welcome to the tribal council." Quam made the obligatory introductions. "You have come today to make a request of our council members. What can we do for you?"

The six men stared solemnly at her. Above their heads hung photographs of men with equally stoic expressions. Past and present members of the council seemed to have sternly judged her before she could even open her mouth. The starkness of the surrounding faces and a chill in the room caused her throat to constrict. Her palms were clammy.

"Miss Jacobs, you do have a request?" the Chairman repeated.

She cleared her throat, determined not to let her feelings paralyze her. This might be her last chance to advocate on the behalf of the Edakees. "I'm concerned about one of the pueblo families."

Joseph Quam riffled through the papers in front of him. "Which family might that be?"

"The Edakees. They're being unfairly

persecuted because of false rumors circulating about them."

Quam stopped to look up at her.

"What do you mean, 'persecuted'?" Robert Tsabi asked.

"They've been repeatedly visited by bogeymen *Kachina*, and their son has been beaten up after school on two separate occasions that I know of."

The chairman went back to shuffling paper. "Can you name who is behind this?"

On the spot. She rubbed her moist palms together. "Whoever they are, they think they can get away with what they're doing and no one will do anything about it."

"So you don't know their names?"

"No..."

"Or why this is going on?"

She tensed. "Not exactly."

Harley Dista rolled his eyes and smirked at her. "What would you like us to do, Miss Jacobs, when you do not even know who is bothering these people, or why?"

Sandy glanced around the table, aware of everyone's eyes on her. She hesitated, suddenly self-conscious. She had to make her case stronger. Harley Dista whispered something into Joseph Quam's ear. The chairman nodded.

She stood, pushing her seat back so abruptly it

wobbled on its hind legs before righting itself. "The Edakees are part of the tribe. As the governing body, they're your responsibility. I had to drive their son, Dixon, to the hospital for stitches the other day. You must stop these attacks before someone's seriously hurt."

"Please sit down, Ms. Jacobs," Harley Dista said firmly. She remained standing a moment longer, then reluctantly took her seat. "The stitches you refer to were a result of horseplay. We cannot prevent children from fooling around."

"I don't believe for one second that the incident was horseplay or an accident, and neither do you. This isn't the first time this has happened. It was a deliberate attack by the same people who are harassing this family."

"Even if that is true," Joseph Quam said, "what can we do about it? We must know who is doing this thing before we can take any action."

"You can...bring the situation into the open. If you were to put out word that you'd no longer tolerate these actions, they'd stop. Someone in authority has to intervene or else we'll all bear the blame for what happens."

The men's expressions remained blank; unmoved by her ardent plea.

The chairman shrugged. "How can you know what caused the child's injuries when you do not even know who did it? And how can you assume something bad will happen?"

"Because my apartment was broken into after I stood up for this family with the *Kachina*. The incidents have rapidly escalated. It's only a matter of time until they get worse."

"Not necessarily, Ms. Jacobs. If this is merely the result of pranksters, they will soon tire of their game." Mr. Tsabi's smile seemed kindly but fixed. "Perhaps you are too involved with this family and it is not in anyone's best interest."

Sandy ignored the implication she had lost her objectivity. Blame the messenger, she thought. "How can I convince you of the seriousness of the situation?"

Joseph Quam stood. "We must consider our role in this. Would you mind waiting in the outer office, Ms. Jacobs? The tribal council needs time to talk things over and come to a consensus."

She rose, knowing she had done her best. She had poured her whole heart into her presentation. Now all she could do was wait out the verdict. "I beg of you to find it in your hearts to help this family."

Harley Dista's voice took on a condescending tone. "That is melodramatic, Ms. Jacobs. We are aware of our responsibility here."

"Without your help I don't know what will happen..."

A uniformed guard stepped in front of Sandy and, after indicating the door, coaxed her from the room. She took a seat opposite the council chambers, praying she hadn't overplayed her hand.

Unable to concentrate on the magazine open in

her lap, she heard a murmur of voices coming from the room, but couldn't make out what was being said. Powerless, she clenched and unclenched her hands, alternately watching the wall clock and the closed council room door.

Finally, Joseph Quam appeared in the doorway and summoned her into the chambers.

The verdict was written on Quam's face before he even opened his mouth. "I am sorry, Ms. Jacobs, we can do nothing. This is the Edakees' personal problem, not a tribal matter. It will have to be handled by the Edakees themselves."

Tears of disappointment prickled her eyes and she blinked repeatedly to hold them back. The tribal council had been her last, best hope. Now all she could do was wait for the bloody hatchet to fall.

She said the obligatory farewells and trudged from the building, then slipped into the alleyway for a couple of minutes to compose herself before she ran into anyone. Thank goodness she had thought to bring tissues along.

On her way home she passed Luci's store, and on a whim, entered to spot Luci's sister on her haunches by a shelf. The woman was as fat as Luci was thin. Her plump face and graying hair made her look years older than Luci.

Sandy came up behind her. "Hello."

Startled, the woman nearly lost her balance and barely stopped herself from falling forward by grasping onto the shelf.

"I didn't mean to startle you." Sandy reached out to steady her. "I'm looking for Luci."

"Uh-huh." The woman backed away from her and disappeared behind a curtain drawn against the rear living quarters.

A moment later, Luci appeared. "What are you doing here, *gringa*?"

"I thought I'd stop by on my way home... Is your sister all right? I seem to have upset her."

"Oh, Ona's okay. Just shy around outsiders. Not used to you whites." Luci gave her a questioning look. "You look down in the mouth. Anything wrong?"

"I just left the tribal council chambers. Got a thumbs down on my request for aid to the Edakees."

"I could have told you so. What are you going to do now?"

Sandy raised her hands in resignation. "I don't know. School break is next week and Ben wants me to go away with him, but I probably won't. I may go to the State and see if there's anything they can do."

Luci made a 'tsk' sound with her tongue. "What do you think you will accomplish? The State can't intervene in tribal matters. We're a sovereign system. They have no authority over us. You're taking this thing too far. Don't deprive yourself of a holiday and waste your time chasing mirages in the desert."

Sandy lowered her head into her hands. "I don't know what to do."

"Nothing out of the ordinary is going to happen if you take a much needed vacation, *gringa*."

"That might be true, but the ordinary has been pretty extraordinary lately."

Luci chuckled. "You're hopeless. I hate to see you give up your vacation for nothing." The late afternoon light sparkled off the snake earrings dangling from Luci's ears. The coils reminded Sandy of the spiral of her uncertainty. Maybe Luci was right, maybe she should go away with Ben. But how would she feel if something unforeseen happened, and she wasn't around to help?

The Thursday before holiday break, Sandy stopped by the Edakee house to see how Dixon was doing. Quinton let her in and she went directly into the kitchen where Cecilia was kneading bread on the table top. Maria was tugging at her skirt and whining.

"Can I give you a hand to free you for a bit?"

Cecilia glanced down at the demanding toddler and smiled. "Sure." She broke off a piece of dough and placed it to the side.

After washing her hands, Sandy took her place at the table and poked fingers into the soft, slightly moist mixture. She inhaled deeply, enjoyed the aroma of yeast and flour and warm melted butter. By kneading the dough and stretching it before folding it back in on itself, she increased its elasticity. She wished she could have shaped the tribal council's decision as easily as she could stretch and mold the dough. She worked it back and forth, over and under, until she pushed it forward and it sprang back unaided.

"We may not be able to go to the sheep ranch next week as we usually do over winter break." Cecilia bounced Maria against her hip. "Dixon still has bad headaches from the bashing. I am afraid to leave town with him feeling so poorly. I may send Tonito by himself."

Sandy had passed Dixon in front of the television on her way into the kitchen. The stitches had been removed two days earlier, leaving behind a zipper-like scab across his forehead. When he turned toward her in greeting, she had the urge to pull open the zipper and learn what secrets lay behind those innocent almond eyes. If she only knew the names of his attackers, she wouldn't be so helpless.

She pinched flour onto the dough. "How about Quinton?"

Cecilia placed Maria in her highchair and joined Sandy at the table, taking up where she had left off. "He'll stay here. With the *Kachina* coming, we need him close by."

"Have they been around here lately?"

Cecilia broke her rhythm, her fingers flexing briefly within their floury cave. "They came again last night, *Tsila*. They were mean. They seem determined to come as often as possible."

Sandy dug deeper into the dough in frustration. It oozed under her nails. She paused to wipe the sticky residue off her hands with a dish cloth. "What threats did they make this time?"

"They said if we do not leave, they will hurt us worse than they hurt Dixon." Cecilia's face was as pale as the white-washed walls. Her obsidian eyes flat. "More people have become sick. Two more have died and no one knows why. So they blame us. I am afraid, *Tsila*."

Sandy picked at scraps of dough, her heart heavy with Cecilia's words. "I have another arrow in my quiver. I won't let you down."

Cecilia had tears in her eyes. "The *Kachina* know you went to the tribal council. They want you to leave them alone. They told us to warn you they will bring trouble to you if you do not obey. No matter what happens, you must not be harmed because of us, *Tsila*."

A fire flared inside Sandy. How dare they threaten her!

Rather than intimidate her as they intended, it only made her more determined than ever. She returned to furiously kneading the bread. Dough oozed between her fingers like white elastic mud. What more could these people do?

"I'm not afraid of them," she said with as much conviction as she could muster. She had to be strong for Cecilia's sake, as well as her own. She didn't know what was next on their agenda, but she wasn't about to let them terrorize her or her adopted family without putting up a good fight.

"They are all-powerful, *Tsila*. They cause the sun to rise and the rain to fall. They can certainly overpower a small person such as yourself."

Sandy smiled sadly at Cecilia. "And what about you?"

"It is different for me. I am San Anselmo. This is my home. It was my mother's home and her mother's home before that. I will not leave. You are an outsider. You do not have to be part of this."

"I thought I was a member of this family. Now you're disowning me?"

Cecilia lowered her voice. "I only mean to protect you."

Sandy felt such love at that moment she would have thrown her arms around Cecilia if her fingers hadn't been thickly caked with dough. "I'm not going to desert my family in their time of need, no matter the consequences."

Cecilia sighed, and turned back to her work. "Thank you, *Tsila*," she whispered, her soft voice barely audible over the wail of the toddler.

Chapter Fourteen

Sandy woke at first light, but realizing it was winter break, forced herself back to sleep. At 10:45, she startled awake, remembering her appointment with Neil. She couldn't believe how late she had slept after all these months of rising with the sun, but suspected her exhaustion was due more to emotional stress than long hours. She put on a pot of coffee before taking a shower. The sensation of hot water as it sluiced through soapsuds running down her stomach and thighs helped to clear her head, but she still felt the need for a cup of coffee before dressing.

Neil was already seated at a table in Ramona's when she arrived. She took a seat across the table from him on a yellow and orange flowered vinyl bench. "Have you been here long?"

He glanced at his watch. "Hours. Where have you been?"

The twinkle in his eyes told her he was kidding. "Sorry I'm late, but you won't believe how late I slept in this morning."

"Good," he said, merriment in his eyes. "You're following doctor's orders." He reached into a briefcase next to his seat and extracted a folded slip of paper. "Before I forget, here's Dirk Taylor's work number. He said to call him any time."

She took the paper, glanced at it briefly, and placed it in the front pocket of her daypack. "Thanks. I'll call him first thing Monday."

The waitress materialized and at Neil's suggestion they both ordered stuffed sopapillas with green chile. Not long after, the waitress returned with plates containing large "pillows" of dough stuffed with meat and covered with chile and cheese. The aroma of spicy chile tickled Sandy's nostrils. The sopapilla had the texture of fluffy filo dough.

"This literally melts in my mouth."

Neil put down his fork. "I'm glad you like it. I'd love to expose you to all kinds of new experiences."

She opened her mouth, but before she could speak, he raised a hand.

"Because I've been here a lot longer than you have."

So Neil's interest in her had not diminished since their discussion. She wanted to dissuade him without hurting him. Whatever happened, her heart belonged to Ben.

Ben. She had not seen much of him since the day of their last argument and she missed him more than she ever thought possible. His avoidance cut to her core. She wished she could see a way out of their impasse.

She sensed Neil's concentrated gaze on her, but when she looked up, he glanced down at his plate. The irony of her interest in Ben over Neil did not escape her. In her mother's estimation, she would be making a terrible mistake to take up with a man as rough around the edges as Ben when a polished, successful doctor was showing even marginal interest. To even consider

Ben over Neil would be preposterous.

She pictured her mother with her perfectly groomed hair, tastefully tinted to deny the gray. In her beautifully tailored suits. If only her mother had been as loving as she was impeccable. Instead, her criticism had diminished Sandy's sense of self. She never failed to point out Sandy's foolishness; the error of her judgment.

But her mother was no longer alive and Sandy had to make her own decision. The one choice she never really had was falling in love with Ben. For the first time, she admitted it to herself. She loved Ben. Her feelings were real and unshakable.

Neil must have noticed her mental absence because he asked, "Where have you gone?"

She gave him an unabashed smile. "Out to lunch."

He shifted his chair around the table closer to hers. "I've done serious thinking since the last time we were together. I know you mentioned your fledgling relationship, but I'd still like to see more of you. I think I could offer you more than he can, certainly more than he has so far. Would you please give me that chance?"

The moment was so delicate. She didn't want to crush him. She weighed her words. "I'm sorry, Neil, but I'm not available..."

He leaned in closer, near enough that she could smell his elegant cologne. "How can you say that without giving me an opportunity?"

"I'm sure you have a great deal to offer

someone, but I'm just not that someone."

"You sound like you're selling yourself short. You need a man who believes in you, thinks the world of you. I know we could have something special going for us if you'd just let me in..."

Before she could respond, he leaned over and unexpectedly kissed her.

Ben's big plans for the holidays all featured Sandy, who he hadn't spoken to in days. The thought of vacationing alone, without her, didn't appeal to him at all. He wanted to fly away with her, escape the reservation, and put miles between her and the source of her problems, but her resistance to the idea seemed more and more insurmountable.

He paced from room to room, restless. His mind worked overtime seeking a solution to their ongoing conflict. No matter how hard he wracked his brain, he couldn't come up with a logical way out. He needed to give it a break.

Since he still had Christmas cards to mail, he tossed his down jacket over his green plaid wool shirt and took off for the village.

At the post office, he spotted Sandy's car parked in front of Ramona's. A chance to "run into" her had just presented itself. He couldn't pass up the opportunity.

He strode through melting snow across the rutted road to the restaurant and pulled open the door. The moment his eyes adjusted to the dim light, he spied

Sandy across the room, kissing a stranger.

The full impact of the image hit him with the suddenness of a sandstorm in the desert. He couldn't believe he was witnessing Sandy with another man. In his arms. Lips on lips. A heart-stopping band tightened around his chest, making it difficult to breathe.

"So this is why I haven't seen you, Sandy!" he shouted across the room.

Sandy disengaged so precipitately that had the man not been grasping her arms, she would have shot back against the wall and rebounded. Her mouth opened and her eyes widened. She began to stand, to say something, but he was out the door before he could listen to her. He catapulted into his truck and tore out of the lot, leaving gullies in the dirt.

Dust rose in furious sheets behind his wheels. He was suffocating. Bleeding. He had to go where he could breathe and heal...and think.

Sandy stared helplessly at Neil.

His gaze fixed on her, his brows knitted in question. "Is that the other member of the relationship you mentioned?"

She nodded.

He looked down at the table. "You want to go after him, don't you?"

Yes, she wanted to rush out the door, push past anyone in her path, forget good sense and decorum. Run after Ben. Her stomach churned. Her head swam. It took every ounce of her strength to restrain herself.

She said with a quiet control that surprised her, "I wouldn't do that to you."

Neil shrugged, unsmiling. "Don't hold back on my account. A minute ago, I would have done anything to convince you to be with me, but now that I see the truth of the matter, I've changed my mind. I don't want you to be with me if you really want to be with him."

"Oh, Neil, I'm so sorry. I didn't want to hurt you, but..."

"You can't help but hurt somebody. So, do what you have to."

He glanced up and her gaze held his. "I'd like to resolve this with Ben, but I don't want to leave you hanging. Are you certain you'll be all right?"

Neil raised his chin, pressing his lips together in a pointedly resolute gesture. "I'm a big boy, Sandy. Go ahead and tend to that rocky relationship, but, if it crumbles, keep my number handy."

"Thanks, Neil, you're a good friend." Sandy stood, and took Neil's hand in hers. His, unlike Ben's, was smooth and soft—unaccustomed to manual labor. "I'll always be grateful to you for this." She squeezed his fingers and fled the restaurant in the direction of Rainbow Mesa. Ben would be there, she felt with as much certainty as the love stirring inside of her.

Sandy struggled her way up the steep trail to the mesa top where Ben had taken a seat on a flat-top rock.

When she stumbled over a pile of loose pebbles, the scraping sound caused him to jerk his head up and glare at her. He immediately began to gather up his backpack as though to leave.

Her heart sank. She rushed to his side. "Ben, please, let me explain."

Although he held onto his pack, he didn't move. "Explain what? I have eyes."

"It's not what it seems. I have no interest in Neil Kramer. He's a friend, that's all."

A skeptical expression sweep across Ben's face. "And how often do you kiss a friend on the lips?"

"That was a first. I wasn't expecting it. I can imagine how it looked, but I don't feel anything for Neil. I love you." *Oh, my God.* The words had escaped before she could consider them. She flung her hand over her mouth.

Ben let the pack slip through his fingers. It fell to the ground with a thud. He watched her through curious but cautious eyes.

It took all her courage, but she forced herself to meet his gaze. "I meant that, Ben. I wouldn't say it if I didn't."

"Then why were you out with another man in the first place?"

"Because Neil's been willing to listen to me and support me in my decision to help the Edakees, support that you have conspicuously withheld."

Ben looked away.

Sandy sandwiched the hand that hung loosely at his side between both of hers. "I still don't understand why you're so opposed to my defending the Edakees. That makes me wonder who you are. What you stand for. I can't believe you'd stand by, permit a family to withstand this kind of harassment, and do nothing. All I'm asking is for you to back me up."

She took his chin in her hand and forced him to look her in the eye. "I'm not here to change anyone or make them more like me. All I'm trying to do is protect them. Can't you extend yourself enough to see my side? Help me out?"

He peeled her fingers away from his face with far more tenderness than she would have expected and walked to the edge of the mesa, his back to her. "I don't know..."

She chose to let him be and took a seat on the rock ledge. "Why, Ben? I need to make sense of this."

Ben stared off into the distance for what seemed an eternity, as though he would rather be visiting some distant galaxy than addressing her. Finally, he whispered, "Because of what happened in El Salvador."

"You never mentioned being in El Salvador."

"I wasn't sure I wanted to. It was a long time ago." He ran his hand through his hair. "After college I joined the Peace Corps. I wasn't ready to settle down and decide what to do with my life, so the Peace Corps sounded like a good intermediary plan. I was stationed as a teacher in a small village called Metapán. Shortly after I arrived I met the woman who would become my wife, Gabriella. She taught in the same school..." His voice wavered and it took him a moment to recover.

An acidic pang of jealousy burned in Sandy, but she ignored it. "What happened to her?"

"At that time, El Salvador was under the control of a military oligarchy that ruled through fear and violence. Most of the people were locked in ignorance and poverty. The only way they knew to fight back was by forming an organization they called the Farabundo Marti National Liberation Front, named for their hero. A civil war went on for years between the rebel FMNL and the military dictatorship. You might have heard about it."

"How did that affect you and...Gabriella?"

Ben hunched on his heels at the rim of the mesa. "Gabriella and I knew foreign aid money was coming into the country, especially from the United States, to shore up the military government. But we didn't have books for our students. The situation frustrated us."

"I can imagine." She was tempted to say something about the inner-city schools, but thought better of it.

"Perhaps. But you'll never know how it felt to see those poor children without a proper education or hope for the future while a few fat cats in San Salvador lived in the lap of luxury on money stashed away in Swiss bank accounts." Ben picked up a small clod and rubbed it to red dust between his fingers.

"My parents had told me how the student protests in the 1960s forced the U.S. government to end the war in Vietnam. I was naive enough to think we could do the same and convinced Gabriella to join me in protesting the unequal treatment. I thought we could shame the government into providing a portion of the supplies we needed to do our job." He flung the remains of the clod over the mesa edge. Self-recrimination coated his words.

His silence lasted so long she knew he would never continue without prodding. "And?"

"We did what we could to organize the other teachers to petition the school board and local authorities for more supplies. We urged others to raise their voices, take a stand, but everyone else was too afraid to act..." Ben hesitated, stared out at the desert below.

"Someone had to do something and that someone was me, since I was the outsider. I approached the town council and they told me they'd consider my request. It didn't take long to figure out that they weren't about to do anything. Frustrated, I wrote a couple of letters to the local paper, which apparently caused quite a stir." He stopped again, clearing his throat. "One night, in November, when Gabriella and I were at home..." His voice broke. "It's hard to talk about this."

"Take your time," she said gently, wanting to encourage him. She hoped her presence would make him feel safe enough, and loved enough, to share his story with her.

"Four jackboots kicked in the front door of our house. I had just enough time to rise from my chair when two of them rushed me and grabbed my arms.

While one of them held a gun to my temple, the other one tied my hands behind my back. The other two had gotten a hold of my wife and were dragging her toward the front door. I'll never forget the look in her eyes." Again, Ben's voice faltered. He took a deep breath.

"I begged the guards to let go of her. Told them I was the trouble-maker...asked them to take me instead. They laughed; said I needed to learn a lesson; told me if I stopped causing trouble, they would release my wife. Since I was getting nowhere, I tried to break free, but the one with the gun whacked me on the side of the head and I fell. All I remember is warm blood oozing down the side of my face, blinding me. One of the guards kicked me in the chest as they left the house. Another spat on my face. It was a demonstration of their strength, meant to humiliate me, and it worked. The guard who kicked me said they would kill my wife if I tried to come after them."

"What became of her?"

Ben ran a shaky hand over his brow. "I never saw her again. Like many others at the time, she disappeared. After the regime was overthrown, I searched for her, but she had vanished without a trace." His voice sounded strained. "That night they took away my wife, they took away my life. Any faith I had in my ability to protect and defend had been beaten down along with my body." He lowered his head into his hands.

Sandy placed a hand on Ben's shoulder. Even though he was facing away from her, his grief proved infectious. Burning tears swelled her throat and blurred her vision.

His shoulders convulsed in silent sobs. "I returned to Missouri, but I didn't feel like I fit in anymore. Everyone seemed to be going about their business, but my life had stopped the moment Gabriella disappeared. I didn't know what to do or where to go, so I moved back to a place I hardly knew but wanted to be, New Mexico.

"San Anselmo has been a refuge for me, a sanctuary. It's taken a long time to heal the wounds, but being here has certainly helped." Unshed tears shimmered in his eyes.

"Then you waltz into my life and bring with you the first hope I've had in years of ever finding joy with another woman."

The look he gave her touched her inner-most core. A wave of tenderness flowed through her.

"But you brought with you the black cloud of another equally controversial situation. How do I know this one won't turn out in the same way as the last one?"

"You can't equate the two, Ben. This is a different time. A different place."

Ben placed his hand over hers and held it against his cheek. "I couldn't stand it if anything happened to you, Sandy. Last year one of the teachers tried to stand up for another kid who was also being harassed. She went before the tribal council to plead her case. As it turned out, the ringleader was a council member's son. Instead of helping the situation, she wasn't hired back another year. That's the job you took."

Her stomach knotted. "I had no idea."

"And I have no idea to what extremes these people will go to make their point. So far they've been willing to break into your apartment and threaten you. What's next?"

Ben wrapped his strong arms around her and crushed her to his broad chest. "I can't afford to lose you, Sandy. You've become...too important to me." Ben captured her with his impassioned gaze. "I've missed you, Sandy. More than I even admitted to myself." He enfolded her in his arms and kissed her.

Sandy's feet were planted firmly on the ground, but her spirit soared. It had been so long since they had been this close. She relished the feel of his firm flesh beneath her fingers, the smell of clean sweat mixed with spicy cologne, and the taste—both sweet and pungent—of his succulent lips.

The kisses, at first tender and loving, quickly became more ardent, more demanding. His urgency echoed her own. She kissed him back with all the pent up passion she had been forced to deny over the past months of conflict.

The heat slowly rose. A tickle which had started between her thighs became a throb.

"Come with me," he said, taking her hand and leading her toward his pack. With a blanket spread on the ground, he sunk with her to the mesa top. Passion born of love mingled with unfulfilled desire flamed in her. He trailed his lips to her nape, teased her with his tongue. His fingers brushed her breasts, followed by his tongue.

She was on fire.

She threw her head back and savored the tension building inside. They undressed each other and before long, he lay naked beside her.

He levered himself onto an elbow and gazed down at her. Naked and vulnerable in the crisp winter air, she trembled beneath his gaze.

"You're beautiful," he said. "More beautiful than I even imagined."

He wrapped himself around her in protectiveness and passion. Answering passion flared in her with fiery abandon.

The weight of his body against hers created a staggering desire. With his strokes, the warmth between her legs quickly ignited. The simple, almost ephemeral, pressure of his fingers provoked sensations so intense she felt as if she might explode. He slipped inside her and she drowned deliriously in a sea of sensations.

Surrendering totally, she lost herself in the delicious dance of desire. Rhythmically, he rocked her into a state of total immersion until the tension in her shattered into a million stars.

Soon he convulsed in her arms and collapsed on top of her.

Afterward, they lay side-by-side, holding onto one another.

When Ben finally sat up, glistening perspiration evaporating from her skin cooled her. The cold air, hardly noticeable moments before, raised goose bumps on her exposed flesh.

"You look as if you're freezing." He grabbed his jacket and threw it over her. "How about we move to a softer spot?"

"Umm." Sandy stretched like a satisfied lioness and sat up. She hadn't really noticed her discomfort until he mentioned it.

Chapter Fifteen

Sandy trailed Ben across the desert floor. Giant tumbleweed and scrub oak dotted their path. The sun slipped rapidly beneath clouds to the west and streaks of red, gold, and violet lit the horizon just above the pillowy plumes. With Ben's hand sheltering hers, she was reminded of their earlier intimacy. A warm, fuzzy sensation swelled inside.

By the time they reached the truck, dusk had descended. "Why don't you leave your car here and we'll pick it up later?" he suggested.

Without hesitation, she agreed. He sealed the deal with a kiss.

The truck shimmied over rutted roads leading toward town and she was buffeted about, but she didn't mind. Sandy basked in the pleasure of being near Ben and nothing would disrupt her contentment.

Then he braked abruptly, throwing her forward. He thrust out his arm to prevent her from hitting the dash.

"Smells like something's burning!" he exclaimed.

She sniffed the evening air. "Where do you think it's coming-" She spotted the glare from the fire lighting the night sky. "Look!" She pointed at the rapidly rising black smoke. "It's in town."

"We better hurry back to see if we can help." Ben floored the truck and she grasped the dashboard to steady herself. Dirt flew in all directions. As they neared town, she could see brilliant yellow flames lick the night sky with serpents' tongues, then retreat, plunge and rise again. Beautiful and terrifying.

The truck plowed down on the normally quiet village, cornered Main Street on two wheels, and raced toward the center of the pueblo. Sandy's hands began to shake. "It's coming from the Edakees' street."

"Let's pray it's not their house." Ben took a sharp left onto the road.

From the turn-off, it became obvious their fears were well-founded. Flames curled out of the Edakee house. Black smoke billowed above. The sight was eerie, unreal.

Sandy bolted from the truck before it had come to a complete stop in front of the house and ran to where Cecilia stood, stunned and dirty, holding Maria in her arms. Over Maria's wails, Sandy asked, "Are you okay?"

Cecilia stared at her through glazed eyes. "Dixon and Quinton are inside! I have to get them out!" She thrust Maria at Sandy.

Ben stopped her. "Sandy, stay here with Cecilia! I'm going in!"

The air had become thick with smoke and heavy with fear. She could hardly breathe. While fire was her most daunting phobia, how could she stand the loss of Dixon, or Quinton? She took a deep breath. Everything inside of her screamed "don't go," but with only Ben going in, one, or both, of those kids might not make it out alive. Time to face her foe. "I'm coming with you!"

"No, stay back." Ben sprinted toward the house.

Sandy handed Maria back to her mother and took off after him. By the time she reached the front door, Ben had rushed in ahead.

He glanced back at her and yelled, "Duck! The flames and smoke are above!"

She could barely see him through the thick, suffocating darkness.

The black smoke swept up her nose and into her lungs, making it impossible to breathe. She choked. All her instincts told her to turn back, protect herself, but the thought of the helpless children inside kept her going. She stumbled forward.

The heat from the fire on the roof forced her to stay low. She hunched over and crab-walked down what she knew was the hallway. Though she could no longer see Ben, she could hear him yell between coughs, "Since you're so damn stubborn, take the room on the right, then get the hell out of here."

Her hand against the wall guided her while she memorized her path to retrace it later. The wall opened into a room. She entered with tear-filled, blind eyes. Smoke filled her head, but she lurched forward and pitched against what seemed to be a bed. Frantically, she ran her hands over sheets, but felt nothing. Turning, she tripped over a large object. On her knees, she felt a mound, but could barely make out Dixon's features.

She pulled him up. "Dixon? Dixon!"

He didn't stir. A wave of terror enveloped her. She tried to hoist his upper body to drag him from the room, but his dead weight worked against her.

A loud crash outside released a tremendous surge of adrenaline. She frantically yanked the prone child, and succeeded in pulling him toward the door. She had no time to find a window in the smoky darkness.

With strength she didn't know she had, she dragged Dixon down the hall. The intense heat seared the inside of her nostrils.

To her left, a flaming fixture tumbled from the ceiling and crashed. She sprang to avoid the flare-up, heaving the inert child with her.

Heat and smoke were beginning to overcome her as she groped for the front door. Unseen objects exploded around her.

Dizzy and disoriented, she knew she had to be inches from the door, but the distance seemed endless.

Pitch-black smoke grew impossibly dark and closed in around her. Precious air escaped from her mouth instead of the scream she heard in her head. Just before she hit the floor in defeat, the door swung open and strong arms gathered her up. First she was being hauled from the burning house.

"Dixon…" she said weakly.

Ben nodded. "Don't worry. He's next."

She choked and gasped as the night air rushed into her burning lungs. Smoke coated her hair and ash-covered clothing, poured from her mouth, seeped from her pores. She could taste it...smell it... feel it.

Safely away from the building, Ben carefully lowered her to the ground with comforting words. Then he carried Dixon to a more open spot. The child lay frighteningly still.

Sandy was dimly aware of Cecilia stooped next to her, tending to Quinton, who was sitting with his head in his hands.

As soon as Cecilia spotted Ben placing Dixon down, she screamed, "Dixon!" and sprang to his side. Maria tottered after her mother, but, for once, Cecilia ignored the baby. Shrieking, she scrabbled at Ben's shoulders as he bent over the boy. "Is he okay? Is he all right?"

Ben didn't answer. Instead, he began administering mouth-to-mouth resuscitation, blowing into Dixon's mouth three or four times, and pushing with the heel of a hand into the child's chest. Dixon remained unresponsive.

A wail rose from Cecilia. A silent but similar cry welled up inside of Sandy. Although still light-headed and nauseated, she pulled herself on trembling arms across the ground to where Dixon lay. Ben took a deep breath and again bent over the inanimate child.

He repeated the cycle of breathing and pressing two more times to no avail. When he sat back, Sandy noticed the welts on Dixon's arms and face.

Cecilia began to wail louder.

"I'm not giving up," he assured her. He tried a

third time, then straightened to catch his breath. All looked lost. Sandy turned away, her heart breaking. She could no longer restrain the tears of loss and frustration that burned in her eyes.

A muffled choking sound came from Dixon's direction. Sandy looked over to see him roll his head from side to side.

"He's alive!" Sandy's hoarse shouts were drowned out by others.

The sound of a siren pierced the smoke-filled night air. A red fire truck with a swirling red beam turned onto the street and headed toward the burning house. Men in yellow slickers and tall black boots jumped down from the truck, pulled a hose off an enormous roll, and signaled another man by the side of the truck. A flash flood of water gushed from the hose onto the house. The squeal of an ambulance quickly followed.

Two paramedics hopped out and raced toward Cecilia, who had bundled Dixon up in her arms and was holding him pressed to her chest. They cleared the area around them. At their prompting, Cecilia reluctantly released him, picked up her toddler, and stood anxiously by while the ambulance crew tended to him.

One paramedic mumbled to another, "I don't like the sound of his breathing. We better get him to the hospital."

Ben slumped next to her onto the ground. "You okay?"

"Better now that I know Dixon's alive."

He placed an arm around her shoulders. A paramedic came up to them. He listened to both of their chests with a stethoscope and asked if they needed any help. He suggested they go to the emergency room to have their injuries checked out. For the first time, Sandy looked down at her arms, covered with ash and scrapes.

A police car raced up the road and stopped in front of the house. Two police officers stepped out, opened the back doors and pulled passengers from the backseat. Virgil Chavez and his brother Duane.

Duane was dressed solely in a short buckskin skirt and red, yellow and green deerskin boots. Virgil wore a black skirt and red and white polka dot gloves. Both had sashes with feathers across their bare chests. Remnants of paint remained on their faces.

One officer with a buzz cut and acne scars dragged Virgil over to Cecilia. "A neighbor called to report the fire. She saw two boys running from the house and these two fit her description, so we picked them up. Do you recognize either of them?"

Cecilia nodded. "Virgil and Duane Chavez."

A woman in a red flannel robe pointed over Sandy's head. "They live behind that house."

The cop with the dermatological problem poked Virgil in the ribs. "That's where we found them. They may be the ones who started the fire."

From the side of the patrol car, Duane yelled over the roar of the fire, water, and milling crowd, "We didn't start any fire. We just meant to scare them."

Sandy pushed herself to her feet. Face to face with Virgil, she could see the fear in his eyes. His hands were cuffed behind his back. "Are you the *Kachina* impersonators?"

Duane mumbled under his breath, but Virgil only stared at the ground and shuffled his feet. "We...we...we never started no fire."

"Why? Why were you out to get them?"

Duane kicked the patrol car tire. In the beam from the emergency light she could see his face was beet red. "They killed our father and sister. We want them off the pueblo."

"The Edakees didn't kill anyone! But you've come close to killing an innocent little boy!"

"Was anyone hurt in the fire?" the tall policeman with the ponytail asked Ben.

"Dixon Edakee, the ten-year-old. They're taking him to the hospital in a minute."

"These boys better hope he's okay," the shorter officer said. "We're booking them for arson. If they're lucky, it won't turn into a murder charge."

"But we did not do the fire," Virgil protested.

"Of course not," the cop by his side said before hauling Duane toward the car. "They're always innocent." He placed a hand on the boy's head and shoved him into the back seat.

Cecilia's aunt arrived as the paramedics were carrying Dixon on a stretcher to the ambulance. "Let me take Maria home with me so you can go to the hospital with Dixon and Quinton."

A paramedic helped Cecilia into the ambulance. Sandy leaned unsteadily against Ben and called after her, "Do you need me to go to the hospital with you?"

"No, *Tsila*, I'm fine. You go home," Cecilia shouted through the open ambulance door. "You need to take care of yourself."

"Cecilia's right." Ben pressed her closer. "You look terrific in soot, but you just may want to go home and wash up."

Ignoring Sandy's protests, Ben maneuvered her into the truck and drove her straight to her apartment.

"Are you sure you're going to be all right?" Ben asked as he pulled up in front. "Maybe we should run by the emergency room."

"I'm okay. I just need a good night's rest." She knew she'd be fine physically, but something gnawed at her. "This was all my fault, Ben. If I hadn't gone to the tribal council it never would have happened."

"How do we know that? There's no proof the events are even connected."

"You *said* this might happen. I should have listened to you."

"Stop berating yourself. I might have been mistaken. We don't know what really went on."

She turned toward him, confused, yet certain his change of heart confirmed the significance of all that had transpired between them. "You certainly don't sound like the Ben Rush I know."

He gave her a sad smile. "This may turn out to be more complicated than we realize. I don't believe those boys started that fire."

How sweet but naive of him. His loyalty to the Chavez boys touched but perplexed her. "If not them, who else?"

Ben stared out the window at the starry sky. She glanced over his shoulder at Orion, the Big Dipper, and the sprinkling of stars in the Milky Way. It always amazed her how many stars could be seen in the New Mexico sky because of the high altitude and lack of city lights.

Sandy had begun to ache all over. A burning spot on her upper arm distracted her momentarily. Her fingers pressed against a hot spot she would have to treat with aloe later. She would probably discover more burns and bruises when the shock wore off.

"All we can do is report what we know to the tribal police. Let them handle this.."

"So you expect me to sit back and do nothing?" She folded her arms across her chest.

Ben's eyes narrowed. "What else do you have in mind?"

"We could at least contact the Bureau of Indian Affairs. That way an outside agency could oversee the locals and prevent a whitewash. After my experience with the Tribal Council, I don't trust it will be a fair and thorough investigation. I'd rather check this out myself."

"That sounds like a Sandy solution if I ever

heard one. Take matters into your own hands." Ben made an exasperated sound. "As amateurs, we might only complicate everything and blotch it up for the experts. We better let the police handle it without our interference."

"Wait a minute. Didn't you just tell me you were burnt—no pun intended—by the authorities in El Salvador? How can you trust them to do their job? If they blow this case, the Chavez boys will probably be sentenced to hard time."

"I see your point. Those boys are in serious trouble, and I want to make sure they get a fair shake. All we can do is serve as advocates and stay public enough with our allegations to keep the officials on target." Ben took her hand. "Let's make a careful report of our suspicions tomorrow morning and see how they're handled before we take any other steps."

Sandy was too exhausted and over-wrought to do more than half-heartedly acquiesce. She gently squeezed his fingers. "Okay, if that's what you think is best."

Ben gave her one of his devastating smiles. "I think what would be best is for you to get some rest. I'll come by in the morning and we'll go to the police station to file a report." He wrapped her in a bear hug she never wanted to break.

Chapter Sixteen

A ringing she mistook for the school bell shocked Sandy awake. She reached across the nightstand, almost knocking over a glass of water, and flipped on the light. The clock read five A.M. What an ungodly time to awaken. She tapped the alarm button to silence the screeching sound.

The chill air collided with her bed-warmed arm and she pulled the covers over her shoulders. She yearned to roll over and snuggle back in her pillow, but had no time to waste if she wanted to reach the Edakee house before the police arrived. While she had promised Ben she would not play detective, she didn't know if she could keep her word. What had happened the night before was partially her fault; she had helped create this disaster. She probably should listen to Ben, but she felt compelled to make things right again, and couldn't do anything unless she knew who started the fire. Perhaps she could find a clue in the remains that would answer that question without stirring up any more trouble.

She pried herself, conflicted and sore, from the comfort of her bed and fumbled painfully into jeans, boots and white tee with the play on words 'KNOW FEAR' emblazoned in hot pink across the chest. With daypack on back, she dashed into the kitchen, grabbed a banana, and rushed out the door. In the dark, she cautiously made her way to what was left of the Edakee house. By the time she arrived, a faint glow lit up the eastern sky.

Even in the dim light, she could make out the blackened and scarred hulk of the house. One side-wall had collapsed, lopsided and misshapen. Pieces of crumbling plaster exposed a skeletal foundation. The ruins looked like a sunken ship, abandoned and rotten. In the charred remains, she saw mute evidence of life as it was before the fire, a table leg here, a broken toy there. The smell of smoke hovered, sickening her all over again.

She stepped around the perimeter of the house in a daze, not knowing what she sought or what she might find. The ground, saturated by the fire fighters, squelched under her boots. Indifferent to the mud, she continued scanning the ruins. An overturned tricycle lay behind what remained of a chair. A blackened toothbrush and soggy, mud-soaked underwear—or what looked like underwear but may have been something else in its pre-fire condition—had washed downstream. Beyond that, the mud ended and the ground hardened to a cracked slab.

She surveyed the area a second time, feeling a little voyeuristic. The early morning rays reflected off a shiny object lying between a charred plate and a lampshade on the ground. She bent and picked it up.

A silver earring in the shape of a snake dangled from her fingers.

Luci's earring!

Bewildered, Sandy stared at it, so stunned it took her a full minute before it occurred to her to wonder why Luci had been there. And what did Luci have to do with the fire? Suddenly, she knew.

The reason for Luci's lies and her adamant opposition to Sandy's relationship with the Edakees became clear. Luci was the one behind the attempts to frighten the Edakees off their land. The one eager to get her hands on the land and its bounty. Only two pieces to the puzzle remained. Why Luci and not Harley? And what did the Chavez boys have to do with it?

She pocketed the earring, knowing Luci had to show up at any moment to look for it before the police arrived, and began to make her way toward the front of the house. On impulse, she stooped to pick up a sharp looking piece of glass for protection. Too late. She heard a truck pull up to the front of the house and doors slam.

Luci's gravelly voice said, "Look over there."

Not wanting Luci to discover her snooping about, she hurried toward the side of the building and hid behind the remains of a wall. When she felt safe, she peered around the corner to watch Luci and her sister, Ona, make their way through mud to the back yard. They were obviously searching for something, because they kept their heads down and their eyes on the ground. And that something was securely stashed in Sandy's pocket. Then she noticed the gun Luci carried in her right hand. A bolt of fear raced through her.

Lots of good her minuscule glass weapon would do against a firearm. She palmed the shard in case she needed it later, making sure not to clench her hand and cut herself.

"Where can that earring be?" Luci muttered aloud.

"We better find it before the police do. Harley will really be mad at us." Ona looked on the verge of tears. "We should not have done this."

"Stop sniveling and look for the damn earring. We can't afford to get caught."

Ona glanced in Sandy's direction. Sandy instantly ducked back behind the wall. A full minute passed before she had the nerve to peek around the corner again. The two women were still busy combing what used to be a backyard. She sighed in relief.

Abruptly, Ona bent over. "What's this?"

Luci rushed to her side and looked at the square object Ona had pulled from the mud. "Aw, it's just a piece of metal. Not an earring." She stood with her hands planted on her hips, a scowl on her lips.

Ona groaned and righted herself. "We better get out of here before the police come."

"Not just yet," Luci said. "Look around there." She pointed to the side of the house where Sandy was hidden.

Ona shook her head. "Why? We did not go over there."

"The earring might have flowed there in the downpour from the fire hoses. We better check."

Sandy jerked back from her vantage point. They were heading her way. She had to retreat. But where?

She automatically stooped lower to make herself small and invisible and backed off, keeping an eye on the corner. Her legs wobbled beneath her. They trembled so much she prayed the women could not hear her knees knocking. She could hardly breathe.

Mud squished as the two women made their way toward the side of the house. The sucking noise became louder and louder until it sounded as though it was a few feet from her. She turned and began to sprint toward the street, but she had only gone a couple yards when her foot caught on an object hidden by the mud. She lost her balance, pitched forward, and hit the mud with a splash. As she tried to scramble to her feet, a hand on her arm stopped her.

Luci's voice boomed. "Stand up slowly, *gringa*."

She did as told, her mind racing with possible escape routes as she slowly turned to stare down the barrel of the gun. She automatically flung her arms before her face. "Don't shoot me."

"Now what are you doing here?" Luci sounded exasperated. "We weren't expecting any help."

"I thought I could salvage some of the Edakees' belongings. That's the reason I'm here. I was just about to leave."

Luci glanced at Ona and sighed. "Too bad, our little friend here overheard our conversation. She now knows too much."

She had to think fast. "I don't know a thing. I was on my way out when I heard a sound. I thought it was the police and knew I better leave."

"Too bad, *gringa*. We can't let you leave now."

"I didn't hear anything, I swear! Just let me go."

"Sorry, *gringa*, but we have no choice. You always did have a knack for being in the wrong place at the wrong time." Luci let out a dry, forced-sounding chuckle.

As emotionally stretched as the skin on a drum, Sandy shivered with fear. "What do you plan to do with me?"

"Take you for a ride." Luci turned to Ona. "We have some twine in the truck. Go find it and tie her hands behind her back."

Ona moved cautiously past Sandy as though she might spring at her. Not with the barrel of a gun pointed squarely at her face. She'd have to find another way out. "I don't know what you're talking about. I just arrived here a few moments ago."

Luci shook her head. "Then why were you running away from us, *gringa*?"

"I told you I thought you were the police. I didn't want to wind up in hot water for trespassing. I didn't know it was you."

Luci shot her a cynical look. "Maybe if you had learned to mind your own business like I told you, you would not be in this predicament."

The squish of Ona's boots behind her made Sandy half-turn.

"Face here, *gringa*." Luci raised the gun and lifted her chin in a movement which demanded compliance. "Place your hands together behind your back."

She followed orders, making sure to sequester the shard.

"Tie her hands together," Luci demanded.

Ona tugged at her wrists with an agility Sandy never expected, whipped the twine around them twice, and pulled until it hurt. Sandy grunted in pain. "That hurts."

"Shut up!" Luci said.

Was it Sandy's imagination, or did Ona loosen the rope a tad?

Sandy made an effort to move her arms, but the rope would only allow the slightest movement. Sandy's only hope of escape lay in her ability to free her arms, which seemed impossible at that moment.

"All right," Luci commanded Ona. "Put her in the truck."

Ona took hold of Sandy's arm and shoved her toward the adobe brown pickup with Luci and the firearm close behind. Pushed into the center of the seat, she sat sandwiched between Luci, who held the gun at her head, and Ona. Ona started the engine.

"Where are we going?" Unwanted beads of sweat dribbled down her brow. She had the urge to wipe it away, but couldn't.

"Rainbow Mesa sounds like as good a place as any. Drive over there, Ona." Luci's face was drawn and pale. It made her look as tense as she sounded.

Since Luci obviously had not anticipated this

complication, she might be more easily convinced to let her go, with the proper persuasion. "You really don't have to do this, Luci. I won't say anything to anyone if you release me. I'm on your side." As soon as Sandy saw the annoyance register in Luci's expression, she knew her argument was useless.

"You've been such a welcome visitor at the store, I wish I could believe that, *gringa*. But I'm afraid I have no choice. Please, don't make this harder on both of us." Luci pressed the gun against Sandy's skull. "Ona, stop by your house on the way out to the mesa."

The truck rumbled down the street, heading out of town. At an orange house on the outskirts of the village, Ona pulled over. Luci jogged around the truck and handed Ona the firearm. "Keep an eye on her until I return."

Ona's hand trembled as she took the gun. The pistol dipped then rose unsteadily. She seemed an easier mark than her sister. As soon as Luci had disappeared into the house, Sandy sprang into action. "Ona, please don't do this. You don't want blood on your hands, do you?"

Ona stared wide-eyed at Sandy, obviously frightened and confused. Sandy saw her advantage and pressed on. "Don't you see the wisdom of letting me go? Why should you have this crime on your hands? What makes you willing to pay for Luci's mistakes?"

Before Sandy could say anything else, Luci opened the truck door and hoisted herself into the cab. She now held onto a hunting rifle, which she bolted to a rack behind their heads.

"Okay, everything is taken care of with Harley. Let's go."

Ona gingerly placed the .22 in the glove box with such care she would have thought it was an easily detonated bomb. Sandy had to fight back tears of disappointment.

The truck lurched forward, jostling Sandy, who was already uncomfortable enough. Sitting wedged between the two women, she maneuvered the glass piece between thumb and index finger and began to saw at the twine between her wrists as inconspicuously as she could. She worked at it and worked at it, desperate to break its grip, but because of her trembling fingers and the awkward position, the knot didn't yield one millimeter. Her spirits sunk lower than the valley on the horizon, but she couldn't give up.

Dust from the road clogged Sandy's nostrils and stung her eyes. The mesa, usually lovely, loomed ominously ahead, the safety of the pueblo and its people left behind. She thought of those she loved, especially Ben, and a pang of regret passed through her. She would have to leave him without a proper farewell. At that moment she wanted nothing more than to throw her arms around him and hold him close. Tears swelled in her throat. She had to force herself to again focus on the job of freeing her hands.

As the truck approached the foot of Rainbow Mesa, the sun broke above the horizon. Dawn streaked the sky and bathed the mesa in a rainbow of colors. Now she knew how it had come by its name.

The vehicle ground to a halt and Luci jumped

out, pulling the rifle from the cab and pointing it in Sandy's direction. "Out, *gringa*, we have a steep climb ahead of us."

A rifle swing to the right indicated the trail to be followed. Sandy had no choice but to cooperate. She again palmed her knife-edged instrument to hide it from Luci's sight. Behind her, Luci bent her head down to the open window and gave Ona final orders. "You stay here and watch for trouble. I'll take care of this."

Whatever Luci meant by "this," the word caused a ferocious knot of panic in her gut. She nearly doubled over, but a rifle poke to the kidneys straightened her out.

"Start up that trail, *gringa*. Now!"

"What trail?" Although she had taken the trail a number of times with Ben, she needed to stall for time.

"Over there." Luci pointed to the clumps of sage brush. "Just start moving. You'll see the trail soon enough."

Luci rotated Sandy around, so she could no longer ply at the rope without being noticed, and pushed her forward. Her legs shook so much her footing was unstable. She stumbled, but quickly righted herself. Behind her the rifle unerringly pointed at her back.

The trail seemed narrower and steeper than she remembered. She stumbled over rocks and roots that seemed to have been purposely put in her path. When the trail rose more steeply, she had trouble maintaining her footing. With bound hands, she could not use her arms for balance. Her limp was more pronounced than usual. She desperately tried to keep from falling, aware of the possible consequences. She soon crumbled.

Luci jerked her upright and shouted, "Get up. Keep going."

"Okay. Okay," Sandy said after a rifle prod to the shoulder. She tried to stand but slipped sideways and had to maneuver her legs while pushing with her shoulder against a rock to right herself.

But not for long. After a second spill she glanced back at Luci, but all she saw was the rifle shaft aimed between her eyes. At the opposite end of the long shaft, a bullet waited. She had no intention of being the one with the bullet's name on it.

"You'll have to untie me so I can climb this hill."

Luci grunted. "Nice try, *gringa*, but your hands stay tied. Move on." Luci grasped her arm roughly and pulled her upright.

Sandy swallowed her disappointment along with tears of defeat. Her one chance to free her arms had failed. Although the twine had loosened a little with her effort, her hands remained securely bound behind her back. She trekked slowly, trying not to incur any more of Luci's wrath, but stalled as long as she could. The sooner she arrived at Luci's destination, the sooner she would meet her fate.

She continued her death struggle up the craggy gallows incline, feeling like a French aristocrat going to the guillotine. Nearer to the mesa top, Sandy slowed her progress so much that Luci spat at her, "Hurry up, *gringa*, or I will shoot you in the knees and you will die a slow and agonizing death here on the trail."

The thought propelled her uphill climb and she soon reached the top. She glanced down at herself. Shrouded in mud and dust and covered with abrasions, she was still in one piece—at least for now. Any hope of escape had diminished to little more than a prayer for a miracle.

"Over there." Luci gestured to her left with the rifle. "Stand over there."

Sandy moved to the spot Luci indicated, but could go no farther because she had come to the rim of the mesa. She glanced at the ledge with its precipitous drop toward the desert floor. Pebbles she dislodged with her boot tumbled over the side, disappearing into thin air, forever.

Time lost all meaning. Despair replaced panic. "I can't go any farther.

Luci watched her through veiled eyes. "You have one more step to take."

Chapter Seventeen

Fear froze into an infinite last minute as Sandy faced eternity. She refused to look over her shoulder at the sheer drop. How could she have survived one of her worse nightmares, only to be flung over a precipice and brutally broken? No matter what happened, she would not take that final step of her own free will.

Luci wore the expression of someone anxious to end an ordeal. "Sorry, *gringa*. I didn't want to do this, but you take that step yourself, or I will help you take it."

If Sandy failed to stop Luci's relentless affront, within moments her body would lie among the bramble at the bottom of the mesa. "So Harley put you up to this."

Luci sneered. "Harley. You have to be kidding. He's about as creative as a paper bag.."

"Then it was you behind all this?" Sandy needed to stretch these moments of redemption to the limit. While she spoke, she could continue to slash at the rope about her wrists.

"Who else? No one else had the guts to do what I've done."

"Is that why you lied to me about your father losing the land to the Edakees? I have a land sale note that shows Harley sold them the land years ago. Is it because you wanted to make the Edakees look bad and deflect any suspicion from you? So no one would think you were behind any attempt to drive them off their land?"

"Since you're such a detective, why in the world would I want to do that?"

"Because you know there's a fortune in artifacts buried on the land and you want the money." Luci's cackle unnerved her.

"And even if there were artifacts on the land, why would I want them badly enough to burn down the house?"

She had to play her hand, even if she wasn't sure it would trump Luci's. "To pay back the money Harley embezzled from the tribe to cover his gambling debt."

Luci gave her a knowing look. "You're pretty good at this, *gringa*." Her face hardened menacingly. "Too good. It's too bad you won't have a chance to work with the police. I'm sure they could use someone like you."

"What good is it going to be for you to do me in? So far you don't have blood on your hands, why start now?" She worked furiously at the rope behind her back.

"That's not entirely true. I saw the Edakee aunt this morning when she stopped by the store to buy milk for the toddler. She got a call from Cecilia Edakee in the middle of the night. They don't expect her boy to live."

A sharp sorrow passed through Sandy, but she didn't have time to dwell on it. She had waited long enough. She had to find out the truth, whatever the consequences.

"With the Edakee boy dying, I have nothing to lose and everything to gain by not letting you talk to the police. Right now no one except you suspects me. I want to keep it that way. From what I understand from their aunt, the Edakees changed their mind after the fire. They're planning to leave San Anselmo. If that happens, there's nothing standing between me and my land—except you."

Damn, her timing was bad. "Perhaps I could be persuaded not to talk to the police."

Luci let out a dry laugh. "You? No, *gringa*. I know your type. Miss Goody Two Shoes. The minute I let you go, you'd be over at the police station. I'm surprised you're not there already."

She wished she was. This was a big mistake. She should have listened to Ben.

"Why would you risk everything to get your hands on the land? Couldn't you just let Harley find a way to pay back the debt?"

"You don't understand how things work around here, *gringa*. If the Chairman were to find out Harley was the one who 'borrowed' the money before we have a chance to replace it, Harley would be out of a job and we'd be out of our land, our reputation, our business, and our self-respect. In other words, we'd be out of luck. We'd be worse off than the Edakees and that's the last thing I want."

She took a step forward, sending a chill up Sandy's spine.

"Harley's desperate, but he's weak. He needed someone stronger to show him the way out of the mess he made. I'd never let my family down like he has." She spat out her words with contempt.

The ropes burned her wrists but she worked on. "Don't do this, Luci. You don't need more blood on your hands."

"Sorry, *gringa*, but I have no choice. You always did have a knack for being in the wrong place at the wrong time." Luci let out another dry, forced chuckle.

Behind her back, Sandy struggled to break the rope's hold, but her efforts were paying off only minimally. "Were you and Harley behind the bogeymen masks?"

Luci guffawed. "That wasn't us."

Sandy shrugged, causing Luci to raise the rifle. "Then who?"

"Those Chavez boys, of course."

"Were they working with you?"

Luci shook her head. "You have it all wrong, *gringa*. I take it back about your working for the police."

Fear caused sweat to bead Sandy's brow. She stabbed at the rope between her wrists. Still, the rope held fast. "If they didn't work with you, what's the real story?" The twine began to give a little. In a matter of minutes, it might loosen enough to free her hands. Sandy had to keep Luci talking. Sweat dripping from her brow stung her eyes. She had to ignore it and work on. "How did they get involved?"

Luci snorted. "They had their own dance to do."

Luci had intentionally implicated those naive boys. The truth turned her stomach and also set her nerves on edge. If Luci would use innocent teens to cover her tracks, it didn't bode well for Sandy's chances. "So you used the Chavez boys?" Sandy stretched her wrists from side to side, the rope definitely looser.

"You ask too many questions. As much as I'll be sorry to see you go, I won't miss all your questions."

The twine eased, but not enough for Sandy to free herself. She continued to strain at the rope. "Isn't it true?"

"Okay, *gringa*, you're on to something. I might as well tell you because you won't be telling anyone else. We waited until those boys had finished their dance before we lit the fire. We knew they would be the logical suspects."

"Did you mean to kill the Edakees?"

Luci's arm drifted downward. "No, we didn't want to kill them. We thought they'd gone to the sheep ranch."

"Please, Luci, I'm not part of your land feud. You don't want to kill me either. This thing is complicated enough. Don't sully your hands with my murder." Sandy could hear the pleading sound in her voice, but it didn't stop her.

Luci studied her through veiled eyes. "I don't have any choice, *gringa*, you know too much."

Desperately, Sandy sawed harder at the rope. "They'll know you did it. If you murder me, you'll put a noose around your neck and Ona's."

"No, *gringa*, they won't know we did this. It will look like you slipped. No one will ever know what happened to you."

"Slipped with my hands tied behind my back..."

Luci frowned. The rifle arm again dipped slightly. With a last tug at the rope, Sandy yanked her hands free. If Luci relaxed her guard a little more, Sandy could make her move. She stared over Luci's shoulder and deliberately widened her eyes. "What's that?"

When Luci automatically looked back,she lunged, shoving Luci to the ground The force jarred the rifle from Luci's hand. It slid off to the side, just beyond her reach.

Trapped under Sandy, Luci struggled. She pushed Sandy aside and scrambled toward the rifle. Sandy grabbed her by one leg and yanked her back. Luci scratched at Sandy with jagged fingernails. A searing pain streaked across her cheek.

Sandy fought back with determination matching Luci's strength. They clawed and pummeled one another, rolling against the pebbles and prickly pears. Sandy's skin tore on the sharp teeth of the cactus. She managed to ward off Luci's blows and secure the high ground above her.

Luci swung her fists at Sandy, but Sandy ducked. In spite of Luci's strength and persistence, Sandy pinned Luci's arms to the ground. Luci lifted her head and bit down with full force on her arm.

Sandy screamed in pain and surprise, losing her grip on Luci's arms. Luci took advantage of her momentary distraction to throw her onto her back.

From this new advantage, Luci held her down. Sandy struggled with every ounce of her will to free herself. With a sudden twist, Luci pushed Sandy aside and scrambled for the gun.

Sandy leaped to her feet in time to stare directly into the rifle barrel.

All hope dissolved.

Luci's face had turned a deep shade of red, a nasty purple bruise spreading across her cheek. "Nice try, *gringa*," she said between gasps for air, "but not nice enough. No more time to waste. Take the walk. Now!" She prodded Sandy with the rifle.

Sandy began to back away on trembling legs. "Please, Luci..." She heard each of a dozen pebbles rattle off the mesa and bounce down the cliff.

Luci's eyes were steely. "No more talking, *gringa*. It's time for your trip."

Luci used the gun barrel like she would a bayonet, driving Sandy to the very edge of the mesa. One more step, Sandy started to slip. The ground began to cave under her. In a moment, she would be tumbling over the side in a hail of rocks.

The earring in her pocket dug into her backside. She had one last card to play. She pulled it out, dangling it before Luci's eyes. "If I go, this goes with me.

Luci gasped, "Give that to me!"

Sandy held onto it. "You'll have to get it yourself."

Luci flung herself at Sandy and grasped for the earring. The impact caused Sandy to lose her footing and, catapult over the edge accompanied by a spray of sand and gravel. She tumbled over and under, the world tossing and turning, blurring her vision. She bounced off a rocky point, but hardly felt the impact. Sharp, jagged objects pierced her skin until her head hit something hard.

Everything went black.

Ben pounded on Sandy's door. "Hey, Sleepyhead," he yelled through the shuttered window. "Rise and shine!"

No answer.

He pounded again and waited, but still no response. He scanned the lot and spotted Sandy's car parked in its usual place. Where could she have gone on foot this early in the day?

She had promised not to play detective again and allow the police to do their job. That she had gone back on her word seemed the only logical explanation for her disappearance. Although this didn't surprise Ben with what he knew of her, it still bothered him. He jumped in his truck and careened toward the Edakee place.

He arrived to find uniformed and plain clothes police crawling over the yard like ants on an animal carcass. The captain he recognized from an incident at school. "Morning, Greyson, where did all these cops come from?"

Greyson chuckled. "The FBI doesn't trust us Injuns to do a good job. They sent some of their own boys over. Maybe they got nothing better to do." Good-natured and unruffled, a broad smile lighting up his lean face, Greyson always surprised Ben. The ugliness of his work didn't seem to embitter him. Ben wasn't sure he could be so upbeat under the circumstances.

"Have you seen a young white woman? I can't seem to locate her. Thought she might be poking around here."

Greyson shook his head. "I've seen no one but those cops over there, but someone else has been here."

He had Ben's attention. "How do you know?"

Greyson pushed the Dodgers cap back from his forehead. "They slipped in the mud by the side of the house. There are fresh footsteps all over the yard."

Ben stared in the direction Greyson pointed. "Any idea who it could be or why they were here?"

"Beats me. Definitely more than one person. Two or three I'd say."

Shivers ran down Ben's spine. Who else besides

Sandy might have been snooping about the place so early in the day? Could it be Harley Dista? Was Sandy in some kind of danger?

"The woman I'm seeking may have run into trouble. It's not like her to just disappear. I'm going into town to search for her."

"The town is pretty quiet after the show last night. Most people must be sleeping in. I didn't see any white woman about."

Ben's throat tightened. If she wasn't in town, where could she be? He riffled through his mental file. "I need to take a look around. Could you spare a deputy for the trip?"

Greyson squinted into the rising sun. "Not right away. I need to impress these wannabe police officers. As soon as I can, I'll send someone to find you."

Relieved, Ben shook Greyson's hand. "Thanks."

Ben headed straight to town. As Greyson had said, the place looked as dead as any town on New Year's morning. Besides two kids lingering outside the closed general store, he saw no signs of life.

On a whim, he stopped by the store. Still shuttered, he tried the knob and the door swung open. At first the store appeared empty, but after his eyes adjusted to the dim light, he spied Harley at the cash register. He quietly sidled up behind him. "Don't move, Harley. Turn around slowly."

Harley waited a long moment, looking down at

the counter, then rotated. "What are you doing here, Ben?"

"I just want answers. I'm looking for Sandy. I thought you might have seen her. Has she been here?"

Harley shook his head. "No, I have seen no one this morning. The store is closed. How did you get in?"

"You left the door unlocked. What do you know about Sandy?"

Harley smiled one of his unctuous smiles. "Nothing. I just arrived to take care of the store. Luci is not well."

"Any idea where Sandy might be at this early hour?"

"How would I know?"

"Because I have reason to believe she's with somebody and that somebody could be Luci."

Harley glared at him. "Why would you think such a thing?"

Time to play his cards. "Because she went by the Edakee house, but she wasn't alone."

"I told you, Luci is not well."

"Then she must be in the back room. I'll check in to see how she's doing and find out if she knows anything concerning Sandy's whereabouts." He began to back toward the curtained doorway, but he hadn't gone more than a few feet before Harley reached beneath the counter and pulled out a 9mm pistol.

"Stop there, Ben. Don't go any farther." Harley

pointed the gun at his chest.

Ben did as told. "Why are you doing this?"

"I told you Luci was ill. You must not disturb her."

Sure. Ben began to back toward the front door. "Okay, I won't disturb her... I'll just head out to the mesa to look for Sandy—"

"Stop right there! You're not going anywhere."

"I don't understand..."

"If you go to the mesa, I want to go along. Wait a minute while I find my keys." Harley stuck his hand in one jacket pocket, than the other, but came out empty-handed. "I must have left them on a shelf."

He made his way over to a row of cereal boxes, keeping one eye on Ben, one on the shelf. "I was here a minute ago..."

The only thing that stood between Ben and a bullet was his superior girth, strength and agility. He sidled closer to Harley. "Maybe I can help."

Harley raised the gun. "Stay back. I must have left them here. I will find them without your help."

The moment Harley looked away again Ben reached for a nearby can of whole tomatoes and rushed at the thinner man. Harley looked up in alarm too late. With all his might Ben smashed the can into the side of his head. Harley crumpled to the ground. Out cold.

Harley's reaction to his simple questions alerted Ben that Sandy must have gone to Rainbow Mesa, but not alone. He had to act fast and find her. He pocketed the gun, jumped in his truck, and peeled off onto the county road.

As he drove up to the mesa, he saw a brown pickup planted at the base, a figure perched behind the steering wheel. He pulled alongside and fingered the gun stuck in his pant pocket.

Harley's wife Ona stared out the truck's window at him. Her skin had taken on a dusty pallor and the pupils of her eyes jumped about like a frightened rabbit's. She began to reach for the far door.

He jumped from his pickup with gun raised, ran around to the truck door Ona was clumsily trying to open, and yelled, "Where's Sandy?"

The rims of Ona's eyes swelled with tears. "I do not know. Luci took her for a walk. I am worried."

So was he. "Where did they go?"

Even though Ona seemed frightened out of her mind already, Ben had no choice but to up the ante. He threw open the truck door, grabbed her by the upper arm, and pulled her out. "Show me which way they went!"

Ona's eyes were unblinking, two enormous flat orbs in her head. "There." She pointed toward the trail.

"Did they climb the mesa?"

She nodded, as though not speaking the words spared her from any betrayal.

He leapt back into his truck and careened toward what he knew to be the quickest trail to the top of the hill. Rounding a bend, he heard a scream and looked up just in time to see a woman with long raven hair plunge toward the valley floor.

His heart stopped and he slammed on the brake. For a full minute, he couldn't move. Then, against every instinct, he pointed his truck in the direction he saw the body fall.

He parked the car near the fallen woman. She lay face down on the ground. Arms and legs sprawled in all directions. Long raven hair in a pool of blood. Unmoving.

Sandy.

A deep throb in his throat escaped in a wrenching cry. He wanted to scream, to flail, to curse the universe, but nothing he could do would ever erase the pain. The magnitude of his grief was too great. Every muscle and joint ached from strain and sorrow.

He had arrived too late to save Sandy, had once again failed the woman he loved. Was this his legacy in life? How could he live with himself after this?

He stumbled toward her, legs buckling under him. The space he crossed to the body, her body, seemed endless. When he finally reached her, he knelt beside her and turned her palm toward him. Took a pulse. There was none.

He lifted her head, gradually turning it toward him, then gasped. Luci stared empty-eyed at him. Although her nose had been flattened and her face was purple and swollen, she was still easily recognizable. How had he have mistaken her for Sandy besides the obvious physical similarities? He must be out of his mind with fear and grief.

Pity for Luci and her violent death mingled with tremendous relief. The possibility Sandy could still be alive galvanized him. He released Luci and sprinted back up the trail to his best vantage point at the top of the mesa, where he could view the entire area. Below, he spied Harley's powder blue pickup pull up next to Luci's. If he had any chance of finding Sandy alive, he better do it quickly. With Harley here, his time was running out.

He circled the rim of the mesa, searching for her, but Sandy had vanished. All he could see clearly was Harley climbing the mesa trail in pursuit. As Ben neared the southern side, a hunch told him to check in the crevice where, months before, the child's body had been buried. He spied an arm draped over the side of the hill. He lowered himself to a rock just beneath the rim where he could get a better view of the ledge and spotted Sandy below. She lay on her back in the crevice, her left leg trapped by a jutting rock.

Since she lay as still as Luci, he could not tell whether she was dead or alive. The drop-off into the crevice was too steep to tackle, so he sprinted down a trail on the opposite side of the mesa from Harley until he was level with Sandy. By traversing the perpendicular, rocky terrain, he soon stood alongside her. He thanked the heavens that sand had built up over the rocks in the crevice. She had landed on a more cushioned spot, which meant she had a fighting chance. He placed a finger under her nose and felt for breath. His spirits soared with the faint movement of hairs on the back of his hand. He grabbed her wrist, checking for a pulse. The steady rhythm of her heartbeat thrilled him. She was alive.

"Sandy," he called to her. "Sandy!" But she failed to stir. Despite concerns she might have broken bones and he could injure her further, he had no choice but to remove her from her cramped resting place before Harley removed them both. Gently he plied her out of the rocks and hoisted her over his shoulder. When he moved her, she groaned.

A voice above startled him. He looked up and saw Harley pass along the rim of the mesa. Instinctively, he ducked beneath the rock ledge. After a moment, Harley moved away. Seizing the opportunity, Ben tore across the ridge and down the trail.

Halfway down, he heard Ona shout, "Over there."

He glanced up. Harley stared down at him.

"Stop!" Harley yelled. "Let's talk."

He didn't know what Harley wanted, but after seeing Luci and Sandy's condition, he knew it wasn't just talk. If Harley wanted to stop them, he might be capable of anything.

He bounded down the rocky trail, Sandy safely enclosed in his arms. Before he had gone more than twenty feet, he glanced up to see Harley racing down the hill toward them. Distracted, he lost his footing and stumbled backward, crashing into a large Yucca protruding from a rocky ledge. A sharp pointed leaf deeply pierced his shoulder, breaking free of the plant. A searing pain slammed across the shoulder and he almost lost his footing, but caught himself at the last moment and shifted his weight so he didn't drop Sandy. Damn! Everything in him demanded he stop to check the damage, but he blindly raced on.

Ben continued to run, his speed enhanced by fear. At the base of the mesa, using the sheer side as a shield, he closed in on his truck. Within feet of his destination, he took a deep breath and sprinted toward the vehicle. He tore open the door, slid Sandy in, and jumped in himself. With a twist of the ignition, he fired the engine and accelerated away.

Only after he had moved out of Harley's range of vision could he take the time to check on Sandy. Bruised and dirty, she lay limp against the passenger-side door, but he could still see the rise and fall of her chest.

He took the bundled jacket from behind the front seat and placed it beneath her head, ignoring the pain that shot down his arm. Her arm dangled at her side, swollen and discolored. An ugly gash cut across her right cheek. Her leg lay at an impossible angle. Nothing he could do now to help her except get her to the hospital, pronto.

As he sped away, he repeatedly checked his rearview mirror for Harley. Sandy would not be safe until she was sheltered in the arms of the Indian Health Service hospital.

He turned off the dirt road, sheets of dust rising behind him, and careened onto the blacktop in a squeal of tires. Just past the village, he spotted Harley's truck gaining on him. He floored the gas pedal and raced through a stop sign, hoping to attract and alert the police. He glanced behind. No such luck.

At Interstate 40, he took the eastbound ramp with so much speed he almost swerved off the road. Harley was gaining on him and his light blue truck turned onto the highway behind him. Sweat ran down the back of Ben's shirt and beaded his forehead. dripping into his eyes. His shoulder ached with such a vengeance he began to lose concentration. A chunk of plant still protruded from his white cotton shirt. With it imbedded in his flesh, he had to transport Sandy to the hospital before blood loss and mild shock got the best of him.

Since traffic ran light on that stretch of road, he gave the engine all the power he could. This offered him no advantage over his pursuer, who seemed to be gaining on him by the second.

The farther down the road he traveled, the woozier he became, until the scenery before him shimmered like a lake on a sunny day. With a shake of his head, he tried desperately to maintain his focus, but it became harder and harder to do. A glance in the rearview mirror clearly illuminated Harley's scowling face. He could not be closer.

Ben again floored the engine and the truck lurched, throwing Sandy's head forward into the dash. He moved her back and her head flopped against the cushion rest. When he again glanced into the rearview mirror, Harley no longer stared back at him. He turned to look to his left. Harley stared him in the eyes. He was alongside!

"Pull over," Harley shouted through his open window.

"Follow me to the hospital. We'll talk there." He tried to pull ahead, but Harley kept apace.

Before Ben had a chance to steel himself, Harley wrenched his steering wheel to the right and plunged his truck into Ben's. Ben swerved and barely avoided being hit. After several near misses, he jerked off the road and onto the shoulder. The truck sputtered and died.

Harley pulled off the road in front of him and began to back up. Ben frantically twisted the ignition. The engine choked and failed to start. He tried to start the truck again. It almost caught this time. The faint scent of gasoline rattled him and he prayed he hadn't flooded the engine. As Harley neared, he tried the ignition once more with his foot pressed against the accelerator. The truck roared, lurched, and flew by Harley.

Ben plied the pedal, hoping to outdistance Harley before he had a chance to catch up, but Harley's newer truck could not be out-run. Harley again pulled up beside him.

Although Ben's head spun, he had enough sense left to know he had to be the aggressor this time. When Harley started to swerve toward him, Ben veered his truck to the left and slammed it into the side of Harley's. To his surprise, Harley slid off the road, but quickly corrected his course and moved back onto the blacktop.

Again, he drove up alongside Ben. Ben's truck

seemed to be on its last cylinder, but he again rammed it into the side of Harley's pickup. sending him flying off the side of the road into a ditch.

The abrupt motion threw Sandy against him, but there was nothing he could do for her under the circumstances. The nerves in his arm had been set afire by the sudden jolt. He glanced behind and saw that Harley's truck leaned sharply into the ditch. A few minutes reprieve might be all he had.

He hurtled down the road toward the Indian hospital and skidded to the Emergency Room door. Screeching to a halt, he cut the engine. For a moment, he could not move, paralyzed by pain and shock.

He looked down at Sandy. Although she seemed to be sleeping, he knew better. Her breathing sounded labored. Her complexion pale.

He opened the truck door, scooped Sandy into his arms, and staggered with her toward the door. By clenching his teeth, he withstood the agony in his shoulder when he hoisted her in front of the admissions nurse.

The bright-eyed, young woman who sat behind the desk dropped her jaw at the sight of Ben with Sandy in his arms. Behind the nurse sat the man Ben remembered from the café. Ben's gut tightened at the sight of his chief rival. He had no desire to turn Sandy over to this man's care, but he had no choice. Sandy's life was far more precious than his petty jealousy.

When the swarthy man in the white coat noticed Ben and Sandy, he jumped to his feet and rushed over. "What happened?"

"She was pushed off a cliff."

"Bring her back here." The man with the tag that read Dr. Neil Kramer, MD, led Ben into one of the curtained stalls in the emergency room and motioned for Ben to place Sandy on a gurney.

Dr. Kramer started to unbutton Sandy's shirt. "Go into the waiting room. I'll be out in a few minutes."

Reluctantly, Ben left. The thought of leaving her alone in her precarious condition unnerved him. She'd been through so much. How could he live with himself if anything happened to her?

He staggered into the waiting room and dropped into a chair. Exhaustion and nausea overwhelmed him. He could not recall a time in his life when he had been so tired and alone, except after his wife's disappearance.

The admitting nurse loomed over him. "We should take a look at that shoulder of yours."

He had forgotten his own wound in his rush to secure assistance for Sandy. "I'll be okay."

"You sure will after we get through with you." The nurse coaxed Ben into a wheelchair and rolled him into an ER stall. "What happened to you?"

"A close call with a maniac," he said as she helped him onto a gurney and shed his boots. "You better call the police."

"I'll call when we're through. First, let's remove that shirt. This is going to hurt."

"I know. Just do it."

The nurse tugged the blood splattered shirt away from the plant, but no matter how gentle she tried to be, lightning bolts flashed before his eyes every time the plant shifted and he had to do everything he could not to pass out from the pain. Finally, she removed the material from the injured shoulder. He grunted.

She dropped his shirt into a basin and studied the wound. "There's still a large chunk of Yucca leaf in your shoulder. I know the doctor will insist on cutting it out. I'll clean you up and have the doctor look at it as soon as he's free."

She wiped the area around the wound with rubbing alcohol. A sharp burning stick might as well have been poked through his shoulder, because that's how it felt. He gritted his teeth to withstand the pain.

When she was finished, he began to rise, but she pressed a strong hand against his uninjured shoulder. "Remain still until the doctor's ready to see you."

"Okay, but I'll wait for the doctor's report on Sandy before I rest." He took the pale green surgical scrub she offered and draped it over his chest and stomach.

Against his will, his head lolled back against the pillow and his eyes drooped shut. Periodically he'd force them open to check the clock. Finally, Neil Kramer emerged through the curtain. Ben pried himself up on his good arm. "How is she?"

The strain on Dr. Kramer's face worried him. "She's alive and that's all I can tell you. She's in a coma with a nasty lump on the back of her head. Her femur was broken in two places. She has a few hundred ugly looking lacerations and contusions, but they're not what I'm worried about."

"What is?"

"Internal bleeding and a concussion. She had quite a tumble." Kramer played with his stethoscope as he spoke. "I set her leg and moved her to a hospital bed. We'll keep a close eye on her. The next couple days are pivotal to her prognosis."

Ben needed to support his weight. Even his good arm faltered. Dr. Kramer knitted his brow. "What's wrong with that shoulder?"

"Yucca bit me."

"I'm sorry I didn't see that earlier. I was too preoccupied with Sandy. It's your turn to be treated. Lie back."

Pulses of pain radiated down Ben's arm when Kramer pressed on his shoulder. Ben had to suppress a scream.

With a frown, Kramer probed again. "Feels like there's still plenty of it lodged inside. Let's remove it before it becomes infected."

Kramer summoned a nurse who helped Ben down the hall into an operating room. She helped him hoist himself onto a table. Greeted by fluorescent lights and antiseptic odors, Ben's stomach cramped. Nausea again flowed through him

A gloved, white-gowned nurse inserted an IV

needle into his arm. "You're going to feel a bit woozy."

Kramer appeared at her side. "That Sandy is quite a woman, isn't she?" He turned a valve and fluid started to flow into the tube attached to Ben's arm.

"Will she be okay, Doctor?" Warm, silent fingers snuck up his spine, relaxing him. "What's the chance she won't make it?" His words grew weighty; his tongue stuck to the roof of his mouth. His eyelids slowly began to close.

"Let's not even consider that possibility. All we can do now is pray."

Ben barely heard the words before darkness descended.

Chapter Eighteen

Ben glanced across the hospital bed at Officer Greyson. Between them Sandy lay, comatose and in traction. Wrapped in a white sheet with only her head and leg protruding, she looked like a battered angel to him.

"Anything else?" Greyson asked.

"That's all I have." Ben wearily rubbed his brow. "One question, though. Whatever happened to Harley?"

Greyson flipped shut the notepad he had used to record Ben's story. "The FBI picked him up a couple hours ago for questioning and got a warrant to search his home. They found evidence on his computer he had been transferring funds from the tribal bank account into his own. I think he has some explaining to do."

Ben stretched his sore back. "Guess you all have your work cut out for you."

Greyson laughed humorlessly. "But your work's done for now. You look tired. Go home. Get some rest. I'll leave a deputy here to keep an eye on things. He'll question the patient when she comes to."

If she comes to. Ben wished he could be as optimistic about it as Greyson, but doubt overshadowed his hope. He rubbed his brow. "I think I'll stick around. She might need me." A fleeting glance at Sandy told him it wouldn't be too soon.

Greyson started toward the door. "Let the deputy know when she comes around." At the door, he moved out of the way to allow Cecilia and Tonito to enter the room. With a nod in their direction, he departed.

Cecilia had a strained look on her face. "How is Sandy?" she asked, moving up alongside Ben.

Ben glanced down at Sandy. "Not very good."

"Oh. I am sorry."

He studied Cecilia's stoic face. Dark moons discolored the skin under her eyes. Lines seemed to have deepened around her mouth in the hours since the fire. She had her own worries. "How's Dixon?"

"No change. He is still hooked up to the white man's machines," Tonito said.

"What does the doctor say?"

"They do not know how badly his lungs were burnt in the fire. They thought he would not live the night." A tear trickled down Cecilia's cheek. "But he proved them wrong. Only time will tell if he will get well."

Ben hated to hear that. "Is there more that can be done?"

"The doctor says to pray, Kyimme." Cecilia lowered her head.

"Kramer prescribed the same medicine for Sandy." Out of the corner of his eye, Ben thought he saw Sandy stir, but when he looked over, she lay quiet as a corpse. The sheet had probably moved as a result of the ventilation system. Momentary hope fled.

"We will be back later this day to see how Sandy is doing," Tonito said as he led Cecilia from the room.

As soon as they were gone, Ben reached for Sandy's hand, willing her to open her eyes. Look up at him. He silently bargained for her recovery, willing to sacrifice everything he had dreamed of and worked for if only she would come out of this alive. Terrified by her precarious balance on the edge of life, he wished he could do something...anything...but he was as helpless with her as the Edakees were with Dixon. Two days had already dragged into three, and still nothing had changed.

He brought his lips to her ear. "Sandy," he murmured, "Sandy, please come back. I have something to tell you."

He watched her face, his mind flashing back to their perilous escape. Something had cemented in him during the time he had searched the mesa and carried her under siege to safety. His feelings, soft as clay before, had hardened under fire like a magnificent pueblo vase.

He leaned closer. "I love you, Sandy. Please come back so I can show you my love."

He ran a hand over her hair, felt its fine texture between his fingers. Guilt pierced him. How could he have tried to stop the one person he cared about from doing what made her worth caring about? Standing up for what she believed in.

"I'm so sorry, Sandy," he whispered. "Please come back to me. If you do, I will always back you up. I will never, ever stand in your way again."

He continued his vigil with a heavy heart. Exhausted from his own ordeal, he flopped into a chair alongside her bed. He ached all over, partly from the shoulder infection, but also from the knowledge he might never be able to share his feelings with her.

By nightfall of the third day, his hope had flickered and faded, and fear had taken the place of anticipation. The creak of the door jarred him from his vigil.

Neil Kramer entered the room. "How's the patient?"

Ben rose to face him. "The same. Nothing's changed."

Kramer consulted the chart hanging from a rope at the end of Sandy's bed, took her pulse, and pulled her eyelids up to look into her eyes.

"You said the first seventy-two hours were crucial. It's past that. Where does that leave us? Is there much hope?"

"Of course there's hope. It's just that it's a little less with each passing day." Kramer refused to meet his eye, but Ben could sense his doubt. "I'm not saying to give up on her. I'm just telling you to prepare yourself for whatever happens. It could go either way."

Even though Ben had expected this, he didn't like hearing it. He wanted to curse at the top of his lungs, to kick the nearby chair, to put his fist through the bathroom door, but what would that do? It would accomplish nothing except guarantee him a bed in the psychiatric ward.

"I'll never give up."

Kramer gave him a cock-eyed smile. "I don't blame you. She's quite special." He turned to leave the room, then turned back. "She thinks you're special too, you know." He left the room.

Ben sagged against the footboard. He despaired of Sandy's recovering with each passing hour, but he had to be strong for her, no matter the outcome.

To clear his head, he took a short break and wandered down the hospital hall to the Intensive Care Unit. A nurse held the door open with her foot while she conversed with an orderly. Beyond her, he spied a small figure swaddled in a blanket. Cecilia's presence convinced him it was Dixon surrounded by long tubes running from pumps and monitors into his small body, his life supported by a respirator, an IV and a feeding tube.

The nurse noticed Ben. "I'm afraid only family can visit the ICU."

He nodded his understanding and trudged back to Sandy's room. Sandy hadn't stirred at all during his absence. He slid into a chair, flipped on the television to watch the national news, and slipped into a much needed doze. Across a great chasm, Sandy reached out her arms to him. Called his name.

"B...B...Ben...Ben."

He flung open his eyes and lurched groggily toward the bed. In the light from the hallway, he could barely see Sandy's half-opened eyes.

"Ben," she said weakly.

"Oh, my God!" Instantly awake, he gathered up her hands, drawing them to his lips. He kissed her fingers one at a time, joy filling him like helium in a hot air balloon. He was light-headed, buoyant, dizzy. "You're back! You're back with me."

"What...time is it?" Her voice wobbled. Her body shaking.

"The question is, what day is it? Don't worry. Nothing matters except that you're back with me."

She attempted to lift her head, but failed. "Where am I?"

"In the hospital, love. It's okay. Take it easy. You've been through a lot. Don't try to push yourself." His heart swelled with happiness. She was conscious. Alive.

"What happened? Why hospital?"

"Do you remember anything?"

"Nothing..." Her voice trailed off and her eyelids fluttered shut.

"Sleep, my darling," he murmured, gently stroking her arm. "You'll be in my arms when you wake again. Then I'll tell you everything." Gratitude filled him, stretched his emotional envelope to the bursting point.

He held onto her hand, unable to tear himself away. As soon as he could he would jog down to the nursing station to report a miracle.

Sandy's leg had been released from its harness

but encased securely in a plaster cast. She lay back in her bed, her head propped against a pillow and a tray of half-eaten food in front of her. Every day, the glow of health stole back into her cheeks and a sparkle had begun to light up her eyes when she saw him.

A nurse entered the room. "Are we through with this?"

It amused Ben that the nurses spoke in plural when referring to Sandy. He certainly wouldn't have touched that poor excuse for food they fed her. He had been sneaking her new found favorites—tamales and other delicacies—when the nurses weren't looking.

The nurse removed the tray, complaining under her breath about how little Sandy had eaten. Sandy had begun to gain back the fifteen pounds she'd lost as a result of her trauma. She made it clear she wouldn't starve to death as a result of not consuming a couple of meals. Not with what she laughingly referred to as her reserve.

She watched the nurse leave. "I can't seem to meet that woman's expectations."

He squeezed her hand. "You can meet mine."

"I thought I failed in that department too."

He removed the tray table in front of her. "What do you mean?"

"You warned me not to stick my nose in the business of others."

How could he tell her he had a change of heart? He no longer saw things the same way. He wanted to make amends. "You did the right thing."

"How can you say that? Look at the results."

Ben bit his lip, thinking of Dixon. While Sandy was on the mend, Dixon had not made similar progress. He seemed to be deteriorating as the days dragged on. "How's he doing today?"

Sandy cast her eyes downward, a pained expression pinching her features. "No change. I think the doctors are beginning to despair of his condition ever improving. He's still not breathing on his own."

When she raised her eyes, Ben could see tears. She cared a great deal about Dixon and his family. It made him realize what a loving woman she really was. A woman he could admire. A woman he could love. He wanted to take her in his arms and make everything go away. "It's not your fault."

Sandy blanched. "If I hadn't interfered, he wouldn't be here now."

"I've heard different."

A quizzical expression passed over her features.

She was finally strong enough to hear the entire story. He went over and sat on the bottom of her bed. "According to Ona, that is. The cop I asked to help me find you found Ona instead, standing over Luci's body."

Sandy gasped. "Luci's dead?"

He nodded. "She fell off the mesa about the same time you did. Don't you remember?"

"Only slipping off the mesa... Wait, I do

remember something. I held out her earring, the one I found at the Edakee house. She lunged at me and I slipped..."

"She must have lost her balance when she pushed you off the ledge, because I found her at the bottom of the mesa, below where you were."

Sandy shook her head. "I don't know whether to feel sad or glad. I thought Luci was my friend, but she tried to kill me..." Her voice trailed off. "What happened when the police found Ona?"

"She was pretty shook up and confessed the whole crime."

"You mean the fire?" Her hand trembled in his.

"Not just the fire, but her involvement in Luci's scheme to run the Edakees off the pueblo."

Ben dropped Sandy's hand and stood. Walked over to the window. "Luci planned her harassment. When the Chavez boys began theirs, she saw her opportunity. She and Ona started by killing the Edakees' sheep. The fire was the next step."

"How did Ona get involved?"

"Ona isn't one to think on her own. It was easy for Luci to convince her to join in."

"How about Harley?" Sandy frowned, making tiny lines appear at the corners of her eyes. He wanted to smooth those lines with his lips. "You know it was Harley who embezzled the missing money from the tribe."

"Yeah, it's all over the Indian airwaves.

Everyone knows that's what this was all about. But Luci was the real ring-leader. Harley just did what she told him to."

"Were they also behind the break-in at my apartment and the arrowhead incident?"

"Not from what I can gather. That was probably the work of the Chavez boys wanting you off their backs."

Sandy placed the glass she held back on the tray table. "Whatever happened to them?"

"The judge gave them a reprimand and released them. I don't think they'll indulge in that kind of behavior again. Ona and Harley are in custody, awaiting trial for arson, conspiracy, and assault. They'll probably be behind bars for a long time." Ben refilled Sandy's empty glass and replaced it on the night stand. "And since you've been in the hospital, two people from the pueblo have come down with what they now call the hantavirus. Same virus that hit the Cochiti pueblo. The experts believe that's what killed the Chavez child."

Sandy sat silent for a minute. "I still feel like I didn't do enough to help the Edakees."

"You didn't fail them. Who did you fail?"

She squinted at him. "What does that mean?"

"You did all you could for them, but you're still not satisfied. Perhaps you were looking for something else."

She let out an exasperated sound. "Here you go

playing psychiatrist again."

"Think about it, okay?" Ben sat again and looked deeply into Sandy's eyes. "If it hadn't been for you, the Edakees may have been run off the reservation. Who knows what might have happened? I hate to admit it, Sandy, but you were right all along."

Sandy tilted her head to the side, a small grin on her lips. "You really believe that?"

In answer, he drew her to him, aware that she might still carry bruises. She responded by placing her arms around him and hugging him closer. Making love had only intensified his need for her. She intoxicated him.

When she pulled back, he held on, never wanting to let go. "I was wrong," he breathed into her hair. "I don't want to stop you from doing what makes you who you are...the person I love. I should have supported you more. From now on, we act as a team."

Chapter Nineteen

Sandy wheeled her chair down the hall toward the ICU. Although only family members were officially allowed to visit Dixon, she had made special arrangements with Neil to see him. Neil had recognized how important these visits were to her. Since making these arrangements, she had seen Dixon almost daily.

Unfortunately, his progress, unlike hers, was painfully slow. Still in a coma and tied to a respirator as a lifeline, he showed no sign of being able to breathe on his own. She often sat beside him, watching his chest rise and fall, listening to the machine pump life into his lungs. The gasp of the respirator and the beep of the monitor were the only indicators he was alive.

Cecilia and Tonito spent as much time as possible at the hospital, but this evening Tonito had stayed home with his other children and Cecilia was there alone. An infectious sadness had settled over the room. Sandy often felt on the verge of tears in Dixon's presence. She reached over and ruffled his thick hair, as she had often done, but it no longer comforted her...or him.

A tear edged its way down Cecilia's cheek. "I wish he would come back, *Tsila*. He has been gone too long. He may already be traveling to our ancestors."

Sandy clenched the arms of her wheelchair. "What do the doctors say today?"

"They say we must wait and see. But how long must we wait? The medicine man was here two days ago. He pulled more hair and rags from Dixon's throat. Still, he does not breathe on his own."

When Cecilia lowered her head into her hands, Sandy maneuvered her wheelchair close enough to wrap her arms around the distraught mother. "I'm so sorry..."

"Pray for him, *Tsila*." Cecilia's voice sounded miles away.

"I'll never stop praying for him."

"I only hope your prayers work better than mine."

At a noise in the doorway, Sandy turned to see Neil Kramer. "I'll be back in a moment," she said to Cecilia.

Motioning Neil to follow her, she rolled past him to a spot safely outside hearing range of the ICU. "I just wanted to know how it looks for Dixon, Doc?"

Neil frowned. "Not good, I'm afraid. He's young and his heart's strong, but his lungs may be too damaged to heal. There's a point of no return in cases like this. He may have reached that point."

Sandy swallowed her sorrow. "I don't believe this. It just seems so unreal."

"I hate to be the bearer of bad news, but I think you better prepare yourself for the worst. Let's hope Dixon doesn't die, but if he does, I'd like to believe what the San Anselmos do: that he'll be joining the

Kachina in their ancestral land and his spirit will come back to visit us." Neil's sad smile offered little consolation.

"Dr. Neil Kramer to Emergency," came blaring over the intercom.

"Have to go." Neil hurried down the hall.

Sandy took a moment to regain her composure before returning to the ICU. Upon entering, she was more aware than ever of an aura of grief hanging over Dixon's bed. Like smoke hovering over a fire, a dark veil of sorrow seemed to drape around him.

She rolled to the end of the bed. Cecilia looked up, her eyes swollen from tears Sandy rarely saw.

"Did the doctor tell you anything?"

Sandy took a deep breath. What to say and how to say it? She wanted to spare Cecilia, but didn't wish to deceive her. Cecilia needed to be prepared too. "Only what you already know: that Dixon's been in a coma for a long time and that concerns Kramer."

Cecilia seemed to falter. She used the side of a chair for support. "Oh God..."

Sandy wheeled over and took her hand. "He added that Dixon is young and has a strong heart. He may still pull through..."

The hand she held trembled.

"I do not know what to do if he dies, *Tsila*." A plaintive tone tinged her words. "He means so much to me."

"I know he does. He's an incredible kid." She

placed her arms around Cecilia and held her.

Sandy stayed with Cecilia as long as her strength allowed, listening to the rhythm of the breathing machine. When she was too exhausted to stay any longer, she said, "I hate to leave you alone, but I still tire easily. I'll be back tomorrow."

"You must take care of yourself." Cecilia grasped the arm of her chair. "What would we do without you, *Tsila*? You have been such a help to us. We are fortunate for your kindness."

Sandy turned from her, unwilling to let Cecilia see the tears pooling in her eyes. "I'm a captive audience," she quipped to lighten the mood. "But I'd be here no matter what." She quickly maneuvered the wheelchair out of the room before the floodgates failed.

Neil Kramer hustled into Sandy's room in his usual brusque fashion. "Cecilia and Tonito are asking for you." He took a seat on the bottom of her bed. "They've made a decision. On the advice of their medicine man, they've decided to shut off the respirator. We've discussed their request in committee and decided to honor it. Do you think you can join us in the ICU as soon as you're dressed?"

Sandy gasped. "Now?"

"We've been weaning Dixon off the oxygen slowly over the last few days. Fifteen minutes ago, the shaman came by and informed us the circumstances were right to remove him completely. He feels strongly about this. Since we're the interlopers in the pueblo, we always try to accommodate the tribal beliefs unless there is reason to differ." He patted her hand. "Don't let this frighten you. I know it's a long shot, but I've been amazed at what the shamans know. I've seen them perform what we would consider miracles. Let's hope that happens here."

"What's the chance?"

Neil knitted his thick dark brows. "Not great, but we have to try. I've let the Edakees know what to expect, but they have such a strong belief in their spiritual leader, I don't think it sunk in. In any case, brace yourself."

As soon as Neil disappeared down the hall, Sandy plucked her robe off the chair and wrapped it around her. After distractedly running a brush through her hair, she wheeled herself down to the ICU. Cecilia and Tonito stood at the end of the bed with arms intertwined around each other's waists. The medicine man stood on one side of the bed with Neil. Across from them the ICU nurse readied a tray of instruments.

Sandy joined Cecilia and Tonito. The mumur of the respirator filled the room as never before. The only sound that vied with it was the beating of her heart. An antiseptic odor permeated the air. Her throat felt tight, scratchy.

What if this experiment failed? What next? She tried to shut off her fearful thoughts, but couldn't quell her uncertainty. Were they making a mistake? Should they wait a little longer? What would happen if Dixon died? Cecilia extended a hand to her and she grasped it like a life preserver.

After Neil scrubbed and stretched on surgical gloves with the help of a nurse, he methodically untied the fabric that held the mouthpiece of Dixon's respirator in place. He took a syringe from the nurse and penetrated the small plastic tubing that extended from the mouthpiece, evacuating air. With a glance at the beleaguered couple and a deep breath, he cautiously tugged the tube out of Dixon's throat. The nurse compressed a button on the respirator; a tense silence followed. No one in the room took a breath, including Dixon.

All they could do now was wait and watch. Moments passed. Nothing changed. Hope mutated into despair. Cecilia dropped Sandy's hand and grasped onto Tonito. He held her close while she sobbed loudly in his arms.

Sandy grabbed the bottom of the bed, pulled herself in closer to better view Dixon. He lay perfectly still, dwarfed by the bedding and the monstrous monitors. His face, typically nutmeg, had taken on an ashen hue from weeks in the hospital.

This family had become her extended family and she grieved along with them. Tears obliterated her vision. A ringing filled her ears. She felt dizzy and disconnected with her surroundings.

Since the accident and the loss of Adam and Tim, she had been afraid to let go, to allow herself a deep emotional connection to anyone else. Instead she had substituted being helpful and benevolent for attachment. It felt safer. She could be close to others without ever having to feel the devastating pain of loss.

But something had gone irretrievably wrong here. She had fallen in love with a child and his family. Once again she lived in morbid fear of losing someone she loved. And suffered unbearable pain as he slipped away from her.

The medicine man extracted another rag from Dixon's throat. From somewhere far away she heard choking and gasping. She saw Neil bending over Dixon.

"Something's happening here," he exclaimed. He held his stethoscope to Dixon's chest. "I think he's breathing on his own." Dixon choked and made large gasping sounds. "Give him oxygen, nurse."

She placed an oxygen mask over his face. He strained for the air. Face red with effort, the muscles stood out on his neck.

The sheet over Dixon's chest fluttered with his struggle. Cecilia grabbed onto Neil's jacket sleeve. "Is he going to be all right, Doctor?"

Neil looked dazed, as though he had not expected this. "There's a better chance than I thought." He nodded toward the medicine man. "Your ways may be mysterious to us, but they work. You must have known that Dixon's lungs were less damaged than I would have thought."

The medicine man merely watched through wise eyes.

Nearby, Cecilia continued to cry, but a small smile illuminated her tear-stained face.

Sandy slipped into a red blouse and denim skirt, savoring the feel of civilian clothes again. The cast meant jeans and spandex tights would be out for awhile, but she could live with that. Anything was an improvement over the open-back hospital gowns she had been sentenced to wear for the last few weeks.

Ben would be swinging by to pick her up soon. She had just enough time to make herself presentable and take one last peek at Dixon before Ben arrived. The progress Dixon had made over the last couple of days sent shivers of joy down her spine. He had begun to regain strength. Neil was even talking about starting him on a liquid diet.

She was so full of enthusiasm she would have skipped down the hall to Dixon's semi-private room, if it weren't for the cast and crutches. She entered to find Cecilia standing over her son, wiping stray hairs off his face. Even from a distance, Sandy could see the love in her eyes. Watching this display of maternal affection touched something deep inside her. She thought about her own son.

Observing Cecilia with Dixon these last few weeks had made her aware of what parenting really meant. More than giving birth—more than blood and contractions, cuddling and caressing—parenting meant long hours of toil, and even trauma. It meant suffering through growing pains and disappointments. Sitting day after day by a sick child's side. Parenting was not only about passing down chromosomes from one generation to the next; it was about passing up one's own pleasures in the service of your child.

The impact of this insight hit her so hard that

she had to step outside the room to center herself. She leaned against the wall and closed her eyes.

Neil's voice startled her. She opened her eyes to see his concerned look. "Are you okay?"

She grinned. "Fine. Wonderful, actually. Probably better than I've ever been."

He raised a brow. "Most people are glad to leave the hospital, but I've never heard such rave reviews."

She pushed herself away from the wall. "I can't say I'm sorry to be leaving, but that's only part of my excitement."

Neil looked over at Dixon's room. "He's doing great, isn't he? We're all pleased."

"Neil, you're a miracle worker."

"No miracles here. Just doing my job."

"I don't buy that. You did so much more than your job. I want you to know how much I appreciate all you've done for Dixon, and for me."

A blush spread down his neck. "Thanks, Sandy. That means a lot to me, especially coming from you. And remember, what I said in the café still applies. Any time you need me, I'm here."

She offered him her warmest smile. "I need you as a friend forever."

"You have that." The flush deepened from blush to burgundy. "I've come to like your friend Ben, so I can't bad-mouth him. But, if you two ever have a falling out, I want to be the first to know. Got that?"

His words touched her. "Ben and I would both like to see you when you come through the pueblo."

Neil smiled, but his eyes were sad. "I'll be by soon. Don't you worry."

"Promise?"

"Promise."

She watched him trudge away before limping back into Dixon's room. Since Dixon slept, Sandy steered Cecilia to the far side of the room. "I came to say goodbye, for now. Ben's coming to pick me up in a few minutes to take me home."

Cecilia looked surprised. "You will be back to visit?"

"Often."

Cecilia hugged her, dislodging one crutch. "You have been such a help to us, *Tsila*."

"How's Dixon doing today?"

"Doctor Neil tells us he grows stronger every day."

What good news. She righted her crutch and noted how tired Cecilia looked. Dixon was not her only concern. Life had altered dramatically for her. "How are you doing without a home?"

"We are staying with my aunt until the house has been rebuilt."

"How long will that be?"

"It will be done by summer."

She stared dumbfounded at her. The house was a shambles the last time she saw it. "So soon?"

"You have not heard?"

"Heard what?"

"The pueblo pipeline must have dried up. Things have really changed since the fire. Everyone in the tribe has banded together to help Tonito rebuild the house."

Sandy couldn't believe her ears. Things really had changed. Goosebumps dotted her arms. If the people in the village were helping Tonito, the family must have been exonerated of the witchcraft charge. They were no longer the pariahs of the pueblo. Joy rushed through her. "That's great. I had no idea."

Cecilia reached in a bag on a nearby table and extracted a *Kachina* doll with an intricately embroidered red, green and black kilt and a gray feather headdress. "I have a little gift for you, *Tsila*, because of all the help you have given us. Everything has turned around for us and we owe much of it to you."

Sandy took the doll from Cecilia's outstretched hand. "It's beautiful, but you owe me nothing, Cecilia." She caressed the doll. "I'll tell you what. I'll accept this doll as a symbol of our friendship."

Cecilia gave her a slight nudge. "Good. Now go. Your Ben may be waiting."

"I love you more than I can say. Keep the stew warm for me, I'll be by soon." She kissed Cecilia on the cheek before hobbling from the room.

Sandy had double checked to make certain everything was packed when Ben knocked on her door. She turned around to see him standing in the doorway. "Come on in. I'm ready and raring to go."

For a guy who had come to help out his girlfriend, he looked pretty damn glum. "Are you okay? What's going on?"

Ben held out an envelope. "I picked up your mail and thought you might want to see this one right away."

She took it from him and turned it over to see the State of Pennsylvania Department of Adoptions in the upper left hand corner. Her bad leg buckled and she couldn't stand any longer. She lowered herself to the bed and Ben took a seat beside her.

"Aren't you going to open it?"

"Sure." She took a deep breath of courage and tore at the flap like a dog would tear at a bone. This might be what she'd been waiting for so long. Her hand shook as she extracted the letter and read it.

Ben waited patiently while she read the letter a second time. "What does it say?"

She looked up in tears. "That Tim's okay, but he's been diagnosed with something called Franconi's Syndrome. It's a disorder that prevents its victims from reabsorbing certain nutrients, such as glucose or amino acids, causing malnutrition. Thank goodness they discovered it early because it's totally treatable if they supplement what's been lost."

"And what do they want from you?"

"Since it can be genetic, they'd like a family history so they can figure out where this originated and whether Tim runs the risk of passing it down to future generations."

"Is that it?"

"For now." She grabbed a tissue off the tray table, blew her nose and sopped up the tears running down her cheeks. "His adopted parents aren't quite ready for me to be in Tim's life, but they promised to write to me on a regular basis and let me know what he's doing and what's happening with him. Maybe someday I'll actually get to meet him, Ben. Until then, I guess this is the best I can expect."

She turned the envelope over and a photo fell out onto the floor. Ben leaned over and picked it up, handing it to her. She gasped, covered her mouth with a hand. "Oh my God, Tim looks exactly like Adam. It's almost like seeing an apparition."

The tears started anew and Ben bundled her up into his arms. He held her close, comforting her, until they lessened. Once she regained her composure, she handed the picture to him.

He stared at it a long time. "Good looking kid."

A nurse appeared in the doorway. "Is everything all right?"

Ben nodded. "We're just about to take off."

Sandy dried her eyes and levered herself to standing with her crutch. She reached for her suitcase, but Ben grasped her arm.

"Let me help you with that. You've got enough baggage to carry right now." He hauled the suitcase off the bed, offered her his free arm and helped her out of the hospital.

After an exhausting first morning back at work, Sandy's leg throbbed. She slid into her chair, grateful to have survived.

Ben peered through the door. "Hi, teach. Welcome home."

At the sight of him her heart did a rain dance. "I'm glad to see you."

Ben grinned. "Why? Do you need help with your light bulbs?"

He hadn't forgotten.

She pulled herself to her feet, grabbed a crutch, and began to wobble over to him. She hadn't gone more than a couple steps when he rushed to her and swept her off her feet into an embrace. Then he lowered her as gently as he would a fine pueblo pot before enclosing her in a hungry embrace. His lips sought hers, and she surrendered all professional decorum to revel in his kiss.

At the sound of kids passing in the hall, he

broke the lip-lock, but his eyes spoke volumes about embraces yet to come. "I have to return to class in a minute, but what about dropping by my place after work? I have something to tell you."

"Can do. Now back to work with you." Sandy gave him a playful shove, then turned her attention to straightening a nearby desk.

Ben grasped her arm. "Whoa, Chester. Let me do that." He moved down the aisle, aligning one desk with another, then halted at an empty one toward the back of the room. "What's this?"

"It's Dixon's. The class is saving it for him. He should be returning to school in a couple of weeks."

"From what I hear, he's doing well."

Sandy's leg throbbed, making it difficult to stand upright on crutches for long stretches of time. She propped herself against the wall for support. "Yeah, Cecilia called to tell me the doctor says he'll make a good recovery."

"Do you mean *Dr. Kramer*?"

She controlled her impulse to smile at his reaction. "I do, but don't fret. Neil's a close friend, but you're the man for me."

"You're sure of that?"

"Absolutely certain, my dear man."

A mischievous grin spread across Ben's face, that wonderful, craggy face she had come to love. "Then how do you feel about being with the school principal?"

Sandy scrunched up her face. "What does Arnie have to do with us?"

"Not Arnie. *Me*. That's what I wanted to talk to you about. I spoke with the superintendent, Elton Begay, this morning. He told me they fired good old Arnie and asked me to take his place for the remainder of the year. I guess he showed up to school drunk one too many times. They had to let him go."

She couldn't say she'd miss Arnie. "Ben! How wonderful for you!" She pushed away from the wall. In her excitement, she straightened too quickly and wobbled unsteadily for a moment before stabilizing herself with the crutch. "What did you tell them?"

"Nothing yet. I wanted to know what you had decided about staying or leaving before I said anything." He leveled his gaze on her. "I didn't want to be here without you."

For a second she thought he might be teasing her, but he looked dead serious. To think Ben would have actually left San Anselmo for her. She knew what that meant. She wrapped her arms around him. "I love you, too." Pure unadulterated, unmitigated elation poured through her. "You're not getting rid of me so easily. Since I can't visit with Tim just yet, it's not time to move back east. I'm staying here...with you."

The bell sounded and children began to filter back into the room, but Ben ignored them. "Does that mean you might consider a San Anselmo style marriage?"

She felt happier than she had been in a long time. Perhaps since she lost Adam and Tim. "What's that?"

He grinned. "The man moves in with the woman and her family. When she's through with him, she leaves his belongings in the front yard."

Simple. Noncommittal. Not for her. "When in San Anselmo... but I'd really like the whole fry bread. White dress, lilies of the valley, champagne. Then you won't have to sweat every time you come home that you'll find your skivvies in the street."

A beaming smile spread across Ben's face. "Fry bread sounds great to me," he said before making his way through the onrush of fourth graders out of the room.

Ben halted his hike at the edge of Rainbow Mesa to catch his breath. He gazed out over the chamisa and sage, contemplating the many changes in his life. Enamored with the southwest ever since he first laid eyes on it, he now experienced a richer, more evolved sense of happiness.

The call of a coyote reached him. In the distance, the village lay sleepy, silent. Soon he would head down the mesa and hike home. Nothing before had prepared him for his new found sense of peace. His restlessness had all but vanished, his gratitude spread as wide as the wings of the eagle wheeling in the updraft of the canyon, and his love knew no boundaries.

He turned to see Sandy point at the bird. "Look what it's holding."

Ben could barely discern the snake held in the

eagle's talons. A rattlesnake, he thought. A symbol of danger. Of disaster. But this snake would soon be the eagle's dinner. It would no longer lie in wait for anyone.

A faint hint of piñon perfumed the air. Smoke rising from roofs beckoned him home. "Let's get going. I'm famished."

He shouldered his pack and sprinted with Sandy down the steep trail, his legs as limber as a colt's in their descent. No longer did he feel like a forty year old. The past placed firmly behind him, the future shone promising ahead. He picked up his pace, anxious to reach San Anselmo before dusk, and eager to return home to the people and the place with the woman he loved.

The End

About the Author

J. K. Winn earned graduate degrees from the University of Pennsylvania and the University of Metaphysical Sciences. Her previous mystery/suspense novel, *Out of the Shadow*, was published on Amazon in 2012 (http://amazon.com/dp/B008dPYM59C). She has had a play produced by the Actor's Alliance Festival in San Diego, and her poetry has been anthologized by the San Diego Writer's Workshop in For the Love of Writing. Her play "Gotcha!" was selected for a reading at the Village Arts Theater in Carlsbad, California in May 2012.

She presently lives by the beach in San Diego County, California.

For more information, please visit http://www.jswinn.com or contact the author at author@jswinn.com

If you liked The Spirit Keepers, check out J. K. Winn's newest Romantic Action Adventure/Thriller, RIVER OF DESIRE at http://www.amazon.com/dp/b00hzd50jg

Made in the USA
Las Vegas, NV
07 January 2022